ALSO BY KIMBERLY MULLINS:

Notebook Mysteries ~ Emma (Book 1)

Notebook Mysteries ~ Decisions and Possibilities (Book 2)

Notebook Mysteries ~ Changes and Challenges (Book 3)

Notebook Mysteries ~ Unexpected Outcomes (Book 4)

Notebook Mysteries ~ Haunted Christmas (a novella)

Notebook Mysteries ~ Suspicions (Book 5)

Notebook Mysteries ~ Parisian Intrigue (Book 6)

Notebook Mysteries ~ A Party to Remember (a novella)

Stand alone novels:

Divided Lives (K.R. Mullins)

1897 A Mark Sutherland Adventure

Notebook Mysteries

Notebook Mysteries

Decisions and possibilities

KIMBERLY MULLINS

NOTEBOOK MYSTERIES - Decisions and Possibilities

Book 2 of the Notebook Mysteries Series

Copyright © JKJ books, LLC 2021

First edition: August 2021

Mailing address for JKJ books, LLC: 17350 State Highway 249, STE 220 #3515 Houston, Texas 77064

Library of Congress Control Number: 202091490

ISBN 978-1-7360104-4-0 (hardcover)

ISBN 978-1-7360104-3-3 (paperback)

ISBN 978-1-7360104-5-7 (ebook)

This is a work of fiction. It is based on historical events within Chicago during the time period 1881-1883.

Edited by Kaitlyn Johnson, Strictly Textual; Cover Art by Miblart

*To Claudia—this book is for you. If you hadn't ask —what happens next
— I wouldn't have written this book.*

To Jonathan and Joshua you are my heart.

CHAPTER 1

1883, CHICAGO - PRESENT DAY

*E*mma looked at herself in the mirror as she smoothed down her white high-necked shirt into her full red split skirt and thought, *Mama would have liked the new rational dress movement, as it allows for a more practical and comfortable fashion. I'm probably one of the few girls who can sit down comfortably because I've never worn a corset. Though you can't really call me a girl at eighteen.* She pulled her long platinum blond hair into a loose bun on her head. The style emphasized her high cheekbones and the dash of freckles on her nose.

She took a final moment to examine her image and swirled to check her skirt for any wrinkles. Her split skirt would be considered too short by most, showing the tops of her black high-heeled boots. She nodded at her image, approving of her clothes selection for the day.

Emma didn't care about looks, though she had them. She gave a bit of an exasperated look at her bun, restraining hair that reached nearly to her waist, and acknowledged it could be hot in the summertime. *A short style would be nice,* she thought, but then she looked again and decided she would just have to put up with it. *Tony probably wouldn't like it short.*

. . .

Narrator commented, "Yes, Tony is still very important to Emma and very much a part of her life. They've been together since she was sixteen and they have remained close."

As Emma did a final examination of her clothes for any flaws, she turned away from the mirror and viewed the room around her. It was her childhood room in the boarding house where she lived with her papa and Dora. Their little family had grown over the past two years with the addition of Tim Flannigan, Dora's husband.

Tim and Dora had been married for a little over a year. She could still remember the wedding, how wonderful the house had felt when full of people, food, and music.

CHAPTER 2

1882, TIM AND DORA'S WEDDING

*M*ama's family had taken over the event and the house for the week. It was a wonderful, joyous time; aunts, uncles, and children were all over the house. Emma spent months making an intricate lace wedding dress for Dora and she looked radiant in it. It was a wedding where everyone enjoyed themselves and no one wanted the day to end.

Emma had felt Mama's spirit that day, especially when she and Dora were alone together getting ready to head downstairs for the ceremony.

With tears in her eyes, Emma helped Dora slip into her dress. They had completed a final fitting a few weeks before, but knowing Dora would be getting married today made Emma emotional.

"Don't make me cry," cautioned Dora, seeing Emma's eyes fill with tears.

"No, no, I won't," she said as she tried to shake them off. "You look beautiful and so much like Mama."

They hugged tightly.

"Enough of that now," said Dora. "I have things to do today."

With that final comment, both girls, looking beautiful in their lace dresses, stepped into the hallway to be greeted by Papa. Emma started downstairs with Dora and Papa following behind. The ceremony was being held in the backyard. Chairs had been set up there with an aisle separating the guest and at the far end, an arch where Tim and Dora would say their vows. Emma entered the yard first and could see Tim waiting for Dora. *He didn't appear nervous, he did appear to be a bit impatient to begin his married life,* she thought.

On her walk down the aisle, Emma glanced at each side. Mama's family took up most of the space. Her eyes found Tony, he smiled as she walked by. Next, she saw Cole and Jeremy Tilden. Jeremy winked at her. She grinned back and had to force herself to focus on where she would stand during the wedding.

The music that was playing was lovely. Chloe, Cousin's wife, had formed a small quartet that performed at different events. Her skills as a violin player were well known. The quartet included Chloe and Lee Sandel on violin, Elspeth Hanson on viola, and Katie Yu on cello.

Amy opened the back door and motioned to Chloe's group to begin playing the music for Dora and Papa's entrance. As they started down the aisle, Emma's tears started to form again and this time she let them fall. Two of her favorite people were becoming one that day.

Once the wedding ceremony was over; the chairs and arch were cleared out. Tables were put in their place and a dance floor was arranged. Day turned to evening with plenty of food, drink, and speeches. Papa stood by the front table with his arm around Dora.

"I'd like to tell you about these two people that we all love so much. Dora is so much like her Mama. Both of my girls are," Papa said, including Emma in his speech. "Mary would've loved to have been here to see this joyous day. I thought when she died, that our family had also died, but I was wrong. Our family continued and is only stronger with the addition of Tim."

He turned to Tim and said, "Welcome to the family."

The crowd cheered and Dora had her face buried in Papa's chest.

It was a memory she would cherish.

Papa had sent Dora and Tim on a trip to New York, but when they returned, they didn't seem to remember much of what they'd seen. *They had returned well-rested*, Emma thought with a laugh.

She moved to her desk and sat down for a moment while she reflected on 1881, that busy year she began investigating.

CHAPTER 3

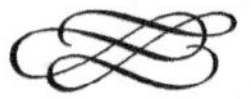

1881 CHICAGO

The cases Emma was involved in over the last two years had involved theft from the Stubing Department store, pickpockets, and smuggling operations involving John Harden. In each case, the clues seemed to be leading in the same direction—to one criminal organization.

The spider web of cases intertwined so that the only way to deconstruct it was to pull the one string holding everything together. Emma thought that string was the head of a local crime organization, but it turned out, it was Mama. Everywhere she turned, Mama was connected. Emma had initially stumbled on the fact that she had been helping a reporter with investigations into illegal activities during the year she died. Mama had inadvertently led the reporter to an opportunity he couldn't pass up, to oversee a large crime organization. That reporter wanted Mama to be part of it, but she had disagreed and he had killed her.

Who was that reporter? Daniel Cooper, local paper editor, and secret crime boss. He believed strongly that, if he could control the news, he could do anything or be anything he wanted. He was right—for a while.

Emma was able to deduce that the cases were probably

connected and were somehow tied to her mama. She also knew Daniel had more involvement than he indicated, but Emma never suspected he was the person who murdered her.

The final clues had unraveled when Thomas, Mama's good friend, and coworker at the bakery, identified Daniel as her killer. Since she died, Thomas had always been there in the shadows looking out for Emma. He knew one day he might have to step in to save her. What he didn't expect was for Emma to end up saving his life when Daniel tried to kill him.

On that final day, Emma had ended Daniel's life, though it wasn't something she'd planned, she didn't regret it. She did what she had to, to save them both.

CHAPTER 4

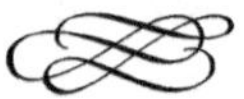

1883, PRESENT DAY CHICAGO

*E*mma pulled herself into the present and opened her desk drawer to find her current case book. She still kept her observations in the black notebooks she always carried with her. As she tried to pull the drawer open, it got stuck and she had to pull forcibly on the handle. When it finally gave way and allowed her access, she knelt to discover what had kept the drawer from opening. It was another notebook, wedged in the back; she reached in and pulled it out.

She sat back on her knees, looking at it for a long moment, and realized which one it was. *It must be a day for memories,* she thought, shaking her head. That notebook, the black cover faded with age, was from another day long ago when she was ten years old and involved her "incident".

The Narrator said, "The incident was when Emma was attacked at the age of ten by a career criminal named Zeke Jones, and it was not the last time he would go after her. He had a personal vendetta against her; he felt she was always taking something from him that he believed was his."

Dear-one commented wryly, "To be fair, she did keep uncovering cases where he was also involved. The Stubing store theft, the smuggling operations involving store owners, and then when he had volunteered to "take care" of Emma for the notorious gangster John Harden."

The Narrator added, "When he did go after her that last time, Emma was ready for him."

Dear-one asked, "What happened to Zeke?"

The Narrator said, "Well, we will get to that later."

Dear one said, "You know you say that a lot."

"I know, but I always plan to go back," commented the Narrator, as she continued to write.

Emma opened the notebook and remembered how it had finally returned to her.

CHAPTER 5

1881, THE "INCIDENT" NOTEBOOK

eremy Tilden, a friend, and a Pinkerton detective had come by the house to see Emma a few weeks after her second attack from Zeke and after she had killed Daniel Cooper.

He asked her to take a walk with him. She happily acquiesced. She liked Jeremy and enjoyed his company.

"I have something for you," he said as they walked down the stoop and onto the street.

She stopped and turned to look at him. "You do?"

He pulled out a faded black notebook and handed it over to her. She looked at him quizzically and took it as he continued. "I don't want to upset you—with this." She looked at him and frowned.

Opening it, she realized immediately what it was. It was the notebook from THAT day when she was ten, and before that "incident". She was very curious about what she had written. Due to the extent of her injuries, she had not been able to recall the events of that morning. Vague flashes came to her, but nothing telling her why she had been attacked. She opened the book and quickly flipped through the pages until she found the last entry. That final day materialized in her thoughts as she reviewed the details her younger self had documented. As she read, she realized she had seen something Zeke Jones didn't want her to see. He had been beating a woman in the alley between the buildings. The last part was written a bit hastily.

"Hmm, so I *was* always where he didn't want me," she murmured.

"Looks like," commented Jeremy.

"So, you read it?" she asked laconically, looking up at him.

"Caught," he said, smiling a bit to ease the tension. "We were concerned about what might be in it, so yes—Cole and I reviewed it." Cole Tilden was Jeremy's dad and in charge of the Chicago branch of Pinkerton detectives. He didn't say, but he planned to look into the details of that day for her.

She closed it, slapping it against her hand. She tried to decide what her feelings were -*was it an intrusion of her privacy? Maybe, but it came from a place of caring.* Coming to a silent decision, she placed the notebook in her pocket and said, "I appreciate your concern."

They started their walk again along the sidewalk. Jeremy took the opportunity to start a new conversation. "Going to keep investigating?"

"Yes, but I'm going to take a step back and work on a few other things first."

"Still seeing Tony?" he asked casually.

She smiled slightly and said, "Yes."

"Well, I thought I would ask," he said, running his fingers through his brown curly hair.

"Still friends?" she asked.

"Yes, friends," he replied.

· · ·

"Are you wondering what happened to Jeremy? His story will continue to unfold in the book. His path will continue to interact with Emma's," the Narrator said as she shot a long sideways glance to Dear-one.

That particular notebook -- many things had come out of it. . .

CHAPTER 6

1881, JEREMY INVESTIGATES THE NOTEBOOK

Jeremy had been assigned to search Zeke's apartment after he had tried to attack Emma the second time. Once Zeke had been taken into custody, Jeremy had been assigned to catalog his belongings. He was loading a box from the desk when he ran across a familiar black leather notebook. *It's the kind Emma always carries with her,* he thought. He was curious enough to want to find out if it belonged to her. He opened it up and, with a smile, noted the girlish handwriting. A ten-year-old girl's writing could be very fanciful. He had no doubt it belonged to Emma.

Skimming through the pages, he realized what the last entry was. He had been told about Zeke's attack on Emma only after they'd locked him up. It was all he could do to not go after Zeke himself.

When he discussed this with Cole, the emotions churned within him again and his fist tightened. Cole grabbed his arm. "Jeremy, he'll get what is coming to him, I promise you."

"Will he?" asked Jeremy in a gruff voice.

"Yes, but we must leave it with the proper authorities to manage," said Cole.

"What if they don't?" asked Jeremy.

"Then we'll step in," he admitted. "For now, we let the system work."

Jeremy continued to read through the observations and realized Emma was always interested in the details of her surroundings; that made him smile. The following information was detailed in the notebook: *Noise coming from the alley on Morgan street, sounding like a woman screaming. A man with dark hair beating on a slender woman with auburn hair and pale skin.* The writing became disjointed after that and there was an appearance of the pencil being dragged down the page.

Jeremy went down to investigate that particular alley; it was located next to an infamous house of ill-repute. He decided to follow up on the lead and knocked on the front door of that 'house'. It opened immediately and two very large men in dark suits blocked the entrance. *Bodyguards*, he thought. He tried not to be intimidated and commented in a cheerful voice, "Hi, I need to speak to the manager."

"What do you want? We're not open until this evening," snapped the one on the left. Neither man showed any emotion.

Jeremy took a deep breath and tried again. "I'm with Pinkerton detectives and I'm looking for someone who was attacked about six years ago in the alleyway next door."

The guard who had spoken first gave him a considering look and then nodded at the other man. He turned and left the doorway without a word. His companion backed up and waved Jeremy into the foyer. Jeremy followed him in, still standing close to the door. He wasn't winning the staring contest with the bodyguard, choosing instead to look around at the foyer and upstairs. The house catered to things he had no experience with, he was curious about what was behind those closed doors.

At that moment a beautiful woman appeared, he assumed was the manager. She walked slowly down the stairs toward him. Two things surprised Jeremy: how young the manager appeared to be

—she couldn't have been much into her thirties—and how perfectly she matched Emma's description.

At least I know I have the right person, he thought to himself.

"Mr. . .?" she asked as she stepped off the last step into the foyer.

"Jeremy Tilden, with Pinkerton detectives," he supplied. "And you are?"

"Clair Spencer. What can I do for you?" she asked a bit formally, keeping her distance.

"I'm investigating an event that occurred here in the alley next door some six years ago."

"Really?" She laughed. "Aren't you a bit late?" Though her lips indicated laughter, it didn't extend to her eyes, they were guarded, showing no emotion.

"New evidence has come to light in the case. Do we have somewhere more private we can talk?" he asked, eyeing her bodyguards.

She looked him over and came to a silent decision to talk to this man about something she would like to have forgotten. She indicated the doors behind him with her hand.

He turned and opened one of them to reveal a library with heavy furniture. A room like that in a house like this was unexpected, but he was glad there was a quiet space to conduct their meeting. Holding open the door for her, he waited while she entered ahead of him, her dress rustled as it brushed past. He pulled the doors shut and joined her on one of the two leather chairs situated across from one another.

"A man named Zeke Jones was seen beating a woman of your description in the alley beside this establishment about six years ago," he began.

This statement finally seemed to break Clair's calm demeanor. She stood up and moved behind the leather chair where she had been sitting. Gripping the back of it so tightly, that her knuckles appeared to be white.

Jeremy noticed her distress and tried to get to the point quickly. "Another attack happened right after that first one, just outside the alley, and led to the serious injury of a young girl."

Clair nodded. "Yes, that was me in the alley," she admitted. "That young girl, she was so brave," she said, an awed look on her face. "She just charged us. I could see her over his shoulder, all that blonde hair. She had a piece of wood and swung it hard at his head. He actually shook after she hit him."

Taking a deep breath, she opened up her fist and set her palms on the back of the chair. "He released me and went after her. Once he let me go, the other girls moved me inside. Last I saw of them, Zeke had her by the ponytail and was going around the corner. I didn't know until later how severe her injuries were. When I could, I found out she had survived and that bum Zeke had gotten away with it again."

"You knew he had done this before?" asked Jeremy gently.

"Yes. I wasn't careful enough and didn't listen to the other girls' warnings. He was good-looking and seemed to like me. I was naïve," she said simply, silently forgiving herself for being so trusting.

"Looks like you got over that." He gestured to their surroundings.

"I was at the right place and time to move up in my career. Why is this coming up now, after all this time?" she asked curiously.

"We finally have Zeke in custody. He went after that young girl, Emma, again," said Jeremy, trying not to show how angry he still was.

"Is she all right?" she asked, looking worried.

He nodded. "She bloodied him this time. He was tied up when we got there."

Finally finding the humor in their situation, she grinned broadly and said, "Met his match, did he?"

"He seemed to hold a grudge against her for a very long time," Jeremy commented.

Growing serious again, she said, "Yeah, he didn't like to let things go. I've been forced to hire bodyguards since that time. You are sure he's finally gone?"

"Yes, he was sent away a few days ago, facing charges in several states."

She let out a long sigh of relief and walked back around the chair to sit down. She looked at him and said, "So, why the visit?"

"To put some closure on the information. I'm looking into things in case Emma wants to investigate in the future."

"When you see her, could you tell her *thank you* for me?" she asked graciously.

"Yes," said Jeremy. "Thank you for making time for me today." They stood and she exited the room ahead of him, making her way gracefully back up the stairs. Jeremy watched her for a long moment and then exited the house.

Later that night, Jeremy discussed the details of the meeting with Cole. He stated with a smile, "I admit, I am curious about Clair Spencer."

"I'm not surprised. She does sound fascinating. What are you thinking?" asked Cole.

"I think a discrete look into her background might be a good idea," commented Jeremy in a serious voice.

"Are you thinking there's something suspicious there?" Cole asked, wondering where he was going with this.

"No, not without more data. But I am wondering about the money. How does someone move up like that and own the business?"

"Hmm," murmured Cole. "Keep it quiet. We don't want to cause her any unnecessary trouble."

Jeremy agreed. "I'll start by looking into the business license for her 'house.'"

"Sounds like a plan. Keep me in the loop." Cole began undoing the top button on his shirt and settling in for the night with a book.

"I will. Toss me my book?" Jeremy requested, ready to relax at the end of a long day.

Cole reached for it on the table beside him and tossed it to him. He asked with a smile, "What's for dinner tonight?"

The next day, Jeremy started looking at City Hall and found that the 'house' where he'd met Clair Spencer was also owned by her. *Surprising*, he thought. *Women don't normally own businesses, especially **that** type of business.* As he dug further, he pulled out records for other businesses and property in the area. He spent the rest of the afternoon looking through a large number of dusty old records, finally finding one attributed to Clair Spence. Possibly a misspelling. *Though*, he thought, *it may have been deliberate.*

Continuing to follow up, he went to City Hall to access the last three census records, looking for Clair Spencer or Spence to determine which one was the accurate name. He found a Clair Spence of about the same age, and it also identified her mother. The first two listed Clair's mother, but the last did not. None contained a listing for a father. He gathered his notes and headed over to the Pinkerton office where he shared the information he'd found with Cole.

"What are your thoughts about the second house? Do you think it's another business like the one I met her in?" Jeremy asked Cole.

"Let's take a look and see." The two personally staked out the house. They watched it closely for two days and noticed very few people ever left. The only people that were seen entering were women. Any men who came to the door were not allowed entry.

Cole stated, "We need to go there at night and check out their activities."

"Tonight?" Jeremy asked.

Cole nodded.

That evening they were in place watching the house as a wagon drew near. Cole nodded at Jeremy to follow behind and see where it stopped. It pulled up behind the house they were watching. Two men jumped down; Jeremy immediately recognized them as the bodyguards from the other 'house'.

They watched silently as the men helped an individual down from the wagon. Given the care they were taking, Jeremy assumed it was a woman. They kept her face and body swaddled in blankets, making it impossible to identify her. "Pops, what's going on in that house?" asked Jeremy in a low voice, bewildered by the events he had witnessed.

"I think it's a battered woman house," said Cole, stroking his goatee consideringly. "Let's clear out. They don't need us to expose their good deeds. They kept the location of the house quiet for a good reason."

"I wonder if the situation with Zeke led her to do this?" mused Jeremy as they left the area and retrieved their buggy a few streets over.

"It might be that or a combination of things," said Cole in a low gravelly voice. They climbed into the buggy and headed toward home.

CHAPTER 7

1881, JEREMY AND EMMA

Several days later, as Emma exited the bakery, she was distracted by the notebook in her hand. She didn't get far when she heard a voice call her name.

She glanced around and saw Jeremy leaning against the wall a few feet from her.

"Jeremy," she said with a laugh. "Just in the neighborhood?"

"No, I'm here to see you," he said cheerfully as he straightened up to his full height, rubbing a hand through his curly hair.

"Okay, walk me home?" she asked.

"Sure," he said. He wanted to delay the reason for his visit so he could enjoy her company.

She looked over curiously and asked, "So, what is the reason for your wanting to see me?"

"I did some follow-up on your notebook," he commented.

Emma stopped for a moment and tilted her head at him. "And?" she said, prompting him.

He let out the breath he didn't know he was holding when he realized Emma was curious and not upset. "I made notes on the last entry," he said, looking at her. "I found the woman you mentioned."

"How did you know it was her?" she inquired curiously.

"Your description of auburn hair and pale skin helped. I also chose to investigate the 'house' to the right of the alley," he reported.

"Hmm," she said noncommittally and started walking again.

He followed up with the details of the attack, the meeting with the lady in question, and her 'house'.

"What was the 'house' like?" asked Emma, extremely interested in mysterious things, and this type of 'house' was definitely that.

"It wasn't what I expected," he admitted, his face turning red.

"Now I really want to know what it looked like," she teased.

Still red and squirming, he answered, "It was nice, with rich colors of browns and blues. Some splashes of gold. I mostly saw the entryway, the massive staircase, and the library."

"What was she like?" asked Emma, enjoying his discomfiture.

"Smart," he said, thinking about Clair. "She seems to be a woman who knows who she is and where she's going. She doesn't apologize for who she is or what she does."

Funny, thought Emma. *He didn't comment on her looks.*

"There is another thing I wanted to share, but I would need a bit more privacy than this," he said, looking around them.

"Home then," she suggested.

He nodded and they headed toward Emma's house. On their way there, they discussed different cases they were working on. As they entered the house, Dora heard Emma and yelled out, "Come into the kitchen!"

"We have company!" Emma yelled back. "I need to meet with him first."

Dora entered the foyer from the kitchen, wiping her hands on her apron. "Hi, Jeremy. Sorry for the yelling."

"That's okay." He grinned, he liked when the house was noisy.

"Would you like something to drink or a snack?" asked Dora warmly.

Jeremy started to say no, but he remembered how wonderful Dora's baked goods were. "Do you have anything sweet?"

"Want me to surprise you?" she asked with a smile.

"Yes, please," he replied quickly.

"I'll have Amy bring you some tea and I'll send a sweet surprise." She looked at Emma and said pointily, "You'll need to eat lunch, so don't fill up on sweets."

Emma saluted and Dora winked at her as she left.

With that, Emma and Jeremy entered the study. "Papa is out of town on a job and won't mind if we use the room. Sit, sit," she said.

He closed the doors and sat down on the couch beside her. "This has to stay quiet; many people could be hurt if the information got out."

She frowned. "Are we still talking about the lady you met at the house, the manager?"

"Yes, her name is Clair Spencer. We were looking into her background as a precaution and found something."

This had Emma on the edge of her seat, but a knock sounded at the door. Emma looked toward it, resigned, and said, "Please, come in."

Amy rolled in a tray with tea and Kuchen, a German pastry. She smiled brightly at Jeremy and left the tea and sweets on the little roll cart near the couch. He scooted closer and asked, "Tea?"

"Please," said Emma. He poured a cup for her and himself and picked out a Kuchen to try.

"Clair Spencer," she encouraged as she took a sip of tea.

Jeremy swallowed the bite in his mouth and continued, "She owns the 'house' she lives and manages, but she also owns another house."

"Is it the same type of place?"

"I asked the same thing," he said wryly. "No, she uses this house as a shelter, to take care of and hide ladies who have been abused by the men in their lives."

She sat a bit stunned; she'd thought he was going to say something illegal. "How does she manage it?"

"We're not sure where the money is coming from, but the main people in that house are there for safety reasons and it is a secret location. Cole and I decided to back off so we didn't inadvertently expose their efforts."

"Jeremy," Emma said thoughtfully. "Could you arrange a meeting for me and Miss Spencer?"

"Yes," he said. He noticed she was drumming her fingers on her lips. "What are you thinking?"

"I'm thinking I would love to meet the lady you have described to me. I'm also thinking of ways we might be able to help her."

"I'll set it up," he promised.

At the front door, they parted with a touch of their hands. She leaned against the door frame and watched him leave. He stopped at the bottom step and turned back to give her one last long, searching glance before he headed off.

Dora came into the foyer and watched as Emma shut the front door. "Did Jeremy leave already? I was hoping to talk to him," she said, sounding disappointed.

"Hm," said Emma, still thinking about Jeremy. Shaking herself out of the mood, she said, "I think we need a team meeting."

"What would be the topic of this meeting," asked Dora, wondering if they had a new case.

"Jeremy told me about a woman who is sheltering a group of abused ladies. "

"What can we do to help?" Dora asked immediately. "Are you thinking food, medical treatment, etc. . ."

"First," she said, "Let me meet with the woman and see what assistance we can offer."

"Yes, that would be the right thing to do."

CHAPTER 8

1881, EMMA'S FIRST MEETING WITH CLAIR

Jeremey set up a lunch for both ladies at a restaurant in an out-of-the-way location. Emma pulled her bike to a stop at its entrance and studied the neighborhood. It had an appearance of quiet elegance, one that was inviting. She climbed off her bike and walked it to the door. A well-dressed gentleman stepped out when he saw her.

"Can I put this somewhere safe?" Emma asked as he approached her.

"Yes, of course. I am Charles, your Host." When the reservation was made, the gentleman had told him they would need to store the bike. "We'll bring it out when you are ready to leave," he said, snapping his fingers at his waitstaff to remove it.

As it was moved, he motioned for her to follow him inside the dark restaurant. A woman was seated at the table they were approaching. *This must be Clair Spencer.* Emma had never met a woman in the sex trade before, she didn't know what she'd expected, but this wasn't it. Taking a moment to observe her, she took in the intricate design of the woman's dress. Her eyes moved up to her hair, it was auburn and pinned up high on her head. Her makeup was also applied with a subtle hand.

Clair was evaluating Emma in much the same manner.

Emma chose not to say anything as she waited for the host to pull out her chair. Taking her seat, she faced the woman. They waited for their host to leave before beginning any conversation. Both ladies were nervous; Emma took a breath and said, "Hello."

"Hello," Clair said back, her tone reserved.

"I'm Emma Evans."

"I figured," Clair said laconically.

"Jeremy mentioned your name is Miss Spencer," Emma said politely.

"Clair, please," she said, in the same tone.

"Very pretty. Please call me Emma."

"Thank you." She nodded graciously.

"I've been wanting to meet you since Jeremy told me about the follow-up from our incident," Emma said as she pulled her notebook from her pocket. It was the original one from the attack on Clair and herself. She felt the need to add the final information before closing the case.

Clair's mouth quirked up at the site of the notebook. "Am I being interviewed?" she teased lightly, slightly softening toward this young girl.

"No, no, I just wanted to add to the facts you shared with Jeremy. He mentioned you remember more than I do from that day," Emma assured her.

"What would you like to know?" Clair asked.

"Do you mind going through it again?" Emma asked gently.

"No, I don't. I understand that you want to know what happened." She took a deep breath and began with how she'd known Zeke and how she ended up in that alley. "He was a regular for me." When Emma frowned because she didn't understand the term, Clair explained, "He would come weekly to spend time with me."

"Was he violent toward you during these 'visits'"?

"Not at first, but after a while, he starting to hit me," Clair said.

"Why did you keep seeing him?" Emma asked.

She explained, "He would apologize and bring me gifts. I let it go on for far too long. He wasn't always violent, so I thought I could handle him."

"What happened to set him off that night?"

"He had been late and this is a business, I had another 'visitor'. When he found out, he entered my room and pulled me out and down the stairs to the alleyway. That is when you saw us."

"What happened then?"

"You were charging at us with your blonde hair flying, brandishing a stick almost as large as you were. You hit him in the back of the head, causing him to drop me and go after you." She finished her story with, "The last I saw of you was Zeke grabbing your hair."

More questions were asked about that day, and Clair shared everything she remembered. Emma closed the notebook, feeling comfortable enough to close the case.

Both ladies remained silent as the waiter approached and set the table with tea and cakes. They began eating the cakes and sipping their tea when Emma broached another topic in a low voice, "I wanted to talk with you about your other house."

Clair's eyes darted about the room, shocked and fearful that someone had heard the comment. Protection was paramount and she would do anything to keep the women that house's secrets.

Emma hastened to assure her in a lower voice, "Don't worry, I'm not going to tell anyone. We—my family and I—want to see if there is something we could help with. Whether that be money or volunteers or food."

Clair smiled, a feeling of relief washing over her. "Money is not an issue at this time. I have some wealthy benefactors who help. We also have all the help we need at the house."

Emma wondered who the wealthy benefactors were.

Clair had done some investigating of her own and knew Emma was a type of detective. One who didn't get a lot of attention, but got a lot done. "What we need is someone to help with moving the women out of town to a safer location so they can start their lives over."

Emma looked intrigued at that response. They sat and talked well into the late afternoon. When they were ready to leave, the two struck up an agreement. When needed, Clair would contact Emma about moving the women to another house or another city.

Before they departed, Clair reached over and touched her hand. "Thank you."

Emma didn't ask what for; she knew she was being thanked for removing Zeke from their lives.

They parted ways, knowing it wouldn't be the last time they would meet.

CHAPTER 9

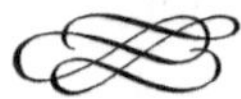

1881, FIRST MOVES FOR CLAIR

It wasn't long before Emma received her first request from Clair to move one of the women from the house to an out-of-state location. They had confirmed the contact, where she would be moved, and the timing of the event. That evening, she met with her team: Tony, Tim, Dora, and Thomas to figure out the best strategy.

Dora said, "Emma, the best way to do this is to dress as a boy."

Tim nodded. "I would agree with that, and I can help with the move."

Emma smiled broadly and reached over to touch Tim's hand. "Tim, out of anyone, I wouldn't want you. You would be recognized a mile away." She paused and looked toward Thomas saying, "I was thinking of you."

A warm feeling washed over him. "Yes, I can help." He enjoyed being part of the team and actively helping with cases.

Tony commented, "I agree. A small operation is better and safer for both ladies."

The group talked the plan through and organized a detailed note containing information on the prearranged evening. Thomas would deliver it to Clair. Emma would dress in boy's clothes, meet at the house to pick up and transport the woman to a safe location via train. They would walk together to a cab driven by Thomas. Tim would arrange for a private compartment in the railcar and Dora would make sure there was food for the trip.

Clair sent back her agreement to the plans and asked for a final date.

Arrangements were made for the plan to be put into effect.

On the agreed night, Emma was ready to head over to Clair's house for the pickup. She kissed Tony goodbye and left the boarding house on her bike. It was stashed behind a bush as she approached the back door of the safe house and knocked. The door opened quickly, a hand reached out and took Emma's, pulling her into the kitchen. That hand belonged to Clair and she was dressed similarly to Emma. Grinning a bit, Clair tipped her hat toward her.

Emma stayed serious and asked, "Is she ready?"

"Yes, come this way." Clair sobered and led her to the dining room just off the kitchen. When Emma saw her first transport, she shook her head. The lady was dressed like a lady, her hair coifed high on her head and a blue dress with a bustle attached to the back. "Clair, do you have any help here?"

Clair nodded, catching on to her train of thought. "Yes, Katy McKenna is still here."

"We'll need to have them exchange clothes," she said. "There's no way we won't be noticed with her dressed like that."

The lady in question started pulling pins out of her hair and said, "I'll do what needs to be done."

They helped her change into the maid's plain clothes and pulled her hair into a tight bun. Emma looked the lady in the eye and asked, "Are you ready."

"Yes," the lady responded.

Emma nodded and picked up the carpetbag. "Follow me, please. Everyone else stay here," she directed. Lights in the house were extinguished and they made their way out to the alley.

Thomas and the cab would be waiting, a few blocks down. The night was quiet and they walked arm in arm down the street. Though Emma was prepared for any unexpected events, she was glad that none occurred. They located Thomas waiting in the shadows, he quickly headed over to take the bag from Emma. He helped the lady into the cab and Emma climbed in on her own. They made their way to the train station and into their private compartment.

She opened the door and motioned to the porter. He walked over, Emma kept her hat pulled down and her voice gruff when she asked him, "Could you make sure we are not disturbed. The lady needs her rest."

He looked curious but didn't question her request after she placed the money in his hand. "I will make sure you are not disturbed," he promised.

Emma shut the door slowly behind her and looked toward her traveling partner. She didn't inquire about her name, not wanting to intrude into her privacy. Instead, she took her book out of her coat and made herself comfortable on the bench. It was a relatively quiet trip that took a few days. They stayed in their compartment, talking quietly and eating the food Dora had prepared. The train was met by the lady's brother. The brother and sister hugged tightly; Emma reminded them to keep a low profile. He assured her that the husband wasn't aware of his location and would not know to look for her here. Once assured, Emma headed back to the train station to confirm when her return ticket could be used to head home. She had balked at the expense of a private compartment on the way back, but Clair and the family were adamant. Emma would also have to buy food on the train. The wait was short and the trip home uneventful.

As she exited at the Chicago station, she was dressed once more in female clothes. Tony waved at her as she descended the stairs and made her way to him. She slid into his arms gratefully, laying her head on his chest.

"Tired?" he murmured in her ear.

"Yes, but I shouldn't be, just sitting and reading for two days. I'm also very glad to be home," she said into his chest.

He kissed her forehead and asked, "Successful trip?"

"Yes," she said simply. "Let's go home."

Emma and her team would continue to quietly transport battered women over the next two years. During that time, Clair and Emma would continue to spend time together and what started as a shared experience would grow into a friendship.

CHAPTER 10

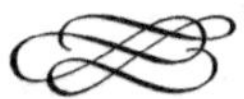

1883, PRESENT DAY

That put a closure to it, she thought as she slid the notebook back into the drawer and closed it.

She continued to get organized for her day and thought, *1881-2 brought so many positive things to their lives.* One of those was the job she was getting ready for this morning. It was part of the temporary employment agency that had been started by her, Dora, and Tim over two years ago.

The business began after a rather accidental burglary that involved their friends Miss May and Miss Marjorie. They were eighty and eighty-two respectively and had been extremely skilled burglars when they were younger. Miss May had additional skills as an escape artist and Miss Marjorie in knife throwing. They were also very close to Emma and had taught her those skills.

While attending an exhibit at the museum, Miss May saw a knife she thought Emma would like; she took it and gave it to her. Emma had explained why she couldn't keep it. Miss May reluctantly gave the knife to Emma and Tony to return.

They met with the curator to explain what had happened and to return the knife. Surprisingly he listened to their story and took them at their word. He seemed more curious about how it happened rather than placing blame on who did it. What interested him was the ladies, who could have taken something from the museum without anyone noticing.

The meeting had given Emma an idea. She approached Tim about a temporary employment agency with Miss Marjorie and Miss May as their first clients. He had taken the idea and developed it, with Emma and Dora as his partners.

Miss Marjorie and Miss May began conducting security surveys for the museum. The ladies couldn't work a full-time schedule but could work part-time for them through the new business. Tim helped set their hours and their pay.

Word had gotten out that temporary jobs were available in the security business; so much so that some Pinkerton detectives applied for side work. The business was strongly security-based in the beginning.

The only sad thing that happened during this time was the original ladies, the reason the business began, had passed away. They had passed together, sitting in the garden, holding hands. Emma missed her two friends.

Emma had moved on from that active year by focusing on completing her education. She'd finished business school and had begun working temporary jobs in various fields. She also tried to stay out of trouble and minded her own business.

Dear-one commented wryly, "Really?"

The Narrator sent a side glance and a slight smile to Dear-one. "Well, I did say try."

CHAPTER 11

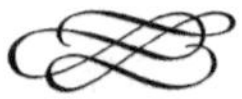

1881, BUSINESS SCHOOL

Tim was planning an expansion to their agency as soon as Emma finished business school. The initial delay occurred because the schools in the area only took on male students. Emma had known about the male student issue when she applied. She applied anyway, wanting the schools to accept her based on her qualifications and not her gender. The process continued and with each rejection letter, she persevered and reapplied, stating her qualifications in detail.

"A letter came for you," called Dora.

"Did it?" she asked as she walked quickly to the small table in the foyer. Flipping through the mail, she found the one she was looking for. She pulled it out slowly, pondering whether or not to open it. *This could be the one,* she thought taking a breath and slid her finger into the envelope to open it. It was the same form letter she had gotten so many times, she sighed heavily.

There has to be something I can do, she thought as she laid the letter back down on the small table. Emma had wanted to do this on her own but it looked like help would be needed. *There was one person that could help,* she thought and ran up the stairs to change, trousers would not be acceptable. She came back down to the foyer and added the new rejection to the ones she was carrying. "I'm headed out, I'll be back soon," she called, not waiting for a response. Striding swiftly to the cable car, she jumped on and rode toward the destination where her friend worked.

She entered his office and waited until he looked up from his desk.

When he did look up, he said, "Emma! What a nice surprise."

The large paneled office with a wall of windows belonged to the Chicago Chief of Police. *Funny,* she thought *that wasn't what he said the first time I visited here.* It was a nice change and she really liked him. "Sir, it is good to see you also."

"Why don't you sit?" he asked as he stood.

"Thank you," Emma said as she sat down. She hesitated before asking her question.

"Are you here for a visit or is there something else," he prompted.

"A visit but also this." She handed him her stack of rejections.

"What are these?" he asked curiously looking at the envelopes.

"Rejections for business schools I'd like to attend."

"There appears to be more than one," he observed.

"Yes. I have tried to get in on my own, but it isn't working. I was hoping you could help."

"Hmm and what do you think I can do about this," he asked looking at her sternly. He held it as long as he could before laughing and said, "I'm sure we can work something out. Is there a particular one you would like to attend?"

"Yes, this one," she said, pointing to a specific envelope. "I'd appreciate your help with this."

"I'll take care of it, now tell me what is going on with your family."

They had an enjoyable hour, and as he walked her out, he told her, "I'll look into the school this week."

"Thank you," she said and leaned down to kiss him on the cheek.

He smiled and watched her leave before going back to his work.

The letter arrived from the school that Thursday afternoon. The mail was on the small table in the foyer, she spotted it as soon as she entered the house. The envelope from the business school was on top, she didn't hesitate this time and tore it open. She started shouting, "Dora! Dora!"

Dora ran in and said, "What happened? What's wrong?"

Emma waved the letter in the air and had a wide grin.

"You got in!"

"I got in," she confirmed.

Dora ran over and hugged Emma tightly. She pulled back and asked, "When does class start?"

"I didn't check," she admitted. She looked down at it and Dora peered over her shoulder. "It looks like a few weeks and I have to go in for an interview."

"That sounds ominous, do you think they could still turn you down?" asked Dora.

Emma tapped the letter on her hand and thought about the police chief, her lips turned up into a wide smile. "No, I don't think so." She looked back at the contents of the envelope and saw it included a cost structure for the program. The reward money she earned from her previous investigations would be enough to pay for it.

"When will you go for the interview?" asked Dora.

"Tomorrow," Emma replied.

"Emma, behave yourself," Dora admonished. "You want this to go well."

"When do I ever not behave," she teased.

Dora sent her a look.

Emma said in a more serious tone, "I will do my best."

CHAPTER 12

1881-82, EMMA'S APPOINTMENT AT THE BUSINESS SCHOOL

*E*mma dressed in a conservative manner to meet the dean. This included a dark blue skirt, white blouse, dark blue jacket, and a smallish blue hat with a white ribbon perched on her head. Waiting outside the office, she forced her hands open, they had been clenched tightly, showing her tension. Taking deep breaths, she watched the door where her meeting would take place.

The dean's secretary looked over and waved Emma to the door. Nodding, she stood and walked quickly toward it. She knocked firmly on it and was called in. As the door opened, she got a view of Dean Randolph. He was a tall slim nice-looking man with dark hair, who appeared to be about thirty and very serious.

"Miss Evans?" he asked.

Emma approached his desk and took the seat in front, "Yes, thank you for seeing me today."

"It wasn't like I had a choice," he muttered. He looked up from his desk, into her eyes, and said, "I will be honest with you, this is a MALE business school and we did not want to accept you here."

Emma kept her mouth shut and let him talk.

"But you are here, so we must make the best of it. You will be given a chance but you must make the grades and pay the fees on time. If you cannot do either, you will be expelled. Is that understood?"

"Yes, it is," she said in a civil tone.

"The term starts in two weeks, can you make the payment now?"

"Yes. I have it with me."

He nodded. "Please see our clerk. You will also be expected to pass a series of test that tells us what level you are at academically. Are you prepared to do that today?"

"I am," she said confidently. "Thank you."

She started to stand and stopped when he said, "Miss Evans, I don't like how you went about this, but I understand wanting to improve one's self. Good luck."

"Thank you," she said as she stood and left the room. Emma went to find the clerk to get her forms organized. The journey she was on was very exciting. She wouldn't squander this opportunity –for her or the women that would come after her.

Emma's test showed that she was well educated but she was still a woman. Against all expectations of her teachers and the dean of the school, she excelled in each course and graduated at the top of her class. During that time, she had an appointment with the dean to discuss her career options. The meeting was a formal step all students took as they prepared to leave the school.

Emma wasn't worried about her career options and had other ideas about the direction she wanted to steer the conversation. Sitting in the dean's waiting room, she waited for the appointment time. At precisely 3pm, the secretary motioned to her and said, "You may go in now."

As she entered the office, she saw the dean sitting at a round table with folders piled around him. "Come in; sit down," Randolph said, indicating the chair across from him when he noticed her in the doorway. She moved quickly across the room, sat in a chair opposite him, and proceeded to open her notebook. He looked over curiously but didn't question it, he was eager to get on with the interview. Opening the file in front of him, he and stated, "Let's begin. . ."

"I have another idea," she said, as she interrupted him.

"What?" he asked, more distracted than ever, sending her a pained look. He had gotten many reports from Emma's teachers on how she periodically interrupted their lectures with her questions. He had planned this meeting to explain that there were no jobs for women available, but as usual, Emma was disrupting those plans.

"Why not bring more women into the school?" she asked a bit forcefully.

"Well, they don't—" he started but was interrupted again.

"They don't do what, perform as well as a man?" she asked, she felt she could guess the answer.

"No, I wasn't going to say that. What I am saying is that they can't get jobs, so it is a waste of our time," he stated, trying to reason with her.

"So, you're saying if I were able to guarantee employment for women, then you would accept them into your school?" Emma asked as she manipulated the conversation.

"Yes," he said, not realizing what he had agreed to.

"Okay then," she said, wheels already turning in her head. Emma closed her notebook and stood to leave.

"Wait, what about you and your position evaluation?" Dean Randolph asked, bewildered by the direction the meeting had taken.

She turned back toward him and said, "I already have jobs waiting for me. Thanks, though." With that, she was out of the room and on her way home.

The dean sat for an additional moment and slowly closed her file. *Women*, he thought. He didn't expect to see her again after graduation and was happy the school could be a professional environment again. She brought too much energy to the class-rooms and was exhausting to the teachers.

That evening, Emma sat down with Tim to develop a business plan for women to work in the offices within their agency. One of their biggest goals was to provide them with more opportunities outside the home.

Tim organized a survey and sent it to the local engineering firms to see if there would be places for graduating women within those offices. Tim spent the next few weeks setting up meetings with other types of businesses to secure additional future posi-tions. Their contacts were enthusiastic about personnel being more available, men or women. Chicago was building quickly and there didn't seem to be enough people to fill the available positions.

Emma and Tim used the data provided by the survey and interviews they conducted to build a detailed business plan to add more women to the workforce. They then went directly to the dean's office at the business school to speak with him about it. When Dean Randolph saw who was waiting for him, he hesitated before inviting them into his office. He hadn't expected Emma to follow up on the promise he'd inadvertently made.

He finally let them into his office and, within a few moments, sat stunned at the job plan they had put together. The opportuni-ties available to women graduates were described in detail; a list with potential contacts was provided for his review.

"So, you're saying you have jobs for people you don't know?" Randolph asked incredulously.

"No, we're saying we have jobs for qualified women," Emma corrected. "You promised that if I could guarantee jobs, you would add more women to your school," she continued deter-minedly.

"Well, I—"

"Are you a man of your word?" she demanded.

"I am," he said rather indignantly

Tim interrupted both, saying, "Look, this is getting us nowhere." He gave Emma a look as he continued. "I think that if we can speak a bit more calmly, we'll be able to iron out the details."

"Yes, well, we always seem to end up here, don't we?" the dean said as he offered a conciliatory smile to Emma.

Emma nodded and relaxed back in her chair, realizing he was listening to them.

In calmer tones, the dean started, "I will agree to this only if you understand that the applicants will have to meet our stringent entry requirements."

"Oh, they will," said Emma, thinking of the ladies she could encourage. There were several she knew who would do well in the school but didn't know there were options outside of marriage. There was also Clair's house, the women there need options to help them get back on their feet financially.

Emma reached across the table to shake the dean's hand. He paused only a moment before shaking it. Tim smiled broadly and stuck out his hand to help seal the deal.

"Tim, I have an idea," Emma said as they were leaving the dean's office. "It would involve women who need more choices in their lives."

Tim had an idea of who she was thinking about but was more pragmatic. "Who would pay? Can they afford it?"

"I think Clair would find a way. I will talk to her," commented Emma.

"Would she do it?" Tim asked cautiously.

"I think she might. I'll meet with her. I'll need to contact Jeremy."

Emma thought about her new friend, Clair Spencer. Their relationship had changed from survivors with a shared experience to close friends.

CHAPTER 13

1883, PRESENT DAY

So many success stories, she thought. Their success rate with graduating females was in the 90th percentile, with most assuming temporary or permanent roles. Emma's hope was that more women would begin their education prior to getting married. It would allow them some independence within the relationship.

Emma reached for her clutch knife sheath and pulled her skirt up, strapping it on her upper thigh, always glad to have the extra protection.

As she gathered her hat, gloves, and satchel from her brass bed, she checked the knife always hidden in her hat. She had to be careful with it; the knife was quite big and was kept sharp. With that final check, she pulled the quilt over the bed and headed downstairs for breakfast.

Her plans for the day included office work in the morning and courier work in the afternoon. The office work was part of the temporary employment business she operated with Tim and Dora. The business had fit in perfectly with Emma's professional plans.

She found she liked temporary work; where she could

continue to develop her skills observing people. It also left her open to take on independent investigations with Pinkerton. Cole had added her to cases when he realized that Emma could get women to talk when no one else could.

As of now, she was working at Baker Engineering as a temporary secretary. There was no case involved in this particular job. Like Tim had told her, "Not everything involved a mystery. Some were just jobs."

Her home was still the boarding house, shared with family and boarders. Boarding houses had come out of making room for families needing a place to live as a result of the 1871 fire.

The 1880s were a time when boarding houses were part of the fabric of life. Private boarding houses like theirs normally lodged single individuals or married couples without children. Theirs was different, they took in individuals and married couples, but they also enjoyed having children around. Dora continued to manage the household.

The family was very particular who lived with them and only took in people who would get along with them. A few things had changed, Tim and Dora had converted two bedrooms on the second floor into one for their use. Another two were being kept empty for Emma's future specialist. In the past, her father had used specialists to build Emma's skills in self-defense, knife throwing, and escape. Her idea now was to have other specialists come in, use their skills, and build a team.

Emma headed downstairs to help with breakfast and heard a booming voice coming from the kitchen. She pushed the door open and caught Dora in Tim's arms. It was not an unusual occurrence, especially since they had married the previous year.

Tim was big, with shoulders that could breach a doorway, ginger hair, and the ruddy complexion that generally accompanied Irishmen. He was always the first to the kitchen, just behind Dora; usually trying to get her to blush or to snag a Berliner. The first one was not hard to accomplish; Dora blushed whenever Tim was in the vicinity. He was currently teasing her about having her hair tucked into her handkerchief. ". . .but it's so pretty—why not have it down?"

Her response, "And have it in my baking or my meals?"

Tim had extra time in the mornings because their temporary employment business continued to be successful; enough so that, in the past year, he had quit his accounting job. He was enjoying being an entrepreneur and loved running a company with his wife and her sister.

Emma wagged her finger at them. "You are being a bad influence on Amy."

Amy, Dora's helper, stood by the sink doing dishes and just grinned over her shoulder at them. She had been with them for many years. She was a solid woman with dark hair and a happy disposition. She also seemed very content with her job and her life. The house was such a happy place to live and work.

Tim gave Dora a last lingering kiss and turned to Emma to say in a more conservative tone. "Morning, Emma. We need to talk before you leave today. Business."

"Breakfast first?" Emma asked Tim, glancing at the abundance of food set out and ready to be moved to the dining room table.

"Yes, always, especially if it's my Dora cooking." Tim sent a wink her way and Dora's cheeks heated. Tim thought, *I love I can still turn her cheeks red.*

Moving into her manager role, Dora said, "Okay, everyone grab something to move." Amy and Tim took their assigned trays and moved them to the table.

Emma grabbed a fresh piece of bread and some butter before she started to move her platters. "Emma, there's plenty on the table in the dining room," Dora reminded her with a smile.

Emma smiled and said, "Stolen ones taste the best." She ate the bread quickly and helped move the platters into the dining room. The long oak plank table had seen better days but provided enough spaces for twelve people to eat. It was already covered with food: eggs, bacon, two types of toast, pastries, pancakes, and oatmeal. Dora didn't let anyone go hungry.

The first ones to the table were generally the Irish widow—Molly and her twin sons. Emma thought, *I am sure there were odes written to her with her blazing red hair and Irish temper.* Her twin boys were mischievous and always planning their next adventure. Running into the room, just ahead of their mom, they stopped suddenly when they saw Emma.

"Good morning, Sister," they said together.

"Morning, boys," Emma replied.

Second to the table were Bessie and Harold Allen, a young couple saving their money to eventually buy a home of their own. Harold was able to find work in building design and assisted Papa in his engineering work now that Emma was busier with her other jobs. Bessie worked different jobs through their temp business as a housemaid, store clerk, and was being trained in typing. She was only working to fill the time until she and Harold had a baby.

Next to the table was Papa, who in his absent-minded way walked by Emma and dropped a kiss on her head. He never looked up from his notebook where he recorded notes for his engineering jobs.

And finally, last to the table, carrying butter, jam, and bread, were Dora and Tim.

Breakfast was a frantic affair when the food started to be passed around. It was best to take what you wanted quickly, or it wouldn't be around again. Being polite could leave you hungry. Occasionally, there were new people at the table, but fewer appeared over the years. The current boarders had long been considered family. *Family who pay rent,* Emma thought with a smile. *After all, it is still a business.*

She took a minute to look at the chairs on either side of her, where the two boys were seated. It was where Miss Marjorie and Miss May had once sat. How she missed their company and advice. She shook off any sadness, knowing they'd had a good life and had died together.

Emma could hear Papa going on about something; it was probably codes or engineering, the only topics that got him stirred up. The rest of the group knew this and were patient with him. Other topics introduced included the day's events, politics, or gossip. Everyone ate their fill and started moving from the table to begin their days; the boys off to school and the adults off to work. Emma, Tim, Dora, and Amy cleared the table and moved the now empty trays to the kitchen. The dishes were scraped and Amy started washing with Tim drying.

Once the cleanup was completed, Amy headed upstairs to start her list of tasks for the day. Dora, Tim, and Emma sat down at the kitchen table and began their meeting.

He had out his ledger and started with a tally of employees. "We currently have thirty-five temporary employees, thirty-six counting Emma," he said, nodding at her. "The staffing includes fifteen men and women in sales at Stubing and Marshall Field's department stores. In other engineering offices, we have ten engineers and office help. At the bakery, we have two, but they will need more once the holiday seasons start. At the museum, we have four security staff personnel. And finally, at the Baker Engineering Office, we have two administrative employees, including Emma. Also, we are down to two there because they hired two more of our people permanently."

"We should let the business school know that we have had two more women hired permanently in the office," commented Emma.

"Yes, good idea. That will encourage them to bring in more women to train," noted Tim.

"Tim, Papa mentioned he may need some additional engineering support on the new building he is working on," said Dora, looking over her notes.

"Noted. Thanks, Dora," said Tim, taking down the upcoming

job. "I'll be getting the checks ready to distribute. Emma, could you pick them up this afternoon?" he asked. The temporary workers were paid monthly after they received their pay from the various companies.

"I can take them around," said Emma. She worked as a courier in the afternoons and could make time to come by the boarding house.

"Any further concerns at this time?" Tim asked. Emma and Dora shook their heads. "No? Okay, we're finished. Emma, please let me know if anyone has any concerns when you drop off their checks."

"I will," she promised.

As the meeting was coming to a close, a knock sounded at the door. Emma looked up to see Tony coming in through the back door. "Good morning, everyone," he said cheerfully. He leaned in and kissed Emma on the cheek. She turned a deep red.

"Morning, Tony," said Emma softly and gazed into his eyes. He gazed back until Tim cleared his throat loudly.

"Hope I'm not interrupting anything," Tim said wryly.

"No," said Tony with a smile. "Nothing I can't do later." He was there to walk Emma to work—or rather, have Emma walk him to the trolley.

Emma gathered up her hat and bag and got organized to leave. "Don't forget to come by for the checks, Emma," called Tim as she was leaving through the kitchen door.

"I'll be here," she promised and they departed the house.

As they were walking, Tony pushed Emma's bike for her. He looked over and said, "Emma, I wanted to tell you about someone that comes to the museum."

"Yes?" she commented, listening.

"He comes and goes each day at the same time."

"Do you think he's casing the museum, planning a robbery?" Her mind was already working on ways to catch this unnamed person.

"No, no, I don't think so." Knowing where her mind was wandering, he said quickly, "His only interest is the photo exhibit."

"Yes, I know that one, the London scenes are very interesting, He has no interest in the other exhibits?" she asked, curious where this was going.

"Never. He comes in and just stares at the pictures in that one exhibit. I think he also carries a camera." He hesitated briefly, then said, "I think he might be one of the specialists you're looking for."

"Really? Photography?" she said. *It's a relatively new field,* she thought to herself. *It might be interesting. The skill would be important because only professional photographers can operate cameras and develop pictures.*

She directed her next question to Tony, "What are your thoughts? For me to learn the skill from him?" That was how the specialists were usually utilized, as more of a supportive role rather than an actual part of the group. They were usually brought in specifically to teach Emma a new skill.

"No," he said a bit slowly. "I was thinking about your idea to develop new specialists with a hands-on role." He smiled and stated in a wry voice, "That is if he actually takes pictures and doesn't just carry a camera around."

"Probably a good idea to check first," teased Emma, bumping him with her hip. "We have been keeping the rooms at the boarding house opened," she mused. "It would be a good resource for new investigations." She turned the idea over in her head, realizing a camera would make it easier to retrieve evidence. "Hmm. Do you want me to talk to him?"

"Not yet. Let me approach him first."

When they got to their stop, Tony turned to her. "Where are you today?" he asked, leaning down to press his forehead against hers.

"Still at the business office," she murmured.

"I have some items that should be sent out today if you want to stop by later," Tony said, lifting his head. Emma had several clients near the museum that she moved around documents for. The city was still growing and paperwork had to be moved from engineers to city officials, suppliers, and customers.

She leaned in closer and said, "I'll come by after I pick up the checks from Tim. I have a few to drop off in that area."

He lowered his head to give her a lingering kiss and said, "See you later." He ran off to jump on the trolley, giving her a final wave.

She waved back, hopped on her bike, and rode off to her office job. Emma had been at her current assignment for a few months, which was unusual for a temporary job, but people were needed. As she pedaled on, the wind wove through her hair, pulling at her hairpins. Her papa had gotten her a Kangaroo dwarf safety bike developed by Hillman, Herbert, and Cooper. He had a contact who allowed Emma to get a model early and she used it to get to and from work; it was most useful for her work as a courier. The bike made riding quite easy.

Emma worked in an office building downtown. It was a bit of a ride but allowed her to see the city before many people were out and about. Slowing the bike as she arrived at the office. She hopped off and placed it on her shoulder to carry as she entered the building. The first thing she had to do was store it in a closet downstairs. After she locked the door, she moved upstairs to begin her day.

CHAPTER 14

JAKE

Tony was walking through the museum, inspecting the displays and taking notes on any changes that might be needed. He was also keeping a tally of the numbers of people attending the different exhibits. That number would help determine when the exhibits should be moved or replaced.

One of the exhibits, where that tally continued to be high, was the photography exhibit. It contained a large number of pictures featuring everyday life in London, England. The curator had a contact overseas who found art subjects suitable for display in the museum. Tony continued to refine his skills there and, in addition to management, was also learning how to evaluate art.

Tony continued his survey and entered the London exhibit. Their regular visitor was already there, having come every day since the exhibit opened. He always carried a camera that he held protectively against his chest. Tony had previously told the temporary security staff to keep an eye on him. They had reported that he would come in at the same time every day, viewed the same exhibit, and then left at the same time. He never deviated from this routine.

Tony decided to approach the man and find out if he could

actually use that camera. As he got closer, he was able to get a clear view of the visitor. He was a young man, slim, in his twenties, with copper-colored hair. The brown suit he wore was always a bit wrinkled and tattered but appeared to be clean. The photos seemed to fully occupy his time and Tony noticed he also seemed to be talking to himself.

Tony approached him quietly and said, "Excuse me." The young man didn't seem to hear him and didn't look over. Tony started again and tapped his shoulder.

This time, the young man shifted his intense look away from the photographs. He looked over for a moment and then returned to staring at the display.

Tony took the initiative and said, putting his hand out toward him, "I'm Tony Marella and I work here at the museum." The young man didn't shake his hand but instead kept looking at the photographs. Tony slowly let his arm drop, realizing his gesture was not going to be accepted. He wondered if he should have had Emma talk to him. He decided to try once again and reached out to touch his sleeve while saying, "What's your name?"

Without glancing over, the man said, "Jake."

Since Jake had finally said something, Tony thought he should push his luck. "Do you like the photos, Jake?"

That seemed to be the key to getting him to talk. He started seemingly in the middle of a conversation. "If you notice the light on these and how the camera was able to capture the different angles. . ." He kept talking about the photos for more than thirty minutes.

Tony realized he hadn't spoken a word since asking Jake about the exhibit. *There had to be a way out of this conversation. How did I get his attention previously?* He reached out to touch Jake's arm and said, "Jake?" Jake immediately stopped talking and looked away from the photos. "I have to get back to work," he told him gently.

Jake nodded and turned back to look at the pictures while

Tony continued his review of other exhibits. Later, as Tony moved on to other things, he realized Jake had gone for the day.

This went on for the next few days. Jake would come in at the same time and Tony would approach him after he'd been there for thirty minutes. He learned that Jake worked as a photographer for the police department in forensics. Tony would need to ask Emma what a photographer in forensics did. "Jake, can you bring in some of your pictures for me to view?" he inquired.

"Okay," he said, happy someone was interested in his favorite topic. "I can bring them in tomorrow."

CHAPTER 15

*D*inner time had rolled around; Tony routinely stayed after to socialize and discuss any cases that might be ongoing. *This was the right time to bring up Jake as a possible specialist,* thought Tony. He described their first meetings to the group and then his focus on photography. Looking over at Emma, he said, "He mentioned he works as a photographer for the police. I think he called it forensics. Do you know what that is?"

Emma looked serious when she answered, "Forensics involves police photographers who are forensic scientists who, like medical examiners, biologists, and chemists, develop and document evidence to help law enforcement solve crimes. After the records are gathered, they can be used to prosecute criminal cases. As cameras are improved upon, I expect they are being used more and more in the field."

"You're saying he has pictures of bodies and such?" That gave Tony a moment of pause. He groaned and said, "Oh, good grief, I asked him to bring in a sample of his work for me to view."

The group sat silently and let that statement sink in for a moment. Then they all laughed. Tim said, "I guess you'll definitely see his work."

"Yes." Tony looked over at Emma and said a bit pleadingly, "Can you come tomorrow and be with me while I take a look at his photographs?"

Emma paused just long enough to worry him and then said, "Of course I'll be there." She reached over to hug him. "And I would like to evaluate him for a specialist position."

Dora asked, "It will be like an interview?"

"More of a pre-interview," Emma quantified.

CHAPTER 16

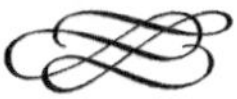

The next day, Tony glanced at his watch and realized it was Jake's normal time to visit the museum. At that moment, he saw him enter the main door with a large box, which Tony could only assume was full of pictures. He looked at his watch and smiled. *Right on time.* The guards stopped Jake at the door to evaluate the large box. Jake grew visibly upset over them trying to take it from him. "Stop, it's mine!" He wouldn't release it to them.

Before the situation could worsen, Tony stepped in and said to the guards, "It's all right. Jake is here to see me." The guards stopped their tug-of-war with Jake and nodded at Tony. Jake looked relieved as he took his box and started to follow him to his office. Tony hesitated and turned back toward the guards saying, "Let Emma know my location when she gets here." They nodded in agreement.

They continued to the office. Once they entered, Tony gestured to Jake to place the box on the desk. He was curious about the types of photographs he had brought with him. *Will it be the forensic ones? Can I stomach looking at them?* he thought, wishing Emma was there with him.

As Jake pulled the pictures out of the box and organized them into stacks, Tony braced himself for the worst. Jake looked over and said, "Come see." Tony moved over to the desk and hesitantly picked up the first picture in a pile. He was pleasantly surprised; one pile involved up-close pictures of people. None of these were posed pictures, which is how most pictures were taken during this time period. Another stack contained nature pictures: trees, grass, and flowers. A final stack involved close-ups of different types of objects: eyeglasses, grass, and carpet patterns. Tony was impressed; these were as good as those on exhibit.

He laughed suddenly and Jake gave him an intense look. Tony realized Jake thought he was laughing at his pictures. "Jake, I'm not laughing at you, I promise. I thought these might be forensic pictures and I was nervous to see them."

"Those are never to be shared outside of work. It is not allowed," he stated in a stern voice. He seemed to be mimicking another person, probably a supervisor.

Tony said gently, "Jake, you're right, I should have known better."

He nodded in agreement.

Tony continued, "You really know how to use that camera."

Jake looked unsure and answered literally. "Yes, I was trained in England on the use of it."

Tony smiled, realizing he needed to be clearer. "Do you sell your work?"

"No, I just take the pictures. The ones at work stay at work. I can't sell those."

"No, no, I wouldn't think so," he murmured, still looking at the pictures. "Do you have a lab at work?"

"Yes."

"Do you have one at home?"

"No, too small; smells too bad." Again, Jake sounded like he was quoting someone.

At that moment, Emma came in through the office door in her

normal rushed manner. "I see you made it on time," commented Tony wryly over his shoulder.

She came up and hugged him from behind and said, "Got stuck at work."

Jake didn't look up from his pictures; he just let the conversation go on around him. Tony reached out and touched Jake's arm and said, "Jake." This action caused him to look up. "Jake, this is Emma. She also wants to see your pictures."

Jake immediately took an interest in Emma and said eagerly, "You like my pictures?"

"Well," said Emma cautiously, "I haven't seen them yet, but I am excited about being able to view them."

Tony and Emma poured over the photos, asking Jake questions about the locations and the items.

"Do you take these with that camera you carry around?" Emma asked.

"Yes, it is a Twin lens reflex camera from the Marion & Co. Academy. It was developed and sold in London. I was lucky to get one."

Emma continued flipping through the pictures and asked without looking up, "Can we keep these for a few days?"

Jake was very hesitant to let them out of his possession and said, "Well, I am not sure."

She looked up at Jake and said in a firm voice, "Jake, we will keep a close eye on them. We want to evaluate these further."

"All right then," he said a bit begrudgingly.

Emma thought quickly. "We would love for you to come to our boarding house for dinner, tomorrow night."

"Dinner? What time? I eat at 6pm."

Emma wiped a hand over her mouth to hide her smile. "Well 6pm is a bit early, but if you come then, we will be close to dinner."

He looked conflicted at the idea and did not seem to be able to decide without some prodding. Tony took the lead and said, "What time do you get off work tomorrow?"

"5pm. I always get off at 5pm, unless there is an investigation and then I have to work late," he stated in a business-like tone.

"We'll worry about that if it comes up. For now, let's plan on me picking you up from your work tomorrow." Jake frowned and Tony immediately understood the issue.

"Jake, is your hesitation because it's a change to your schedule? If it is, I think you'll enjoy having dinner at the house,"

Jake had focused back on his photos and said, "I can wait for you at my job."

Tony smiled and said, "Okay, where can I meet you?"

"I will be in the basement of the police station."

"I'll be there at 5pm and will take you to meet my friends and have dinner," said Tony. He could already tell he was dismissed as Jake started organizing the pictures in front of him. "Jake, I'll do that if you want to head back to work."

Jake noticed the time and said, "I just have time to view the exhibit before I leave."

"Thanks for bringing these in for us to see," said Emma in a sincere manner. Jake nodded and headed out to the exhibit. Tony knew he would be back on his schedule and back to work on time.

He walked over to the desk where Emma continued to look at the photographs in wonder. "He is an amazing photographer," she said, thinking of how this new technology could be applied to her investigations.

"Yes. What do you think about Jake becoming one of your specialists?" he asked.

"I think I like the idea," she said with a smile. "Let's see what the family thinks." She laid down the pictures, kissed him, and headed out to finish her afternoon jobs.

CHAPTER 17

That night after dinner, the group inspected Jake's pictures and discussed his skills. "I think Jake's skills would benefit us," said Emma. "I have a few jobs he would be helpful on."

"Also," commented Tony, "I think we would be good for Jake."

"What are you thinking, Tony?" Dora inquired softly. "What type of help could we provide him?"

"I think we could help him socially; he doesn't understand social cues at all. He also tends to only talk about what he's interested in." He looked over at Emma and asked, "Did you notice he doesn't make eye contact?"

"I did," she responded. "Do you think it's something we could help with?"

"Yes, in the short time I've been talking to him, I see that interaction with me has made him open up. He also tends to speak very little except about photography." Tony warned, "We need to not overwhelm him when he gets here. If we want to get to know him, we'll have to draw him out."

"A small group dinner, here in the kitchen?" suggested Dora, thinking about how to best meet Jake for the first time.

"Yes, we can help you with getting the boarders fed. Tony can bring Jake in through the kitchen and avoid some of the noise," suggested Emma.

Everyone agreed on the plan.

The next night, the kitchen was quiet with just Amy and Dora working on dinner when Tony knocked on the kitchen door. Dora wiped her hands on her apron and let them in.

"Hey, Tony," she said as he leaned down to kiss her on the cheek. "Who do we have here?" Dora asked, turning her gaze on Jake. She noticed right away that he did not make eye contact with her.

"This is Jake."

"Welcome, Jake. I'm Dora and this is Amy." Amy nodded over her shoulder at him from the stove. "As you can tell, dinner is almost ready. Would you like to sit at the kitchen table and have some bread and butter?"

Jake looked at Tony, then at Dora, and said in a somewhat monotone voice, "Yes, please."

"Have a seat," Dora said and indicated the kitchen table. They sat and watched while dinner was completed. When platters started being pulled out, Tony jumped up to help load them. "We will move these into the dining room and then we'll start our dinner in here after that. Okay?" she asked Jake.

He nodded. He had been told they would eat in the kitchen, so he stayed put.

"Tony, could you call Emma and Tim? They're in the study," requested Dora.

"Sure," he said as he went off to get them.

The boarders were at the table talking about their day and enjoying the food. The family had told them there would be a guest eating in the kitchen.

The family sat with Jake at the kitchen table to eat dinner. Once the food had been consumed and cleared away, Emma and

Dora handed out pie to everyone. Tim decided to ask Jake some questions. "Jake, where do you live? Do you live on your own?"

Jake looked up from his pie and answered, "I live two blocks east of the station and two turns off the main road."

Tim frowned. He knew that area. "Jake, those are very nice houses. Are you sure that's where you live?"

"Yes," stated Jake.

"Do you live with your parents?"

"No, they died," he said simply.

"Oh, Jake, we're sorry," said Dora, immediately feeling for the young man. "Was it long ago?"

"Mom passed about ten years ago and Dad about a year ago. I was in London and then I was allowed to come back home," he commented, looking around.

Emma wondered at the expression and asked, "Did someone tell you that you couldn't come home?"

"Yes. Dad said I was just a nuisance since Mom died and he had no time for me. I came home after he died."

"What were your parents' names? We might know them," she pointed out. Tim, Tony, and Emma had worked delivering to that neighborhood.

"Martha and Daniel Cooper," he stated.

Emma looked sharply at Tony. She had known Daniel lived in that area but had not considered him having a family. She followed up with a question and hoped they were wrong, "Jake, did your dad work at the paper?"

"Yes," he said absently, unaware of the turmoil he was causing. "He was the editor."

Tony looked as shocked as Emma felt. She stood in an agitated manner and indicated for Tony to follow her. Once in the dining room, he said in a low voice, "We should probably talk about this outside."

She nodded and accompanied him out to the front stoop.

Once there she sat heavily on the first step, looked up at him, and said, "Tony! Good grief, what now?"

"Emma, I honestly had no idea," he said, throwing up his hands.

"I know, I know, but what do we do? Do we tell him I killed his father?" she asked, bewildered.

"I'm not sure what he knows since Pinkerton and the police chief kept your name out of it," commented Tony.

"But is it right? To not let him know?" She paused a moment. "I don't regret my actions, but I regret that he's alone now." She put her head in her hands. "Before we consider him as a specialist, I think we should have Pinkerton do a background check and confirm who his parents are—or were."

"Agreed," Tony said.

They went back in and found Dora and Tim talking at length with Jake about his job. They seemed to genuinely like him.

"Jake, let's get you home," Tony said.

Jake nodded and stood up to leave.

Dora stood also and approached him. She touched his arm, and said, "We would like to see you again."

"Can I come over tomorrow?" he asked quickly.

That caused Dora to laugh out loud. It was hard not to like him. "Well, let's wait a few days," she commented with a smile.

"So, Thursday," he said, taking everything literally.

"Yes," she said, giving in. "Thursday for dinner. Tony, can you pick him up again at work?"

Tony nodded and sent a worried look to Emma. She nodded it was all right. "We'll be going then," he said to Jake and the group.

Jake spoke up at that time and said, "Nice to meet you Tim, Dora, and Emma."

"You, too," they said almost simultaneously and laughed. Jake smiled back in response before following Tony out.

"Wow," Tim started, "is he Daniel's son?" Dora shook her head in response.

"I just don't know." Emma sat back at the table, looking down at her hands. She looked up at Tim and Dora and said, "I'll send a note over to Cole and ask him to look into this for us. I think until we hear more, we don't offer him a specialist position."

"Yes," Dora said. "I understand we have to wait to confirm his identity, but the main question is what will we do if he is Daniel's son?" Emma pondered that for a moment and Dora gently prodded her. "Emma, can you work with someone related to Daniel?"

She frowned. "If there's a connection, we'll have to see. I'm going to get the note written and over to Cole." That was not something she was ready to face until she had to.

Emma went upstairs and wrote out a detailed note to Cole about Jake, mentioning she would like to stop by after lunch tomorrow to discuss any findings.

CHAPTER 18

The next morning was slow to come around, as Emma spent most of the night thinking about Jake and Daniel. She kept dwelling on the question, *Can I work with Jake knowing that I killed his father?* She tried to push the thought out of her head until she spoke to Cole.

The clocked tinged seven times, it was time for breakfast. She went downstairs the next morning to help and have her regular morning business meeting with Dora and Tim. Breakfast was served and their morning meeting was completed just as Tony knocked at the kitchen door. He was waved in by Emma. A knock on the front door interrupted his good morning greetings. "I'll go check the front door," Tim offered, exiting the kitchen.

Dora caught Tony before they departed and asked, "How was Jake last night when you took him home?"

Tony shrugged. "He was Jake. He talked about different types of cameras and exposures the whole way."

"Did he live where he said he did?" she asked, worried about the young man living alone.

"Yes, it was exactly where he said it was. Staff met him at the door. In my opinion, they weren't very nice to him and they didn't like me dropping him off."

"Do you think he's okay there?" Dora asked worriedly.

"For now, but I think we should look into it," he said, also concerned that it was not the best place for Jake to live.

"I already asked Cole for further information on his background and his current home," commented Emma, still not sure how she felt about Jake being in their lives.

"Good," said Tony. "Ready to go?"

Tim came in from answering the front door with an envelope in his hand. "Emma, this came for you," he said and handed it to her.

Emma opened it and read aloud. "Have data you requested. Please come by at the requested time. Signed Cole." She looked to the group and said, "I'll follow up with Cole and we can meet tonight to discuss how we would like to move forward. Agreed?" The three nodded, and Tony and Emma headed out for the day.

Tony didn't feel the need to discuss Jake on their way to work. Instead, he tried to steal kisses from Emma as they walked. She didn't put up much of a fight, she enjoyed the attention.

Thoughts of Jake pushed their way to the front of her mind as Tony kissed her goodbye. He noticed her preoccupation and said, "You're quiet and look a bit tired." He traced the dark circles under her eyes with the tips of his fingers. "Are you all right?" he asked, worried.

She laid her head against his chest for a moment, then tilted it up to look at him. "I'm okay. I just need some time and information before I can make a decision."

He nodded, knowing she would consider everything. He leaned in and kissed her quickly. "Promise me you'll come to see me later if you want to talk."

"I promise," she said as she stepped back and took her bike from him. "You're about to miss your ride." He looked over his shoulder, panicked, and started to run toward it. She waved at him as he ran to catch the trolley and laughed when he almost tripped trying to run and look back at her at the same time.

Her current job was located 10-12 blocks from the trolly. She biked over to her current job location and pulled to a stop in the front of the building. The smile she had from watching Tony earlier, lingered on her face.

A boy's voice called, pulling Emma out of her musings. "Emma!" a young boy of about ten ran up to her. She recognized him immediately as Henry, her coworker Lauri's younger brother. A quick observation took in his clothes as cheap but clean, his face and hands washed, and his brown hair unruly. "Emma, I need to talk to you," he said in a rushed tone.

Emma paused, getting ready to lift her bike on her shoulder, and said, "Hey, Henry. What are you doing here? Where's Lauri?" Lauri had begun her position at the office as one of their temp employees and was now a permanent employee of the Baker Building Co.

"Lauri is running late; Ma needed her this morning. She's hoping you can cover for her," he continued.

Emma looked pensive at the idea and said slowly, "Okay, I will, but tell her to hurry." She continued to frown as she watched him run off. Emma knew she could do the work, but her concern about covering for Lauri was that their jobs at the office were kept separate, with no two people working on the same project or material.

The position Emma held at Baker had been on and off for the past six months. The office manager, Mr. Tracy, was very picky about who worked on what projects and didn't encourage socialization between the employees—particularly the female employees. Discussions over projects were only to be undertaken with team leads but not individually by the administrative staff.

Taking her bike into the building, she stored it in the closet before heading to the second floor to start her day. Once in the office, she changed into a more appropriate outfit, replacing her split skirt with a longer one. She folded the skirt and put it away in a bag she kept under her desk.

Emma stood from her chair and headed to Lauri's desk to pull her daily folder. Lauri liked to have her work prepared for the day; Emma was thankful for that. There were several bills to type and file. The work was to have been completed when Lauri first got there.

Jobs for women, especially permanent ones, could be hard to come by and Lauri's mom and brother depended on her income. Emma wanted Lauri to keep her job, so she would cover for her. She started reviewing the invoices in Lauri's file and noticed they were different from the ones she handled. These were the customer invoices and Emma handled were from the vendors.

The numbers seem a bit odd, Emma thought, realizing they were different from the ones on her invoice from this company. "Stop with the observations. I have to get her typing done first," she muttered to herself. Emma sat down at her desk and went to work on the paperwork. She was a fast typist and finished Lauri's work in a short time.

Is there time? she wondered and glanced at the clock. Fifteen minutes was all she had to evaluate the customer/vendor invoices. She pulled her file and found the same invoices to the vendor and compared the two. The invoices indicated the amount of structural steel, cement, and sand. Laying them side by side she saw there was something wrong between the customers' and vendors' numbers for steel and concrete components.

Feet could be heard echoing on the stairs as someone ascended to the second floor. There was just enough time for her to put the completed work into the file and replace it on Lauri's desk. *I'll have to reason out any discrepancies at another time.*

She moved back to her desk as the door opened, revealing the office manager, Mr. Tracy. His hair was combed over, greased and glistening in the morning light. His suit was too tight on his skinny frame.

Emma had pulled her file out and was inserting paper into the typewriter as he walked past. He didn't say a word as he entered his office, barely glancing her way. The management staff treated the women as furniture, a necessary function but not important enough to acknowledge.

Baker was one of the first offices to allow women, even in a temporary capacity, to begin working in full-time jobs, an opportunity occurring due to the shortage of male typists. The men working in Chicago could make more money in the booming construction industry.

As he retreated to his office, Emma pulled out her notebook and documented the discrepancies she had seen and follow-up questions. She slipped it into her skirt pocket and got back to work. If the notebook was found by anyone other than her, it could not be read. It was written in a modified Pitman shorthand, something she learned in business school and adapted.

Emma heard more people arriving and kept her head down, working on her typing. The women murmured, "Hello," as they entered and the men shuffled quietly to their offices. She was transferring her completed work into individual files when Mr. Tracy stuck his head out of his office and said, "Miss Evans, has Miss Taylor been in yet this morning?"

"Oh, yes, sir. She was here before me and mentioned she completed her morning typing. She stepped out for a few moments but said she would be back soon." That seemed to mollify him and he pulled his head back into his office.

Luckily, Lauri came in about that time. Her eyes darted to Emma, who gave a slight nod.

Mr. Tracy heard her come in and stepped out of his office. "Where have you been, Miss Taylor?"

"Here, Mr. Tracy. I went downstairs to check on today's bills and when they will be sent out in the mail," she replied innocently.

Good cover, thought Emma.

Mr. Tracy frowned but nodded and went back into his office.

Lauri reached behind her and brought out a bag containing her jacket and lunch. She slipped it under her desk as she sat down. She mouthed a silent *Thank you* to Emma.

Emma winked back, indicating it was okay.

Everyone settled in for the day's work and the sound of type-writer covers being removed and the click-clack of typing filled the office. While she continued to type, Emma thought about the possible discrepancies in the paperwork.

In Chicago, the soil was wet and unstable, and the best support was structural steel and well-mixed cement. It was only two invoices, so it could have been a localized mistake. The trouble was, she was never supposed to see them next to each other. There was no way to tell her office manager that there might be a problem without disclosing that she'd seen something she wasn't supposed to see.

The possible discrepancies would need to be investigated, but she was hesitant to involve Lauri because of her family situation. She would have to do this on her own and secretively determine if this was a one-time mistake or indicative of a more intricate criminal activity.

Her work was completed and Emma got ready to leave at noon. The last thing she had to do was file her work and set up her desk for the next day. As she covered her typewriter, she quietly got ready to leave and stepped away to the lavatory to change into her split skirt. She pulled out her notebook and detailed her concerns for the day.

The papers, I need more time to evaluate them. There was an ability to make copies, but that would require the hectograph, gelatin duplicator, or jellygraph. The printing process involved a transfer of an original, prepared with special inks, to a pan of gelatin or a gelatin pad pulled tight on a metal frame. It would also require her to take the papers from the office, and that was something she didn't want to do. The only viable alternative was a camera. It was becoming apparent that, regardless of Jake's parentage, she would need him on the team. His skills would give them the ability to grow. *Jake would come in handy as a specialist in this situation. Pluses and minuses,* she thought ruefully.

She nodded her goodbyes to her friends and stepped out with her bag, heading to the Pinkerton office to meet with Cole.

CHAPTER 19

Emma arrived at the Pinkerton offices and hopped off her bike. Taking a moment before heading in, she admitted her hesitancy in determining the truth about Jake's parentage. Maybe she should just go home and tell them she didn't want him as a specialist. She started to turn and do that.

She stopped and thought, *No, you have to find out and make a decision based on the facts, not emotion.* Straightening her shoulders, she picked up her bike and put it on her shoulder to carry it up the stoop. When she reached the doors, one of the agents recognized her and ran over to help.

"Emma, you should tell us when you get here so we can help," he scolded.

Emma said simply, "No reason I can't do it myself."

He just shook his head as he took the bike from her. "I'll keep this here; Mr. Tilden is waiting for you."

She nodded, distracted by her thoughts, and said, "Thanks for the help." Heading back to Cole's office, she knocked and heard him call, "Come in."

When Cole saw her in the doorway, he said, "Emma, come in and sit down." He walked around his desk toward her in an unhurried manner. He was in the typical Pinkerton black suit, black tie, and white shirt. He indicated the chair in front of the desk and he took the one opposite to hers.

"Did you find anything?" she asked once she'd sat down, committed to hearing the news, good or bad.

"I didn't have to look far," he said as he tapped the thick file on the corner of his desk. "We did a background check on Daniel's family after he passed away. Jake is Daniel's son." He could see she had questions, but he held up a hand to stop her. "Jake hasn't lived with Daniel since he was about ten. He didn't have much patience with the boy and, after the mother died, he had shipped him off to boarding schools in England. Judging by the timing of the move and the distance to his school, we think he blamed Jake for his mother's death."

"But why?" she asked, astonished a ten-year-old boy would've been sent from his home and family.

"There was a fire, I know," he said, seeing her expression. "Another fire. Jake's mother was asleep in the living room and died of smoke inhalation."

"Was Jake home?"

"He was," he acknowledged, "but the statements given by the maid detail that he was in his room when she left the house."

"Could they determine where the fire started?"

"The chemicals in the basement," he said simply. "Someone or something knocked over several chemicals near a lit burner."

"Someone?"

"The maid indicated that Jake was always very careful with them and wouldn't leave a hazardous environment. The basement filled with smoke and covered the first floor."

"Where was the maid? Why didn't she wake up Jake's mom?"

"She had been given the afternoon off."

"Who arranged that?"

"The maid said the request came from the mom."

"But what about Jake? How did he survive?"

"As I understand it, he climbed out of his window and jumped down."

"Was he hurt?"

"Broken leg."

"Poor little boy." Emma sat silent for a moment, then asked, "Are we sure Daniel didn't set the fire himself and kill her?"

Cole shook his head and said, "He was in New York at the time and we have confirmation from several people who were there. "

"So, someone did this. Do you think it was related to his illegal activities?"

"Yes, it's probably related."

She pondered that. "Cole, I was wondering. . . is there something wrong with Jake?"

"Wrong?" he asked, looking a bit puzzled. "I understand he can be a bit absentminded."

"No, it is more than that. He doesn't make eye contact; he talks about certain topics all the time and seems to have a timing issue."

"Timing?"

"Yes, he wants to be on a set schedule all the time."

"No, I can't say I know anything about that, except the police indicated he's very professional at work."

Emma let the topic go and asked, "Cole, we have been thinking about making him one of our specialists."

"I do have notes that he is a gifted photographer."

"Yes, I'm just not sure how to explain to him what happened to his father."

"Emma, it's not necessary for you to explain anything."

"But I killed Daniel," she said starkly.

Cole acknowledged that comment with a nod of his head. "Yes. But no one knows that outside of the police chief and this office. Is it fair to limit his opportunities based on who his father was?"

She hadn't thought about it that way. "You're right. Okay, we'll give him a chance."

"Also, Emma, he's very alone. He's in that big house of Daniel's with no family."

"We'd wondered about that. Tony mentioned the staff is quite cold to him. Dora has already been thinking of having him move into the boarding house."

"That would be a good thing for him," he acknowledged.

"His talent with the camera will be a huge benefit to us." With that comment, she closed her notebook and stood, prepared to leave.

"Emma," Cole said, delaying her exit. "I have a second thing to discuss with you." She sat back down and waited as he reached for another folder on his desk. "It's about the shelter Clair runs." Emma was startled at the topic but listened intently.

"We've had some information that someone is selling the location of the safe house to one of the abusive husbands."

She gasped in shock and asked, "Which one?"

"It appears to be Alison's," he commented. "The note was anonymous but it did give her name and shared that they were concerned for her safety. Have you had any trouble moving the ladies lately?"

"No, but we haven't moved anyone in a few months. We have three ladies in the house, but only one who is probably going to want to move."

"Which one?" he asked.

"Alison," she admitted.

"What about the help?"

"No one new."

Cole had been contributing Pinkerton's services for background checks on personnel wanting to work there. They didn't put anyone in the safe house without a cleared background.

"Has anyone been hanging around who shouldn't be? Deliveries showing up that haven't been ordered. Anything unusual?"

"I'm not sure," she admitted.

"We'll have to check them out."

Emma sat stunned for a minute, then asked, "Do we need to move the women to another safe house?"

"No, but we do need to find out who's selling their location. If there are any moves scheduled before we find out, contact me immediately. Also, I'll have agents do some reconnaissance to see if anything stands out. Don't worry," he said when he saw her expression, "we'll keep a low profile."

"You've given me plenty to think about," she said wryly. "Let me get with the team and evaluate our options for interviewing the women."

"I'll let you know if we find out anything."

She nodded and said, "Thanks, Cole. Tell Jeremy hello for me." She left the office and paused just outside his door and laughed suddenly. "Life is never boring."

CHAPTER 20

At the boarding house that night, dinner had been cleared and residents had moved to the sitting room to relax. Tim, Dora, and Tony sat around the kitchen table at Emma's request. Amy had completed her duties and headed home with a cheerful, "Goodbye."

They all looked at Emma to begin. She paused a moment and then said, "I'm sitting here wondering what to discuss first." Coming to a decision, she started again, placing her hand on Dora's. "I'll begin with Jake since I know he's on your mind."

"He is Daniel's son," Dora guessed, not sure she wanted the answer.

"Yes," stated Emma with no expression in her voice.

As Dora took a breath, Tony and Tim looked at one another. Dora withdrew her hand from Emma's and inquired, "Well, what does that mean? We can't like him or have him live here?" Her tone hardened a bit as she continued, "Emma, you need to face what you did to Daniel and that boy." Emma looked hurt at Dora's tone. Dora's voice softened as she continued, "I don't mean for you to tell him. I don't think he would understand the circumstance—"

Tony interrupted, "Not understand? He's a forensic photographer and is on crime scenes all the time."

"Yes, but this involves an emotional element; at least, we think it might. I just don't think he would understand the circumstances," Dora explained.

"Emma, it comes down to this: can you work with him or not?" Tony asked.

Emma sat pensively for a moment and then broke out in laughter. They looked at her like she had lost her mind. Emma said, with a laugh still in her voice, "We've been so worried about if he should live here that we haven't bothered to ask Jake if he wants to live here and work with us."

The group realized what she was saying and soon the room was filled with laughter.

Tony sobered and said, "Emma?"

She knew what he was asking and responded, "This isn't about me or my feelings. I think my only hesitancy is that someday he might find out and not trust us."

Tim said, "I don't see how he could. The Pinkertons kept it quiet and even the police changed the reports."

"Should we just tell him?" Emma asked.

Dora, feeling protective of Jake, said, "I would like him to get to know us. Also, knowing he's so alone, I'd like to have him here. We could give him something Daniel couldn't or wouldn't. A family."

Tim said in a conciliatory tone, "Let's have him over for dinner this week and approach him about moving into the house as well as helping with future investigations. Is that acceptable to everyone?" They all nodded.

"What's our next topic, Emma?" asked Dora, catching how she had closed the notebook containing Jake's information and opened another.

"It relates to Jake being a specialist on our team." She started to explain the possible discrepancies she'd found on the two sets of invoices at the Baker job.

"That doesn't sound like much to go on," said Tony.

Emma nodded. "Agreed. I need to get a look at more accounts to help me determine if this one is a mistake or an ongoing conspiracy. The other thing that bothers me is that the shortages are on the orders and not on the invoices to the customers."

Tim asked, "How do you plan to move forward on this?" He was worried it might affect their contracts with Baker.

"Jake," she said simply. "I need to discuss using a camera to record the data. Any other way, I would have to take the paperwork out of the office, and I don't want to do that."

Tony said, "If Jake accepts, we can review this with him. Is there any reason we can't take our time with this case?"

"I don't think so. Most of our buildings are in the planning stages," Emma commented.

"Okay, so we wait for Jake on that one?" asked Tim.

She nodded.

Tim cleared his throat and said, "Emma, please let me know before you do anything that could jeopardize our contracts. We have people relying on Baker for a paycheck."

"I understand and I promise to check in with my partners," she glanced at Dora and Tim, "prior to doing anything other than investigating."

Tim seemed satisfied with this response. "Thanks, Emma."

"Was there anything else?" asked Tony, glancing at his watch. Time was going by quickly tonight.

"Well, I have another topic, if everyone can stay a while longer?" Emma asked. She looked around the table for confirmation. When she received a nod from each, she opened her next notebook and started describing her conversation with Cole about Clair's safe house. "He indicated there has been an anonymous report that the location of the house is for sale. Alison is listed as the person of interest."

The room went silent. The safe house was a place battered women took shelter to heal. They stayed for different lengths of time before they decided on where or not to move or stay. If they stayed, they would be entering school or looking for a job. "I was thinking of going to the shelter and interviewing the longer-term residents," Emma said.

"Are you thinking one of the women at the house is involved?" asked Tony.

"Yes, it just feels like an inside person is providing the information."

"Emma, I would like to go with you," said Dora, calmly but firmly.

That statement surprised Tim. "Dora. . ." He started, concerned about her being involved in the business at the house.

"Tim," she said, squeezing his hand and looking deep into his eyes. "I want to see it for myself. I also want to see if there's some additional support I can offer."

"All right," he said, accepting her decision, knowing he could deny her nothing. "How are we going to get you both there safely?"

A knock sounded on the kitchen door from the dining room. "Just a minute." Emma opened the door and saw it was Thomas. "Come in," she indicated.

"I asked Thomas to see us when he got home," she explained. She gave him a quick recap of the activities involved with the shelter.

"I have some ideas on that," Thomas said. "I have been making deliveries in the area for Clair." His face went red at this statement.

Dora looked at Emma questioningly. Emma shrugged at the silent question.

He continued. "Emma and Dora would go unnoticed in my wagon. We could have them lie in the back under a blanket."

That could work. "Dora, we could make some pastries to take over for them," Emma suggested.

"That would be nice, it would be more like a visit than an interrogation," said Dora.

The group pulled together their plans and decided they needed to act the next day. Emma would get a note to Clair to set up a meeting. "I'll firm up the plans in the morning."

"Given we have this scheduled for tomorrow night, let's ask Jake about moving in this weekend," suggested Tim.

"Agreed. But, Tony, could you let Jake know he is welcomed to dinner anytime? In addition, let him know we have a special dinner for him to attend on Saturday night," said Dora.

While Dora was arranging Tony and Jake, Emma was writing out the note for Clair. She signed and folded it before giving it to Thomas to deliver that night. "You don't mind?" she asked him. "I could get Jeremy to deliver it."

"No, no," he said a bit hastily as he took it from her.

She looked at him curiously but didn't say anything.

He said, "I'll wait for a response."

"Thank you, Thomas," Emma said gratefully.

He nodded and headed out.

Emma walked slowly into the kitchen where Tony, Dora, and Tim were talking quietly. "The note is off."

"What was up with Thomas?" asked Tony.

"I'm not sure," she said with a shrug. "He hasn't mentioned anything, but he did color a bit when Clair's name came up."

"I don't think we should be talking about this," said Dora.

"You're right. It's their business, not ours," commented Emma.

"Yes," they all agreed.

"Tim, I am heading up to bed," commented Dora.

Tim realized what she said and jumped up. "Oh! I am a bit tired," he said eagerly and grabbed her hand to rush her upstairs.

Dora paused on the stairs and called down, "Emma, I need you up early to make the pastries for tomorrow evening,"

Emma called back, "Okay. I'll be up early with you. I'm going to walk Tony out now." She reached out her hand to him. He took it, and they walked to the back door and outside. He'd had enough conversation and pulled her close for a long, sweet kiss. She was shaking a bit when he raised his head. He glanced down at her, wishing they could go to their own room in the boarding house. Pressing his forehead on hers, he said, "I'll see you tomorrow."

"Yes," she said. "Tomorrow."

She returned to the kitchen and up to her room. As she walked upstairs, she saw the light under Tim and Dora's door. For a moment, she was a bit envious that Dora had someone with her through the night. She still had no want of marriage but she would like to experience the closeness that came with that type of relationship. *Does it have to be only in marriage?* She mulled that thought over and headed to her room.

CHAPTER 21

Early the next morning, Emma heard a quiet knock on her door. She called out softly, "I'm up."

Dora stuck her head in and said, "Okay, meet us in the kitchen."

Emma nodded as she laid on the bed and yawned widely. Dora closed the door quietly behind her.

Time to get up, Emma thought as she got dressed and headed downstairs to help with pastry preparation in the kitchen.

As they were finishing the pastries for that night and starting breakfast for the boarding house, Thomas entered the kitchen looking tired. He sat down with a sigh and Amy got him a cup of coffee.

"Pastry?" asked Dora.

He shook his head. "Not just yet, thank you." He looked at Emma. She lifted an eyebrow at him as he reached into his pocket and handed her a piece of folded paper.

As she took it, Dora said to Amy, "Can you see if the towels are dry and bring them in? They've been left out overnight."

"Will do," she said and headed to the backyard to retrieve them.

"Thanks, Dora," Emma said absently as she unfolded the note and started to read. "Clair wants to meet me today." She directed her gaze at Thomas. "Did she have any idea who might be sharing the information?"

He shook his head slowly and said, "She said she hasn't noticed anyone unusual hanging around the house or seen the women leave the house for any reason."

"We have backgrounds on all of the help and they are aware of how important their silence is," she said, tapping her fingers against her lips. "That still leads us back to the women living in the house."

"Yes," agreed Dora

A worried look crossed Thomas' face. "I don't think Clair likes the idea of you questioning the women."

"I know she's protective, but if it isn't the help or someone connected with the house, it must be one of them," Emma mused out loud. "Her note also indicates she wants to meet in the same place we met initially. Thomas, can you confirm with her that I'll be there?"

"I can. I'll stop by on my way to the bakery." He paused for a moment and asked, "Do you want me to take you to the meeting this afternoon?"

"No, I'm working as a courier around that area and I have my bike," she said, absently tapping the letter on her hand. Presenting her case to Clair would be difficult; she would have to show she wasn't deliberately targeting the women. This needed to be handled carefully.

Thomas readied to leave, but Dora stopped him by saying, "Time for some breakfast, Thomas?" She didn't want him going without food; he meant too much to them.

"I'll stay," he said, easing back down in his chair.

Dora smiled at him and said, "Good."

They went back to baking while Thomas watched.

Amy tapped on the kitchen window and he jumped up to help

her with the basket. He asked, "Do you want me to take this to the upstairs closet?"

"Please," said Amy with a smile. He took it upstairs while she moved to the stove to start the eggs and sausage for breakfast.

While the pastries cooled on the table, Emma grabbed some bread and butter to eat and headed upstairs. It was time for her to get changed into her office clothes and head to work. She wanted to arrive a bit earlier than normal to compare invoices. Brushing her hair into a high ponytail, she continued thinking about her day. She was pulling on her boots when a knock sounded on her door. "Come in," she called out.

The door opened and Amy walked in. "Emma, Tony is waiting downstairs."

"Okay, thanks for letting me know. I'm on my way down now," she said as she gathered her notebook and stowed it in her jacket pocket. Slipping on her shoulder bag, she did a final check to confirm it contained her skirt, then headed down.

Tony was in the foyer and looked up when he heard her boots on the stairs. Grinning, he watched her walk down. She returned his smile and increased her pace to get to him. He lifted her off the last step and gave her a deep kiss.

"Wow," she said.

"I missed you," he murmured.

"It was only one night," she reminded him with a laugh in her voice.

"Yes." He said and kissed her again.

When they finally came up for air, Emma said, "I need to get my lunch. I want to go in early today." As she stepped away, she looked at what he was wearing and commented, "You look nice."

Tony glanced down at his attire. He wore a dark brown suit with a burgundy tie. "Several important clients are coming in today to meet a few of our up-and-coming artists. I'm hosting the event."

"That's wonderful," she said sincerely.

"Did you want to stop by after your morning job and eat lunch with me?" he asked hopefully.

"What time is your meeting?" she asked as they walked to the kitchen.

"This morning. I should be done around noon."

"I'll stop by," she promised. She lowered her voice. "I do have to meet with Clair at 3pm."

"Tell me about it once we're on the way," he commented to her in a similar tone of voice.

They stopped by the kitchen to get her lunch. Dora noticed him eyeing the cooling pastry and tossed him one. He caught it deftly. "Do me a favor?" she asked.

"Sure," he grinned, "if I can get another one of these."

She grinned back and tossed him another one, saying, "Remind Jake that we want to see him for dinner. Do you think you could bring him with you when you come over this evening?"

"Sure, it shouldn't be a problem," said Tony after swallowing the final bite of the second pastry.

"Now, on your way, both of you. Didn't you say you wanted to be in early, Emma?" Dora reminded her.

Emma nodded and gestured at Tony to head out.

"Have a good day, both of you. Emma, let me know if our plans for this evening change," Dora said, knowing she would be meeting with Clair.

"I will," she promised.

Tony held out his hand as they exited through the back door. Emma accepted it and squeezed.

As they left, they went to the small building on the side of the house where her bike was located. Tony inquired, "Did you hear from Clair?"

"Yes," she said simply.

"Going to tell me what she said?" he asked as they made the turn onto the sidewalk toward the trolley.

"She's unhappy with my inquiries and wants to talk this afternoon before anyone is interviewed at the house."

"Do you think you can convince her this is from a reliable source?"

"I certainly hope so. If it is true—and I believe it is—we have a leak. Any future moves could be in jeopardy."

"Emma." He stopped her with his hand. "I know this is your operation, but if you can't convince Clair how dangerous this is, I think you should tell her all future moves are out of the question until it's safe."

Emma nodded slowly. "That's what I have in mind. I certainly love adventure, but I will not knowingly walk myself and someone else into an unsafe situation."

They went quiet for the moment and continued walking toward the trolley stop. As they drew closer, Tony offered, "I can take your lunch with me today."

"Oh, thanks," she said, pulling out her lunch pail and handing it to him.

He leaned down and kissed her. "See you at noon?"

"Definitely," she said while climbing on her bike. "See you then!" she tossed over her shoulder as she rode off.

He watched her depart. He knew she would consider all the facts and not do anything rash. With that thought on his mind, he spotted the trolley and ran off to catch it.

Emma rode on through the city to her office building. Arriving early, she hurried to put her bike up and change out of her split skirt. After her belongings were stored under her desk, she glanced around to make sure no one was there. Once she confirmed she was alone, she made her way over to Lauri's desk to review her daily work folder. Pulling it out, she laid it on the desk and pulled out her notebook to copy down the invoice numbers, materials being ordered, and amounts. She returned the file to its proper location, then moved back to her desk. Sitting down, she quickly compared her notes with her invoices, adding the information from her files to her notebook.

I'll review these later, she thought. *I won't have time for a detailed evaluation now.* With a snap, the notebook was closed and was stored in her jacket. She would have preferred the actual invoices to compare side by side. *The camera. Follow-up would be necessary with Jake, his talents with it were the key to this case. I hope he accepts our offer.*

The office started to fill with personnel as she put paper into her typewriter. Lauri said a quiet hello as she entered and began her work. Emma watched her from the corner of her eye. When Lauri did not seem to find anything wrong with her daily work folder, Emma went back to her work.

A few hours later, after applying herself diligently, Emma checked her watch and realized the morning had flown by. She closed her files and covered up her typewriter. Standing, she made her way to Mr. Tracy's office and knocked on the door; he opened it quickly. He didn't say anything, knowing what she needed. They walked to the file room, and he pulled out his keys to open the door, watching her carefully as she completed her filing. The door would then be locked until it was needed again. Without saying a word, he headed back to his office. Emma rolled her eyes at Lauri, who hid a smile as she watched. The daily files were set up on her desk for the next day.

"Goodbye," she said to Lauri and headed to change into her split skirt.

After she changed, she retrieved her bike and rode toward the museum. It wasn't close to her office, but the bike allowed her to get there in a short amount of time. She arrived and placed the bike on her shoulder as she climbed the front steps of the museum. As she entered, the guards took it and placed it in the side storage room as usual. The guard pointed to where Tony was speaking to a woman. *A beautiful woman*, she thought to herself. She appeared to be a bit older than him; her dress was very stylish on her trim figure. Emma continued to watch them; curious but not at all jealous.

Tony saw her and gave a nod as he started to wrap up his conversation.

Emma noticed the woman place a hand on his arm to detain him. Tony smiled at her and disengaged himself. He waved the administrative assistant over and said, "Could you accompany Mrs. Smith to her cab?"

The admin nodded and offered her his elbow to escort her out. She paused for a moment and stared directly at Emma. Emma stared back, not understanding her interest. The lady broke the rather intense eye contact and turned a charming smile on the assistant walking her out.

Emma put the matter out of her mind and greeted Tony. He leaned over to kiss her hello. "Want to eat in my office?" he suggested.

She nodded, and they headed there. It was small but had a nice desk and chairs. They sat next to each other and unpacked their lunches.

"How did the event go this morning?" she asked curiously, taking a bite of her sandwich.

"Really well," he said with a serious tone. "There's a lot of interest in our new artist."

"Who is he?" she inquired.

"His name is John Singer Sargent. He is a powerful artist and well known for his portraits. We have one of his landscapes on display. It is entitled: *Street in Venice*."

"Venice? Italy? Can I see it?!" she asked excitedly. Travel fascinated her.

"Let's finish lunch first," he suggested as he nabbed her hand in his. They continued to eat and spoke about her afternoon meeting with Clair.

When they finished, he took her to the room where the landscape painting hung. It was an exquisite picture, one that made Emma yearn to see Venice for herself.

"We hope this one does well with visitors," commented Tony.

Emma didn't want to take her eyes off of it. *So many places to see*, she thought. They parted and she continued to her courier jobs' delivering drawings to companies located near the restaurant where her meeting was located.

After she completed her deliveries, she made her way to the meeting with Clair. Despite very much liking Clair, Emma wasn't looking forward to the tense meeting. Gritting her teeth and setting her jaw, she entered the restaurant. The manager greeted her at the door and waved at a busboy to take the bike to storage until she needed it again. He said, "I believe your party is already waiting for you, miss." He motioned for her to follow him.

They went in the opposite direction from the dining room to a door located down a long hallway. He opened the door and indicated she should enter. As she made her way into the room, she glanced around and noted it was brightly lit with high windows. Across the room was a small table set up with an afternoon tea service. The manager excused himself and shut the door quietly on his way out.

Clair stood near the table, looking out the window. As she turned to Emma, the girl noted the older woman's strained features.

"Clair." She acknowledged her with a nod and started without any pleasantries, but kept her tone pleasant. "We need to talk openly about the information Pinkerton has provided."

"Yes, that's why I requested a private room," she responded and seemed to relax a bit when Emma didn't sound accusatory. "Why don't we sit down? I ordered tea."

"It looks nice, thank you." She watched as Clair poured it for them. She took the cup and took a sip before starting. "All right, let's talk about what was communicated to me. Cole indicated that the shelter location and women's names are for sale to the highest bidder." Clair's face lost some color, but she nodded. "Cole and I thought about the workers at the house, but all have had background checks and clearances."

"Couldn't it be someone outside the house?" Clair asked, hoping it wasn't one of her women.

"We thought of that, but the information is too specific. They're in contact with one of the husbands of a woman at your house."

"How did Cole find out?" she pressed, still clinging desperately to hope it was from another source.

"There was an anonymous note sent to the Pinkerton office. It indicated they were worried about the lady getting hurt."

"Which one is it and why hasn't the husband come to the house to try to get her?"

"It's Alison who was mention in the note. We don't think money has changed hands yet, so we don't think the address has been shared. One of my concerns is that we haven't been keeping the movements quiet from the other residents. We've only kept the method of movement and final locations quiet. When we schedule her move, they'll probably try to take her."

"You think it's one of my women selling information. Already victims, maybe now victimizing the others," Clair said, reeling with that information.

"I'm not sure; we just need to look at each one and confirm their stories. One may be a plant, put into the house to get the locations of the other women. I've also been thinking, is there anyone who has been avoiding a move?" asked Emma.

"We have two, other than Alison, who has not indicated a desire to move out of the city or haven't made any inquiries about attending school," Clair admitted.

"I'll need both names so I can have Cole look into their backgrounds. Though, we may not be able to find out much, especially if their names have been changed."

"It looks like we may have a traitor in our midst," said Clair, her face hardening at the thought.

They both went silent at that thought. Then Emma continued. "Dora and I had thought to come over tonight and bring pastries. She has wanted to start spending time there, possibly teaching cooking classes and listening to the women who need to talk."

Clair said quietly, "I'd like that, as would the women." She paused. "I know it's important, but we must go about the quietly. I want them to continue to feel protected."

"We also need to evaluate our next moves for changes and different routes. Perhaps by buggy instead of trains. Until we find out who this is, we'll have to be creative or delay them until we can assure their safety."

"It was going so well," Clair said absently.

"Yes. It will be so again; we just have to find who is trying to sabotage us," Emma said vehemently.

"Agreed," she said finally. "You and Dora will be by tonight?"

"Yes, Thomas will bring us dressed as boys."

"Thomas, it will be nice to see him," she said, looking happier.

Again, Emma didn't inquire, allowing their personal lives to remain personal.

"What time will I see you this evening?" Clair asked, wanting to be there when they arrived.

"Our thought is 8pm. We'll bring in the treats and start speaking to the ladies at that time."

"There are three," Clair admitted. "Lily, Ann, and Alison. They have been with us for a while. They don't have a family for support and don't seem capable of living outside the house -- safely. I would assume that, since Alison's husband is involved, we can remove her from the list."

"Yes, I agree. So, it's Lily and Ann we need to look at. I'll get the information to Cole. Can you write down their first and last names? He may be able to track down their histories."

"Will we be able to tell from the background checks who might be involved in this?" Clair asked hopefully.

"Maybe, but I think I should still observe them." Emma paused for a moment, thinking. "Who gets the mail or deliveries?"

"The housekeeper answers the door for all reasons, but I don't think we receive any mail there," said Clair.

"I can confirm that tonight," said Emma.

"Okay, we'll see you there. Oh, tell Thomas he can come in the kitchen to wait for you," Clair said innocently.

"It will be a chilly night; I'm sure he'd like to be inside while we're visiting," commented Emma in the same tone.

They had their tea and cakes as a quiet end to their meeting. Clair and Emma briefly touched hands as they left the room. Emma retrieved her bike from the manager and headed to the boarding house to help with dinner.

Tim was already in the kitchen "helping" Dora with a dessert when she entered. "Hey, Emma," Tim said absently.

"Hey back," she responded.

He arched an eyebrow in a silent question. "Later," she said, glancing at Amy's back. They trusted her, but the women at the shelter needed to know they would not share their private information.

He and Dora nodded and continued to work on dinner. They pulled together to get the food to the table. Tony arrived with Jake as they were starting the evening meal, and he sat in the chair next to Emma. She grabbed Tony's hand under the table and squeezed. He squeezed back and gave her a sweet smile.

After prayers were completed, Dora asked, looking over at Jake, "Did you have a good day?"

"I did. We had some interesting cases, but I can't talk about them," Jake said hurriedly, looking around.

Tim said in a calming tone, "That's okay, we understand. Were you mostly in the office?"

"No, I was out a few times today and then I spent time developing pictures this afternoon," he replied. Dora was glad that Jake had not balked at eating in the dining room that evening. The conversation went on around the table, a noisy but comforting sound.

They finished eating and started to clear the table. Emma told Tony in a low voice that they would meet after dinner in the kitchen.

"Papa, you had mentioned you wanted to show Jake something downstairs this evening," Dora hinted to him.

"Does it involve photography?" Jake asked hopefully.

"No, but it does involve similar chemicals, and you might use your camera to investigate some findings for me," said Papa.

Jake looked interested in this development and accompanied him to the basement. The other boarders moved into the sitting room to settle in for the evening.

Amy, Dora, Tim, Tony, and Emma pitched in to clean up after dinner. As plates were cleaned and the kitchen table scrubbed, Dora said to Amy, "You can go home a bit early, if you like."

"That would be nice," she said happily. "I'm reading a new book and I would love to get home early to finish it." She started out and almost ran into Thomas. Laughing she stepped aside, so he could enter.

"Thank you and good night, Amy," Thomas said with a smile.

"Good night," she said and headed off to her house, thinking about the evening in front of her.

"Thomas, you missed dinner. Would you like me to fix you a plate?" asked Dora.

"That would be nice, thank you," replied Thomas.

Dora was handing Thomas his dinner plate when Tony came back into the room. "Good evening Thomas. I checked and confirmed everyone is in the sitting room."

Tim, Tony, Emma, Thomas, and Dora sat around the table. "Emma, you met with Clair?" Dora prompted.

"Yes, She was unhappy that we might be targeting one of her

ladies. But she agreed we could do background checks on them and we can subtly interview them tonight at the shelter."

"Was she okay with me accompanying you?" Dora asked, hoping she could still go.

"Yes, she was happy to hear that you wanted to start coming to the shelter. The ladies need some sort of distraction from their situations," said Emma.

Dora smiled. "Good."

Tony said, "We need to get you both organized and the wagon ready." Emma nodded and indicated for Dora to follow her upstairs.

Tim and Tony took a moment to speak with Thomas. "You'll watch out for them? We want you to come back here if anything looks suspicious."

"I will," promised Thomas and stood up to take his plate to the sink. "Let's go."

The three went to get the wagon. They set up blankets and placed the boxes of pastry in the back. "Thomas, meet them at Stevenson Street in the alley," directed Tim.

"I'll be there," he said as he climbed into the wagon and made a clicking sound to get the horses moving, while Tim and Tony headed back to the boarding house.

Emma and Dora entered the kitchen as Tim and Tony were coming in from outside. Even with all the seriousness of their current project, when Tim saw Dora in her pants and a loose shirt, he let out a low whistle; she turned red, enjoying the attention. "Enough of that now," admonished Emma with a slight smile. She helped Dora tuck her hair into her newsboy cap, it was made of cloth with a rounder puffier design, topped with a button. Giving her a once-over, she approved her look. Emma handled her hat carefully. It was her bowler with a special slot for her long knife.

"If you're ready, Thomas is waiting on Stevenson Street in the alley," Tim said, wanting to get them moving.

Tony had started to worry and stated a bit loudly, "I can go with you."

"No," said Emma, moving to him and hugging him tightly. "Better to keep the group small."

He looked down at her for a long moment and nodded his head in agreement. He squeezed her hand before letting her go.

Tim also took a moment with Dora. He tilted her head back with his fingers to look him in the eyes and said, "Be safe."

"I will," she said softly. They shared a long kiss.

For once, Emma didn't tease her. Giving them their moment, she cleared her throat after a few seconds and said, "Let's go." They exited out of the back door.

"Dora," Emma muttered out the side of her mouth as she noticed how her sister was walking, "don't swing your hips too much. Be a boy." Emma slipped into the boy's skin easily and showed no outward appearance as a female. They took a circuitous path to meet Thomas, making sure no one was following them to where he was waiting patiently.

He saw them approach and said quietly, "Hey, in you go."

Emma and Dora climbed in the back of the wagon with Thomas' help. After he covered them with several blankets, he leaped into the driver's seat and moved the wagon out of the alley in an unhurried manner. He wouldn't be suspicious; he made deliveries to the shelter routinely.

Once he had the wagon out of sight behind the shelter, he uncovered Emma and Dora. Emma exited by jumping down and Dora followed her lead. *I can see why Emma likes these adventures,* Dora thought.

Thomas took the pastry boxes out and handed them to the girls. As the three approached the back door, Clair opened it to let them in. She looked a bit pensive but seemed happy to see them. "Come in, come in."

They went into the kitchen. The housekeeper, Katy, was there and rushed over to hug Emma. "Visit or move?" she asked.

"Visit only, and we brought something with us," she teased, indicating the boxes she carried.

"Oh, Emma, did you bring us something sweet?" asked Katy excitedly.

"We did," she said with a smile and set her boxes down the table. She indicated for Dora to do the same. "And I brought someone to meet you." Emma turned and grabbed Dora by the arm and dragged her over to Katy. "Dora, this is Katy. Katy, this is my sister Dora."

"It is so nice to finally meet you. We have loved the pastries you've sent us," Katy said sincerely.

Dora blushed and said, "I'm glad you enjoyed them."

Clair spoke to Thomas in a low voice and then approached Emma and Dora. "Dora, I'm Clair. It's very nice to meet you. I appreciate you wanting to help our little family." Dora and Clair shook hands, rather formally.

Emma knew she used "our little family" to highlight her protectiveness of the women in the shelter.

Clair said to the housekeeper, "Katy, please take the pastries and put some on a tray for the sitting room. Also, prepare some tea." She then turned to Dora and Emma. "Let's adjourn to the sitting room."

Thomas would stay in the kitchen and read while the women conducted their business. The women living in the shelter knew he was a good person but some were skittish around men. He couldn't blame them, knowing what they had been through.

Before they exited the kitchen, Emma stopped Clair and asked quietly, "Where are the three ladies?"

Almost reluctantly, Clair said, "Alison and Ann are in the sitting room, and Lily is in the study reading."

"I'll start with Lily," said Emma, checking her pocket for her notebook.

"I would like to visit with the ladies in the sitting room," said

Dora, breaking the uncomfortable pause that had settled between Emma and Clair.

Clair nodded and accompanied her down the hallway. Emma followed behind but broke off from the group at the study entrance. Clair and Dora continued as Emma took a moment to observe Lily before entering. She was a smallish woman in her late twenties, with thick brown hair and a rather plain dress.

As she walked in, Lily looked up from her book and said in a surprised tone, "Hello, Emma. How are you? What are you doing here this evening?"

"I'm well," Emma commented, sidestepping the question of why she was there. "What are you reading?" she asked.

She gave Emma a brief frown before showing her the spine. Emma read out loud, *The Count of Monte Cristo*. That's a good book. I love all of the intrigues."

"Me, too," Lily commented, studying it.

Emma let the silence settle around them. It was a tool that could be used to force people to talk. She moved to a chair near the couch where Lily sat. Pulling out her notebook, she started asking questions, "Lily, we were wondering if you had plans for your future outside of the shelter."

She looked a bit panicked at the abrupt question and asked with a nervous tenor in her voice, "Am I being asked to leave?"

"No, no," Emma assured her. "We want to know if you would like us to relocate you to another environment or would you like us to arrange for you to attend business school here. We would like to help you move forward with your life."

That statement didn't seem to mollify her. Standing suddenly, she started to pace in front of the fireplace. Finally, she turned to Emma and asked, "Why are you trying to get rid of me? Did I do something wrong?"

Emma studied her behavior, watching for signs of deception. She had worked on this skill for the past two years with Jeremy as her primary instructor. Prior to this, she'd had a bad experience when someone she trusted turned out to be lying. It almost cost her and a friend's life.

There were specific signs to look for: no eye contact, changes in voice, unusual body language, something sounding off, and being overly defensive. And Lily was hitting all five. Emma made notes without showing any emotion. Lily would stay on her list until she got further information on her background.

Emma decided to back off and end the conversation there. "Lily, think about what you might like to do with your future. It doesn't have to be decided tonight. We just wanted to let you know we are thinking about you." She used the word thinking, knowing it could be taken in two ways.

Lily didn't take that as a threat and seemed to calm down. She crossed back over to her chair and sat down with her book. "Okay, I'll get back to you."

"Okay. There are pastries in the sitting room; my sister brought them to share. You're welcome to join us," Emma said, wanting to end the meeting on a positive note.

"No, I'm good here," she said, holding onto her book tightly and sounding relieved the questions were ending and Emma would be leaving.

She smiled slightly, knowing she wasn't wanted and exited the room. There was enough data on Lily to form some conclusions and she was ready to move on to the next person on her list. She walked down the hall to the sitting room and paused in the doorway to observe the people there. There were four women in addition to Clair and Dora. Emma didn't recognize the two sitting on either side of Clair, but she was able to see new bruising on their young faces. Her heart plummeted a moment, thinking of all the hurt girls out there; they were only helping a small percentage. She shook the thought off and entered the room.

All the ladies have tried the pastry, judging by the empty platter on the table, Emma observed. Dora sat talking quietly to Alison; Ann was in the corner reading. Emma wanted to continue her interviews with both Alison and Ann. Clair glanced up and indicated with a wave of her hand for Emma to enter. She stepped in, and Clair quietly introduced her to the two new women seeking shelter in the house. They didn't say much and she understood they were still too skittish to speak with anyone but Clair.

Emma moved closer to Alison and Dora. She had known Alison for the last month and had had many conversations with her. Emma had a gut feeling that she was ready to move on and her next statement confirmed this. As she sat next to Alison on the small settee, she leaned over and quietly said, "I think I'm ready to leave the shelter. Can we speak for a moment?"

Emma nodded and said in a low voice, "Kitchen?" She had made sure to keep Ann in her line of sight. The other woman had straightened up when Alison had moved toward Emma. She didn't appear to be listening, but in fact, she was. *Interesting,* thought Emma.

She motioned to Dora that she and Alison would be leaving the room. Dora nodded, understanding Emma wanted her to watch for anyone who chose to leave the room while the interviews were ongoing.

Emma stood and indicated that Alison should go ahead of her into the hallway toward the kitchen. As they entered, they saw Thomas was speaking with Katy. Alison hesitated a bit before entering; she seemed to be okay with him but didn't want to get too close.

"Thomas, I think there are some books that might hold your interest in the study," Emma said. "I'm sure Lily wouldn't mind the company." Lily wasn't skittish around Thomas and wouldn't mine him in the room with her.

Thomas got the underlying direction and said, "I'll check it out." He would keep Lily busy so her conversation with Alison was kept private.

Katy, seeing that she needed to give them some space, said, "I think I'll go up to bed. Just have them leave the cups and plates in the sink."

"I'll tell Clair. Goodnight, Katy," said Emma, hugging her.

With the kitchen empty, Alison pulled an address out of her pocket. "I have a distant cousin who would allow me to live with him. This is his address. He has a farm out in the country."

"Can I see it?" Emma asked as she sat down at the kitchen table.

"Yes," said Alison, handing it over.

Emma looked at the address and thought about this cousin. She asked, "What is your relationship like? Why are you sure he would take you in and help with transport?"

"I spent most of my summers there as a child. We grew up together," she said simply.

Emma asked, concerned for her safety, "Has your husband been to the farm or met the cousin?"

"No, he was very jealous of any men and would not even let me invite my family to our wedding," she assured her.

Emma frowned. *That would have deterred me from marrying him, but this isn't about me.*

"My husband had me cut off contact with all of my family as soon as we married. I wasn't even allowed to attend my parents' funerals," she said, suddenly tearful.

"No communication of your cousin or these trips you took as a child?"

"No, he only wanted to discuss him. I went along with it because I thought he loved me," she said, looking lost.

"Have you shared this information with anyone in the shelter?" Emma asked.

That question seemed to help bring her back to the present. "No, I just decided I needed to keep moving forward and that means leaving the safety of this shelter. Do I need to be secretive?"

"I would say not to share any information about your possible move at this time. We want to add a layer of privacy to the moves, even from other women in the shelter."

Alison frowned, not saying anything, and finally nodded.

"Alison," Emma said, touching her hand, "could you write the letter to your cousin, asking if you can go live with his family?"

"Yes, I can do that," she said, happy they were setting things into motion.

"Let Clair know when it's ready to be sent. This is important - don't let anyone see it and keep it on your person at all times. Give it to Clair. She will get it to me to be posted," Emma said, stressing the need for her discretion.

Alison would do as she was asked. She had seen Emma get women out of the shelter to safety; she trusted her. Feeling relieved, she said, "I'm looking forward to the future for the first time in a long time."

"I'm glad." Emma decided she needed to ask Alison some hard questions. "Alison, your husband, tell me about him."

Alison took a deep breath to steady herself before answering.

Emma saw the question disturbed her and continued, "We normally don't ask but, in this case, I need to know everything so we can protect you."

"Charles Lewison." Emma felt a jolt at hearing the name; she immediately knew who that was. She would need to let Cole know as soon as possible. He hadn't been able to find much on the women, since they had hidden their last names.

"He's a very powerful man here. He's also very unstable out of the public eye. He could control his public behavior, but once that bedroom door closed, he changed, became violent. On the outside, I had everything but. . ." She trailed off.

"What finally happened to get you out from under his abuse?"

"I would like to say that I escaped," she said sadly, "but I'm not that strong. I hope I can be one day." She paused before continuing, lost in her memories. "I had help. Our maid, Wendy, came to check on me. When I didn't answer, she realized I must be hurt.

She left and came back with her husband; he was able to take the door down. They found me on the floor. Wendy had worked for Clair at her other 'house' and knew we could trust her."

"Where is this maid now? Not still with your husband," Emma asked, suddenly worried.

"No, Wendy has an ability to survive. She and her husband decided it was time to move on," Alison said, wishing she was just as strong as her rescuers.

"Yes, that was probably the best decision," acknowledged Emma.

"How long do you think it will take to get things moving?" Alison asked, ready for the next step, whatever that might be.

"I think I have enough to get things set up. It may take some time to organize," Emma said, jotting down notes in her notebook.

"How long do you think?" she repeated, a little apprehensive.

"An estimation?" asked Emma, still jotting down her notes. "Probably a few weeks, if your cousin agrees," she cautioned, not wanting to be overly optimistic.

Alison was very relieved to have a date to plan for. She nodded, feeling secure that her cousin would be there for her.

Emma sat forward at the table, leaning on her elbows, clasping her hands together. "Alison, I have to stress again, please don't share information with ANYONE. In fact, if anyone is too curious, send a note to Clair or me."

"Who do you mean?" Alison asked, bewildered.

"I mean, *anyone* other than Clair or myself. We want to make sure you're protected."

"Yes, I can do that," Alison said, still curious about this request.

Emma reached out to touch Alison's hand. "We will get you somewhere safe," she promised.

Alison gripped her hand and nodded. She used her other hand to wipe a tear before standing and moving toward the kitchen door. She hesitated a moment and turned around. "Emma, I appreciate everything you and Clair are doing here. I will not allow myself to be placed in this type of position again," she insisted.

Emma watched her leave and had a moment to reflect on their conversation. She completed the documentation in her notebook and thought, *I have requested backgrounds on the ladies from Cole but, without a husband's name, the women are nearly invisible. Also, since these are runaway wives, the husbands might be covering up their disappearances.*

At that moment, the kitchen door swung open to reveal Clair. She hesitated in the doorway a few moments and seemed to come to a decision about something saying, "Emma, did you get what you needed?"

"No, not completely," she admitted. "I have an idea but, without more information, I don't want to accuse anyone."

Clair smiled slightly. "I think I can guess the two you are concerned about: Lily and Ann?"

"Yes." Emma smiled back. They thought along very similar lines. "They've been here the longest and have not asked for a placement or help moving on."

"You spoke with Lily; do you want some time with Ann?"

She nodded and stated, "Yes, can you ask her to come in here?"

Clair said casually, looking down at her nails. "Thomas mentioned you asked him to go to the study for a book to keep him occupied while you were talking to Alison."

"Yes," she replied just as casually, studying Clair's face. "I was hoping that book would keep him inside the study until I completed my conversations."

Clair continued, "I also noticed that Dora seemed to be keeping a close eye on Ann while you were talking to Alison."

Emma made a point to take a moment and wait for Clair to make eye contact with her. "You caught me. I just want to keep the conversations private with each woman."

"Yes, I understand, and thank you for keeping the interview

nonconfrontational. I'll get Ann now," she said as she walked out of the kitchen.

A few moments later, Ann peeked her head in the door, smiled timidly, and asked, "You wanted to see me?"

"Yes, Ann, have a seat."

She sat down and Emma watched her closely, studying her body language for signs that she was lying. There was no eye contact, she observed as Ann sat down at the kitchen table, she kept her eyes lowered demurely toward her hands.

"Ann." When she didn't look up, Emma prompted her again in a firmer voice, "Ann." She finally looked up and looked her straight in the eye. That startled Emma. *Why would such a timid woman make such direct eye contact?*

Emma hid her response as she noted that; she knew the hardest ones to detect were the practiced liars who were aware that lack of eye contact is a tell. *I'll have to watch for more subtle responses—behavior pauses or delays and breathing patterns,* she thought.

Emma began, "We've been talking about your future. You haven't mentioned to Clair if you would like us to start planning for your future outside the shelter."

Ann's gaze remained steady. She delayed speaking for a moment. When she did start talking, her voice came out timid. "Does a decision have to be made now?" Emma noted her tone.

"No, of course not, but we would like to know if you're thinking of staying here in the city and going to school or if we need to look into relocating you to a safer location."

"Why now?" Her eyes had a harder look and her voice a deeper timbre.

"Could you think about it? I can come back to discuss it at a later date."

She lowered her eyes and fell back into her timid voice. "May I go?"

She assumed her timid persona purposefully, Emma thought.

"Yes, and thank you for speaking with me tonight," she said.

Ann kept her head down as she left the room.

Emma immediately opened her notebook to document her conversation and observations. She waited in the kitchen for Dora and Thomas and thought, *I've accomplished what I wanted to this evening.*

Thomas and Dora entered the kitchen with Clair. As the group got organized to leave, Emma communicated Katy's message to Clair. She sent a questioning look at Emma. Emma caught it and said, "I'll talk to you soon."

With that, the group exited. Emma noted Thomas and Clair shared a long look as they were leaving.

Dora and Emma lay quietly in the back of the wagon on the way home. Thomas stopped the cart in the alley they'd started from. Emma and Dora felt the wagon come to a stop and took off the cover. After they jumped down, Emma asked softly to Thomas, "Headed back home?"

He cocked his head and said with a soft smile, "No, I think I'll be out for a while."

She smiled, certain he was returning to see that Clair got home safely. They waved him off and started the walk home. Dora couldn't wait to start questioning her. "Well, which one did it?"

"I've narrowed it down to Ann and Lily," she said, thinking of the three conversations this evening.

"Do you favor one over the other?" Dora asked, trusting Emma's instincts.

"They were both lying, but I think it's Ann informing on the house."

"Why Ann? She seems to be such a mouse of a woman."

"She is pretending to be something she isn't. Her demeanor is a disguise." Emma went on to describe her voice changes and her eye contact.

"Where do we go from here?" Dora asked, knowing they had to tread carefully.

"Data," she said simply. "We'll need to build a file on each lady with as much information as we can find. I'll continue to work with Cole on background checks and keep watch on the shelter. I'll notify Clair of my plans in the next few days."

They fell silent as they made their way around the last corner and entered the house through the kitchen. The light was still on. Dora had expected that Tim would be waiting up for her, but Emma was surprised to also see Tony there.

Dora hugged Tim hello.

Tony came over to Emma and gave her a quick kiss.

"Did it go all right? Any clues as to who might be involved?" he asked, more curious than concerned.

Tim wanted to hear what happened as well, so the group sat at the kitchen table while Emma recapped what she had learned. As she finished, Tim and Dora headed up to bed, leaving her and Tony alone.

Wanting to spend some one-on-one time with him, Emma asked, "Do you want to move to the sitting room. Is it too late for you?"

"That would be nice," said Tony softly.

They moved to the living room, sitting quietly enjoying each other's company, not wanting to discuss their respective work. They stayed together for a while and then he could see she was starting to drift off. He kissed her lightly and said, "Up to bed with you."

"Yes," she mumbled sleepily. "Sorry."

"No need to be. I love being with you, sleepy or not," he teased her.

"See you in the morning," she said as she yawned.

"Definitely."

She walked him to the door and kissed him one more time before he left. With the locks secured, she slowly made her way upstairs.

CHAPTER 22

The morning came around quickly. Emma laid in bed, wishing she didn't have to get up. She rolled to her side, pushed her hair back off her face, and moved to sit on the side of the bed. The note for Thomas to take to Clair had to be written this morning. Standing, she walked over to the dresser and splashed some water on her face before beginning her day.

Once she felt more awake, she quickly dressed and sat down at her desk to jot down the note. *Also,* she thought, tapping the pencil on her notebook, *it might be best to drop by and see Cole and Jeremy and let them know what's happening.* She finished and folded the note, placing it in her pocket as she headed downstairs.

When she entered the kitchen, Thomas was just preparing to go to the bakery. "Do you think you could stop by Clair's and deliver a note for me?"

"I think I could make time to see her this morning," he said with a smile, aware Emma knew he and Clair were seeing each other.

"Great," she said with a laugh, handing him the folded note. "Thanks."

Tony was already there as well. Emma walked over to where

he stood near the back door and kissed him hello. Breakfast was in the works and the kitchen was a bit crowded. Dora's leadership took over and she said warningly, "If you're not here to work, then I need you out of my kitchen."

"I have an early appointment," said Emma, scrambling to grab some bread and butter.

"Take an apple with you. Your lunch is packed and it is on the table," Dora directed.

She grabbed both and said, "Thank you."

"Tony, do you want something to take with you?" asked Dora, always wanting to feed her family.

"No, Mom took care of that before I left the house this morning," he said, holding up his lunch bucket with a chuckle. As they left, he asked Emma, "Are we in a hurry this morning?"

"I want to stop by Cole and Jeremy's house before work and see if they have some time to discuss the shelter situation with me."

"Do you mind if I accompany you?" Tony asked.

"No, of course not, but it will be a little out of your way," she warned.

"That's fine." She looked at him and couldn't tell why he might want to go along. She shrugged and retrieved her bike. Tony hailed a cab to take them to Jeremy's house, as it was a bit far to walk and the trolley wasn't close to the area.

The cab stopped at Jeremy's house. Tony helped Emma down and retrieved her bike before paying the driver. He placed it on his shoulder and they climbed the stoop to Jeremy's house.

Emma knocked. The door opened and a nicely dressed woman of about Emma's age with long brown curly hair appeared at the door. "Yes?" she asked.

Emma felt a bit puzzled as to who this woman was and why she was at Jeremy's house so early in the morning. "Is Jeremy here? Or Cole?"

The woman looked at her with a curious expression before

calling over her shoulder, "Jeremy, company." She looked back at them and said, "Come in, I'm just on my way out." She called as she headed down the stoop "See you later, Jeremy."

Emma absently frowned at her but kept her questions to herself. Tony noticed the frown and tried not to read into it.

Jeremy appeared in the doorway and waved his guest on her way.

"Emma, good to see you. Tony, welcome. You're both here early this morning. Everything okay?" he asked, looking concerned.

Shaking off her thoughts, she said, "Yes, I wanted to follow up on what we learned at the shelter last night. Do you and Cole have a few minutes?"

"Yes, Pops is out on the back patio. Join us for coffee and some breakfast?" asked Jeremy.

"We ate, but we would love some coffee," said Emma, answering for them both.

They followed Jeremy out to the back patio. Cole was sitting reading the newspaper when they exited the house. "Pops, Emma, and Tony stopped by."

He looked up and immediately stood. "Welcome both of you. Emma, I am assuming this is about the shelter. What did you find out?"

"Pops, let them sit down and have some coffee," Jeremy said with a smile.

"Oh, yes, please sit. Jeremy, pour them some coffee," he directed.

Jeremy poured it and Cole started the conversation. "Emma, can you give us an update?"

Emma pulled out her notebook and Jeremy's mouth quirked up as she started to go over her observations of the behavior of both Ann and Lily.

After she finished, Cole sat back in his chair and pondered the facts. Finally, he said, "I agree that it is most likely Ann and we should keep the shelter under surveillance. What are your thoughts on what Lily might be involved in?"

"I think she is hiding something. I'm just not sure what it is."

"What is the timeline on this? You mentioned Alison has somewhere to go?"

"Yes. I'm going to get her letter posted in a few days. That should allow us to finalize the timeline for her departure," commented Emma.

"You should use the Pinkerton office for the return address," suggested Jeremy.

Cole nodded. "I agree."

"That's a good idea. Thank you," said Emma, grateful for the suggestion. "Did you need us to work on how to pay for your services?" she asked, knowing the additional men would be expensive.

"No, we care about the women in the shelter. We'll take care of it," said Cole firmly.

"Thank you."

"No thanks are necessary."

Jeremy spoke up, "Pops, I can lead the surveillance effort."

"That's a good idea. Report any suspicious activity, but tell the men it should be subtle. Don't approach, just surveil."

"I'll take care of it."

Tony said, looking at his watch, "Emma, we best be on our way."

"Yes," she said. "Work calls and I started on another case."

"Anything you need help with on that one?" asked Cole.

"Not yet, but I'll let you know," she promised.

They thanked Cole and Jeremy for their time and headed out.

Tony hailed a cab, but Emma declined the ride. "I have my bike and I don't mind the extra time to get over there. Miss you," she said to him, lifting her face to his.

"Miss you, too. I'll see you this evening," he said as he kissed her before climbing into the waiting cab. She jumped on her bike and headed off to her office job for the morning.

Emma got there on time, but not early enough to make any additional notes on the invoices. The office was fairly routine that day, typing contracts and filing. She closed her files as noon approached. She was going to head straight to the restaurant for her meeting with Clair.

When she arrived, her bike was taken and the manager escorted her back to his office, where Clair waited patiently.

"Emma."

"Clair." She nodded at her,

"Sit, please." Clair sat down at the round table; lunch was already set up. She said, "I thought you might be hungry."

"I am," commented Emma. "Thank you." She ate her sandwich quickly while Clair sipped her tea.

Clair said, "So, where are we on this investigation?"

"I believe it's Ann or Lily. At this time, I truly believe it's Ann."

"Of all people, that little mouse of a girl, you think she's behind this?" she asked incredulously.

"I do."

"Why?"

"It was her behavior. She appears to be a practiced liar. We're still investigating Lily, but we do feel it's Ann."

"I'll have to get her out of the shelter and away from my other women," she said, feeling protective.

"No," Emma cautioned. "Not just yet. We want to catch her in the act and find out who's paying her to do this."

"So, how do we go about it?" asked Clair determinedly.

"First, Pinkerton has set up surveillance on the shelter to watch any comings and goings. Any deliveries will be monitored and each person, especially those who come around often, will be checked out."

Clair nodded. "That sounds appropriate."

"Second, we'll wait for a response from Alison's cousin. Let her know we'll need the letter as soon as possible and that we'll post it."

"What then?" asked Clair.

"Well, for that," Emma said, "I have a plan." She went on to describe how to move Alison and catch Ann.

As they were wrapping up, Clair asked, "What about Lily? You said she's lying about the reason for being in the shelter?"

"I do. I don't know why yet, but I'll work on it. Do you know where she was before coming to you?"

"She said her husband beat her up and she did have significant bruising to her face when we took her in."

"How did she arrive at the shelter?"

"You know, that's an odd story. Normally, we're contacted at my business and usually by friends. That's how this operates—a friend of a friend. She just appeared on the doorstep and, once I saw her, we didn't question her motives for being there." She paused a moment, thinking. "I had forgotten about that."

"Did she arrive with anything?"

"Another odd thing. She had a bag with her."

"What was in it?"

"Books," she said simply.

"Books?" Emma frowned heavily. "If you were trying to get away from someone, would you take something like that? What kinds of items do the girls normally have?"

"Normally? The dresses on their backs. Most are lucky to get out alive, much less with belongings."

"Curiouser and curiouser," murmured Emma, drumming her fingers on her lips. "We'll continue to observe her. Any idea of where she was before the shelter?"

"She claimed to not want to talk about it. I believed her then, but I'm unsure now," she admitted.

"I'll investigate her and we'll keep that separate from this case." She closed her book and opened another, asking, "How did Ann get to the shelter?"

"It was one of the girls at my business. She knew her and brought her to us."

"Hmmm. More to think about. Can you give me her name?"

"Yes, but she has moved on, I doubt we will be able to find her for questions."

Emma noted that.

"Emma, one more question, who is paying Pinkerton to do this for us?" Clair knew few things in this life were for free.

"They're not being paid. I found out from Jeremy and Cole that the detectives have volunteered their services."

Clair teared up. To see such a strong woman, struggle with her feelings made Emma also tear up. She cleared her throat, laughed, and said, "We need a lighter topic."

Clair brightened and she wiped the tears from her cheeks. "Well, I do have one. I think you know I've been seeing Thomas."

"Yes," Emma said, not allowing any emotion into her voice.

Clair bristled a bit when she couldn't read her tone. "Well, we don't need your approval, but Thomas would like you to be aware of our friendship."

Emma grinned suddenly and said, "Clair, we love that you and Thomas have found each other. Our only concern ever is that Thomas is happy. You make him happy."

"Oh, well then," said Clair, relieved the family didn't disapprove of their relationship.

Emma checked her watch pin on her blouse and, as she picked up her courier pouch, said, "I have some deliveries to make before heading home."

"Of course. Thanks, Emma, for everything."

"We still have lots to do," Emma commented. "Contact me as soon as you have the letter."

"I will," promised Clair.

And with that, Emma headed out.

CHAPTER 23

It had been an active week with two cases being worked simultaneously. Emma allowed herself to sleep in that Saturday morning. There was a knock on her door, and she called out, "Come in."

Dora entered and jumped on her bed. "Going to get up today?"

"Eventually," Emma said as she stretched. "Did you bring me something to eat?"

"Is that all I am good for?" she teased.

Emma thought for a moment and said, "Well, yes."

Dora slapped her hand lightly to scold her and they both started laughing.

"So, did you bring me something?" Emma repeated.

Dora looked at her wryly and said, "Of course." She stepped outside the door and picked up a tray of goodies and brought it back to the bed.

"Mmm, my favorites," Emma murmured as they lounged on the bed and ate off the tray. They discussed their men and other topics.

"Jake will be here tonight; are you still okay with us inviting him to join our family?" Dora asked.

"Yes, you're right. He'll be a good fit for us, and he doesn't need to know what happened between me and Daniel."

Dora teared up and hugged her tightly. "Get dressed and come downstairs." Gathering the items from the bed, she headed to the door.

Emma called after her, "I will. I think I'm just going to hang around here today and read."

"Is Tony coming over?" Dora asked, pausing at the door.

"No, not until tonight. He's running a special exhibit at the museum today," said Emma, stretching and enjoying her lazy day.

"Will he bring Jake or should I send Tim?"

"Tony told me he would bring him."

Dora knew the family would be asking Jake tonight if he would like to join them as a specialist. She was making a special meal for them to eat together in the kitchen.

The day wound down slowly, and the family started entering for the dinner hour. As the whole group arrived—Tim, Tony, Jake, Papa, Dora, and Emma—they sat down and relaxed around the kitchen table. Tim sat next to Dora, Tony, and Emma across from one another, and Jake had a place next to Papa.

Jake was dominating the conversation with his favorite topic—cameras. He was moving into the types of exposures when Emma nodded at Dora. She was the best with him and the most patient. She reached over and touched his hand. He stopped talking and shifted his gaze to her.

"Jake, we would like to speak with you."

When it seemed she had lost his attention, she tapped his hand to remind him to look her in the eyes.

He stayed quiet and watchful. He seemed very nervous being the center of attention.

Tim took up the conversation from there. "Jake, we—" he paused, glancing around the table for confirmation and, as he received a nod from each, continued, "—would like you to move in here at the boarding house."

"Really? I can bring my things over tonight!" he exclaimed.

His response caused the group to laugh, and Emma took up the conversation from there. "Jake, we love that you're excited. We also want you to have a role in our investigations."

Jake had been around enough to hear about the different cases she had led. He was very curious and sat still as a statue, waiting for more information.

"We believe your photography could be very important to future investigations. We've seen your pictures and know you're very talented. Also, your knowledge of overall photography will come in handy."

Jake couldn't wait any longer and said loudly, "Yes! I would love to."

"I don't think he needs much convincing," Emma commented wryly to the group, and they laughed in response.

The group broke up for their evening activities.

"I will be in the study," commented Tim.

"I will meet you there soon," said Dora and looked at her menu for the next day.

"Dora?" asked Jake.

Dora looked over and saw Jake in the doorway. "Yes, did you need something?"

"I have a question – about my living here."

"Of course, sit down." He sat and she joined him for a talk.

CHAPTER 24

JAKE'S MOVING DAY

Emma sat with Dora and Tim at the kitchen table, they'd completed their morning business meeting.

"Jake wants to move today," stated Tim.

"He was certainly eager last night," commented Emma. She saw Tony at the back door and waved him into the kitchen.

"Good morning," Tony said to the room. He leaned closer to Emma and said a low, "Good morning."

"Morning Tony. Tim mentioned Jake wants to start his move to the boarding house today," said Emma.

"Did you need some help?" asked Tony. "I can make some time this morning."

"I would appreciate the help. Can you meet me at Jake's house?" asked Tim.

"I'll be there," he promised.

"I'm ready to go," Emma said and stood up, gathering her things to leave.

"See you there," Tony said.

"We have to go," Emma said firmly.

"Bye!" called Emma.

"Bye!" called Dora and watched as they exited. She stood and went over to Tim and said, "Tell Jake we have his room ready and Papa cleared out a room in the basement for his equipment. Also make sure you move more than just his photography equipment," she warned. "He'll also need clothes and other personal items."

"I will," he promised and bent to kiss her. When he continued to linger, she pushed at him and said, "Go on with you."

He kissed her again quickly and said, "I will be back soon, with Jake."

As he turned to leave, she said, "Tim one more thing, Jake mentioned something odd to me."

"What was that?" he asked, pausing at the door.

"He asked if the furniture in the boarding house would start disappearing after he moved in."

"Disappearing?" he asked with a frown.

"Yes — I asked him what he meant and he said that the furniture in his home has been disappearing for the past year."

"When did he mention this?"

"Yesterday when I was confirming that he needs to bring his bed over. He was worried that the same thing would start happening here."

"I'll look around the house to see what is missing," he promised and left the room.

Heading down the stoop, he made his way to his wagon, parked in the front of the house. He climbed up, clicked at the horses, and headed over to Jake's house. *The furniture would have to be inventoried and sold, then the house could be put on the market. It would provide a savings account for Jake's future.*

The neighborhood was quiet as he pulled the wagon to a stop in front of Jake's home. Jumping down, he tethered his horse to a post and made his way up to the front door. He knocked briskly on it and waited. The door opened but it wasn't Jake that greeted him, it was the butler. Tim frowned, his unease didn't stem from him answering the door instead of Jake, but the fact he appeared to be in street clothes. *What's happening here,* he wondered. He didn't voice his concerns, instead, he asked, "Is Jake upstairs?"

"Step in please . . . sir," he said seeming to add the "sir" as an afterthought.

The attitude and clothes worried Tim. He frowned as he stepped into the foyer and looked up the staircase. Not turning, he asked, the butler more forcibly, **"Where is Jake?"**

Something hit him on the head--he turned to the butler and saw him holding a shovel. Tim reached up a hand to touch his head, looking bewildered.

When the hit didn't result in Tim collapsing, the butler screamed and tried to hit him again. This time, Tim saw the shovel coming at him and he intercepted it before it could make contact.

Tim looked at him in disbelief. "Give me that!" Tim wrenched the shovel out of the man's hands. "What do you think you're doing? How would you feel if I hit you with this?" He swung it at him in a threatening manner.

"That's enough," a woman's voice said from behind him. Turning he saw the maid on the stairs, holding a gun on him. She gestured to Tim with her gun and said, "Drop that please."

He did as he was told and she gave further instructions. "Now, I want you to move to that closet behind you."

Tim was considering if he should rush her to get the gun.

Reading his mind, she said, "Don't test me -- I will shoot you."

Tim took her threat seriously and moved to the closet she referenced. He stepped in and heard the door lock behind him. Leaning toward it, he listened, trying to find out their plans. "Get Jake, we're leaving," the maid's voice said.

"But what about the house," The butler whined. "It belongs to us, Daniel owed us for taking care of his wife."

Tim stood very still and thought, *It wasn't an accident, Jake's mom was murdered. Was he supposed to die in that fire? How long would Jake have lasted if Daniel were still alive?*

"We have to let that go, it's more important that we get the money from the bank. He is the only one that can do it."

"What about the big guy?" the butler asked.

"We leave him locked up, no one will be here to get him out," she said simply. "Get Jake."

Tim heard feet on the stairs and he looked at the door. He leaned on it to see if he could break it open. *No help there,* he thought. It was too thick and he had no space to ram it. Bending down, he examined the lock. *She had left the key in it.* He felt around behind him and found some paper. He would put his plan into place as soon as they were out of the foyer.

"Get your things and bring him down, we are leaving now!" the maid commanded loudly.

He heard Jake's voice, it seemed to be getting closer to the foyer.

"I don't want to go!" yelled Jake.

"You'll go," said the butler, his voice sounded strained.

Jake must be putting up a fight, thought Tim. *Good for him.*

"No! No! I won't, I am waiting for Tim. I am moving to the boarding house."

"No, you're not-you're coming with us to the bank!" the butler yelled back.

"Bank? I don't want to go there. You can't make me!" answered Jake. Tim heard a bang, that sounded like someone or something had fallen.

"Yes, it is time to get the money. Get up off the floor!" the maid said, quickly losing the last of her patience.

"Why?" he asked, still argumentative.

"Just shut up Jake," Tim heard the frustration in the woman's voice.

Tim didn't hear a response from Jake.

"Jake what is this I am holding?" the woman asked.

"My camera, hand it to me!" Jake demanded.

The woman's voice continued as if she hadn't heard him, "If you do not cooperate, what will I do with this?"

"You will break it," he said in a low voice. Tim had to strain to hear it.

"So, what are you going to do?" she asked.

"Go to the bank," he said in the same tone.

Tim heard the front door open.

"That is Tim's wagon, is he here?" asked Jake excitedly.

"No, he isn't," the butler said shortly. "Just go."

Tim heard the front door slam. He slid the paper under the closet door and kicked the lock. The key dropped onto the paper, he pulled the paper under the door to him.

He inserted it into the lock and opened the door looking quickly around the foyer. They appeared to be gone. A knock sounded, he went to opened it and saw it was Tony.

"Hey-I'm here ..." Tony said and he stopped abruptly when he saw Tim's head. "Is that blood? Are you okay?"

Tim touched his head tentatively, "It's ok for now, the help has taken Jake."

"Taken him!" he said nonplussed. "Why would they take him?"

"Theft. They want his money. They are headed to the bank—probably to clean out his accounts before they leave town. We need to head over there."

Tim stumbled a bit going down the stoop. "Are you sure you're, okay?" Tony asked.

"Yes, we need to get to the bank."

"Let's go," Tony said.

They headed out, climbed on the wagon and Tony took the reins. Quickly making their way there, they pulled the wagon to a stop in front of the bank. They jumped down and rushed up to the entrance, Tony pulled Tim to a stop. "We need to think this through, security should be involved."

Tim continued to move forward, wanting to barge in and get

Jake but Tony grabbed his jacket, pulling him to a stop, and said again, "Let's get security involved."

Tim nodded, taking a deep breath to steady himself. They entered and looked around taking in the large tiled room with a staircase leading to a second story. Tony was able to locate the guards nearest to the door. They went quickly to them and explained what was happening. The guard called to his men to join them and said, "Can you tell me where they're located?"

Tim and Tony looked around quickly, and Tim said, "Over there at the second teller's window. The dark hair heavy-set woman with the slim young man. Be careful Jake may not understand what is happening."

"I see him. Stay back we will take care of this." The guards spread out and approached the butler and Jake.

Where is the maid? Tim wondered, looking around. There was no way she wasn't here, she didn't seem to trust the butler to get the project done. He continued to look around and finally saw her speaking with a bank officer. They were in the area with the lockboxes were kept. *The furniture they sold, that must be where they kept the money.*

She hadn't noticed the guards approaching Jake and the butler. They quickly took him into custody and Tony stepped up to speak with Jake to reassure him.

Tim didn't wait for the guards and headed toward the lockboxes alone. He waited outside the room and when she came out with a full bag, he moved into her path. "Going somewhere?"

She seemed shocked he was there and didn't move.

"Is something wrong miss?" the bank officer asked when he noticed she stopped suddenly.

Tony had seen where Tim was and send a guard over to assist him.

The guard asked, "Sir, do you require assistance?"

"You'll want to take custody of her bag, I believe it's from stolen property sales," Tim indicated the bag she carried.

"No," she said pulling the bag to her. "This my money."

The security staff took custody of the bag and said, "Please come with me."

She followed him, clutching the bag close to her.

Back at the boarding house that evening. The family was in the kitchen listening to Tim's story. "What happened then?" Emma asked, wanting to hear all of the details. *How did I miss out on this adventure? I wish I could have been there.*

"They took them into custody," Tim said simply. "Kidnapping, assault, and theft." He didn't mention the additional murder charges that would be applied after an investigation.

"Am I still moving in?" asked Jake.

Laughter rang out through the table. Dora took his hand and said, "Of course, you can stay here tonight."

"We'll try again tomorrow," Tim promised.

Emma said, "We will all come over to help."

CHAPTER 25

About a week later, just after lunch, Jeremy and Emma were on a stakeout of the shelter. Emma was dressed as a boy and leaned against a wall near Jeremy. They both appeared to be relaxing and taking in the sun. Their location was the alley of the apartment building adjacent to the shelter; which allowed them to monitor the incoming and outgoing activities.

Emma was humming a bit when Jeremy started a conversation. "So, Jake has moved into the boarding house?" He had been over for a few family dinners and had the opportunity to meet the young man.

"Yes. Finally." She explained what Tony and Tim had to deal with during the move. "I helped with the inventory, the thieves had sold almost everything on the first floor. The money and Jake's mom's jewels were recovered. It didn't happen as we expected, but he is safe with us now. We all pitched in and got him settled the next day."

"What does he want to do with the house and remaining items?"

"He only cares about his photography things. Dora thinks we

should keep his mom's jewelry for him, in case he wants it later. The house and remaining items are to be put up for sale, soon."

"I am glad he is safe and at the boarding house. His family home is very nice, it should sell fast. Were they able to charge the maid and butler with the murder of Jake's mom?"

"The police used Tim's statement to charge them. The butler confessed and stated that the maid formulated the plan."

"I'm glad. There should be consequences to taking his mother away."

"Yes."

The conversation dwindled and Emma thought she would ask about something that was bothering her. "Who was that girl we saw at your house this week?"

"This past week?" he asked, delaying his answer for a bit.

"Yes," said Emma.

"She's a friend," he said simply.

"A close friend?" she asked, treading carefully.

"Getting there," Jeremy said, looking at her facial expressions. Savannah was only a friend, but he was fascinated by Emma's response to his answers. *Could she be jealous?*

"What is her name and where did you meet?" she asked, not willing to admit to herself why she was so curious.

"Savannah Woods and she works in the theatre. Her parents are actors there. She does the costumes and makeup."

"Really?" Emma asked, pushing down the feeling she had no right to have. "Can I meet her? I would love to see what she does." She started drumming her fingers on her lips, thinking about costumes and makeup.

"It seems I'm always facilitating meetings for you with interesting ladies," he teased.

"That's true," she admitted and teased back. "You do seem to know a lot of interesting ladies. I have an idea that she might help with."

Jeremy noticed a delivery wagon approaching and pulled his

hat down over his eyes. "Emma, we've documented that delivery driver here at least twice a week."

"Same person?" she asked intently.

"Yes," he murmured.

"What's he delivering?"

"Flowers."

"Can you tell where it's from?" she asked, not looking toward the wagon.

"Yes, it says The Flower Shop."

Emma smiled and said, "Well, guess what? I have a person I can contact in that establishment."

Jeremy nodded and asked, "Do you need any help?"

"No, I can handle this one." She glanced at her watch. "I need to wrap it up and get home for dinner. Want to come with me?"

"No," he said surprisingly. "I'm going out."

"To meet Savannah," she teased lightly.

"Yes," he said, watching her.

She hid her feelings as she pulled herself to her feet. "Let me know when I can meet her."

Before she could go, he took her hand and said, "Emma, Cole wants to meet soon and probe our potential suspects."

"Tell him later this week. I need to follow up on the flower vendor first."

"I'll let him know." She noticed his hand lingered on hers before he strolled away.

She rubbed where he had touched her, wishing she could figure out why she had such strong feelings for him. She shook her head. *Let it go, just let it go.* She walked away slowly, making her way home and starting to plan her next day.

CHAPTER 26

*E*mma was thoughtful the next day while preparing for work. *I'll have to pick up some Berliners for my meeting later today.*

Noticing the time, she hurried, knowing Tony would be there soon to pick her up. As she made her way downstairs, she absently touched her hand, remembering yesterday's conversation with Jeremy. Feeling uneasy and disloyal to Tony, she battled with herself on how to handle these new feelings. She stopped at the kitchen door, put a smile on her face, and entered. It was business as usual with Dora and Amy preparing breakfast and Tim conducting business at the table.

"Morning, Tim, Dora, Amy," greeted Emma.

"Morning," called everyone.

Tim looked up from his books and said, "Emma, Jake has something for you this morning."

"He does?" she asked absently while putting together the bread and butter for her breakfast.

"Yes, after you went over your office case with him, he thought he had an idea for a camera that might work."

At that moment, Jake pushed open the door from the dining

room. "Emma, I have this for you." He handed her a box camera. It was smaller than the ones she had seen prior to this.

"Jake, is this yours?" she asked curiously.

"Yes. It is a prototype of a spy camera. I met the inventor, Professor Bolas, while I was at school in London. He said it would be good for law enforcement and gave it to me when I left there."

Emma turned it over in her hands and asked, "Will I be able to use it and bring it back for you to develop the pictures?"

Jake was silent for a long moment, then he said, "I think so. We can practice together."

"Sounds like a plan. Can you show me how to use it this evening?" she asked, happy with his initiative.

"Yes, I can make time," Jake said, glad he could offer support for a case.

"Thank you," Emma said sincerely.

Tim smiled at Dora and she responded by nodding. They were both happy she was taking steps to include Jake in their group.

Jake sat down at the kitchen table to have his breakfast while the rest of the family moved the breakfast platters into the dining room for the boarders. Tim, Emma, Papa, and Dora moved back to the kitchen table to join Jake. Since he had moved into the boarding house, the family had started having more private time for breakfast. Papa went to the basement to work; the rest of the family were all still there when Tim started his business meeting.

As they were wrapping it up, Tony tapped on the kitchen door and Jake let him in. "Morning, Jake," said Tony.

"Morning, Tony," answered Jake pleasantly.

"Morning, everyone," he added, speaking to the entire room. Different hellos and good morning greetings came from the group in the kitchen.

"Just a moment; I'll go get my bag," Emma said to Tony from her position at the table.

"No rush." He bent down and kissed her hello. "I always enjoy the mornings and a treat," he teased and Dora tossed him a pastry in response. Tony sat to talk with them while Emma stood up and went to get her bag. She jogged back downstairs and they said their goodbyes to the family. Tony held the door and they exited through the back door to retrieve her bike.

As they strolled toward the trolley, Emma and Tony shared their plans for the day. He inquired, "How did the surveillance go yesterday?"

She mentioned that it involved Jeremy and went on to comment, "I think we have a new lead. You remember Karl?"

Tony got the reference and asked, "The florist? Is he involved?" He hadn't gone with Emma to meet him, but he knew they were friends.

"No!" She laughed. "But I think his delivery driver might be. I plan to meet him today to ask him some questions."

Tony was quiet for a moment and asked, "So, your surveillance was with Jeremy?" There was no expression in his voice.

She looked at him oddly and said, "Yes, he is in charge of all the surveillance for this case and my shift was with him yesterday."

"Hmm," he said noncommittally.

Emma had to let the conversation go. They didn't have time for this particular topic on a workday. The silence settled around them as they continued to the trolley. As they reached the stop, she went to kiss him and, at the last minute, he turned his head, so she kissed him on the cheek. "See you," she said quietly, knowing something was bothering him.

"Yes," he said and turned to catch the trolley.

In all the times they had walked together, Tony always turned around to give her a wave goodbye, but that day he didn't. *What has changed?* she wondered. Shaking off the feeling that something was wrong, she continued to make her way to the office.

Nothing unusual occurred that morning; the noise of type-writers filled the room. As the noon hour approached, she thought, *Just what I needed, a day with no drama.* The day's folders were put into the file room and her next day's work was organized on her desk. *The camera,* she thought. *I'll bring it in tomorrow.* She would have to be early, though it shouldn't be a problem because she knew the building manager would let her in early. Waving goodbye to everyone, she exited the office.

She rode her bike, enjoying the wind in her hair as she made her way to the bakery for the Berliners she knew would be required for her afternoon meeting. She entered the bakery through the kitchen back door and was immediately yelled at by one of her cousins. "Emma! Are you back with us?"

"No, just picking up something," said Emma. She stopped by Chloe's workstation to chat. "How are things? "

Chloe rubbed her very pregnant belly and said, "We are wonderful." Cousin had finally admitted that he saw a future with her and didn't waste time asking her to marry him. Chloe continued to work at the bakery after they were married and would probably do so until she had the baby.

"How are you and Tony?" asked Chloe.

"Funny you should ask. I'm not sure," Emma admitted.

"Why, what happened?" Chole asked, edging closer and dropping her voice to keep their conversation private.

"That's what's odd. Nothing really," she said in a confused voice.

She didn't get a chance to say more before Cousin spotted her and walked over. He leaned in and kissed her on the cheek and asked, "Anyway I could get you for a dessert?"

"As long as it isn't. . ." she teased, referencing the dessert favored by a local gangster.

"Yes, well, I have banned that one. Too many bad memories," Cousin responded.

"I appreciate that."

"I need an order of German Cinnamon Star Cookies," said Cousin.

"I think I can arrange that. When would you like me to have the order ready?" asked Emma.

"We need them for Tuesday delivery. Thanks, Emma."

"I will make them tonight."

"Perfect. I will send over the ingredients to the boarding house for you. Now, what are you here for?" Cousin asked curiously.

"Can't I just stop by because I miss everyone?" Emma teased.

He gave her a look until she relented. "Okay, I need some Berliners for a meeting today."

"I think we can arrange that." He snapped his finger at a younger cousin to get them for her.

While they were compiling the Berliners, Cousin started discussing family business about his next expansion plans. "Emma, would you like to participate and be a larger partner in our next bakery?"

She tilted her head, thought of her savings, and knew she had no plans for it at this time. "Interesting offer. Can I think about it and get with you later?"

"Yes," he replied.

Chloe ran over as fast as her pregnant body could carry her and hugged her. "Come and have dinner with us soon and bring Tony."

"I will, I promise," she said, hugging her back.

Getting the box from her younger cousin, she hugged her and headed out to the florist shop. Her mind was focused on the task in front of her as she rode around the neighborhood where the shop was located. The delivery wagon was not in the area. It was normally parked on the side of the shop. *He must be out on a delivery,* she thought. *Good.*

She entered the shop and heard the familiar twinkle of bells announcing her entry. The area was filled with flowers and smelled wonderful. As she stood there, waiting for Karl, she thought about how they had met two years ago when she was researching her mama's past. That event brought them together, she was happy they had continued to build their relationship and become close friends. She was wandering around the showroom, admiring the lovely flower arrangements when Karl came out of the back.

He smiled broadly and immediately went over to hug her. "What a nice surprise! I didn't expect you today." He noticed the box in her hands. "And Berliners! Come sit," he said, gesturing to the stool by the counter. "I have to stay up front today. I have a few orders being picked up and my delivery driver is out," he said, confirming Emma's observations.

"I had something to talk to you about, if you have time for me?" she inquired.

"Of course, I have time for you, always. What do you need?" he asked jovially.

"Your delivery driver, how long has he worked for you?" Emma asked in her typical blunt style.

He frowned, surprised at the direction of the conversation. "About six months. Is there a reason you're asking?"

"Would he come in the front or the back when he enters?"

He looked at her in a canny manner and said, "He'll be out for a few hours."

"And?" she prompted.

"He'll come in the front," he admitted. "We should be able to see him when he arrives. So, girly, are we wrapped up in another adventure?" he asked, a twinkle in his eyes, rocking back on his stool with hands-on his rounded belly.

"Yes, we have a suspicion that your delivery driver. . .?"

"Pete Langston," he supplied.

"Maybe working with someone to carry messages that could lead to a woman being hurt and possibly killed," she stated the facts without emotion.

"Hmm," he murmured thoughtfully.

"You don't appear surprised," she said, gauging his expressions.

"Well, you know good help is hard to find," he admitted

laconically.

"Can you tell me what you know about him?" she asked, ready with her pencil and notebook.

"I can tell you what I know. Pete Langston is his name, and he is about twenty years old. He keeps to himself and gets deliveries completed on time," he said simply.

"Does he talk about his personal life?"

He pondered the question and answered, "No, not really. He usually talks about the weather or the required deliveries he has scheduled. He stays out most of the day, doesn't keep money that's not his, and he's on time."

"Does he have parents?" she asked.

"I have never inquired," he said and shrugged.

"Could you inquire for me?"

"It's that important to you?" he asked, reaching over to take her hand in his.

"Yes," she answered, letting emotion into her voice and squeezing his hand.

"Then I think I can do that for you," he said warmly.

"How come I haven't met him before this?" she asked.

"It never came up, and he's usually on deliveries this time of day," he said, shrugging.

She nodded.

"Now, let's have some of these." He eagerly opened the box of Berliners. He ate one and, as he reached for another, asked, "Would you like one?"

"Just one?" she teased and took it out of the box to eat.

He grinned at her as they both took a bite of the sweet snacks. They completed their meeting with an agreement that he would send her a message if he turned up any information. She hugged him and said, "Goodbye."

She was exiting the shop when the delivery driver was coming in. He seemed to pause when he saw her but brushed past in a hurry. She raised an eyebrow at Karl, who nodded as she exited.

CHAPTER 27

That night, dinner had wrapped up and Emma accompanied Jake to the basement workshop. Tony was having a late night at the museum and wouldn't be coming by to see her. She found herself relieved that she wouldn't have to endure a conversation she knew was coming.

Putting him out of her head, she tried to concentrate on what Jake was saying about the proper way to hold the spy camera. "You will need to practice holding it steady and make sure there is plenty of light on the paper," he said.

"So, I hold it very steady and I will need to hold the paper up, maybe tack it on the wall. I'll take it tomorrow and try it out in the morning. I sent a note to Tony to tell him I will be leaving early. Thanks, Jake," she said sincerely.

"When you come back, place the camera in my workspace here," he directed.

"I'll bring it by after my office job," she promised.

That satisfied him and he started talking about film and development. Emma stayed and listened, enjoying the discussion about the technical side of the camera she would be using. They walked upstairs together, with Emma heading to her room and Jake joining the others in the sitting room.

Emma carried the camera, handling it carefully as she opened her door and entered her room. She sat on her bed, looking down at it as she planned on how to use it in the office in the morning. Standing up, she walked to the desk to lay out some papers to practice taking pictures. *Jake was right; it has to be vertical.* He had explained that to her, but she hadn't realized the challenge this presented. The paper couldn't be tacked up because the holes would be noticeable and lead to questions she didn't want to answer.

She sat in her chair, drumming her fingers on her lips. *Where was that packet of chewy candy?* she thought as she pulled open a drawer on the left side of the desk. She moved stuff around, looking for the packet Papa had gotten her while traveling.

As she searched, she remembered what he had told her about it. Just a few years ago, in 1880, Henry and Frank Fleer experimented with chicle from the sapodilla tree. The Fleer brothers made cubes of the chicle substance and overlaid the cubes with sweet material.

"Ahh, here it is," she said as she found the small, flat packet. She looked at the cube and put it in her mouth and chewed until it got sticky. She grimaced, thinking, *I much prefer my sweets in the form of baked goods.* Pulling it out of her mouth, she tore it into two pieces. The chewed cube stuck to her fingers and did not easily come off. There would be some trouble with splitting one piece when it was already chewed. *I'll probably need to chew a much smaller piece, one at a time.*

She removed as much as she could from her fingers and used the small amount remaining to attached it to the back of a paper on her desk. *Definitely sticky, very little will be fine,* she thought as she attached it to her wall. She set the camera up and move the paper around until she was able to get the optimum range.

Okay, that should be it, she thought as she documented the height of the paper in her notebook and put it back on the desk. She reached up to take the papers down and started to try to remove the sticky material. It wasn't coming off easily. *Water*, she thought, she went to her dresser, poured some into a glass, and pulled a handkerchief out. Wetting the edge, she rubbed it. When she finished, she looked at both sides of the paper and thought, *A little less tomorrow should do it.*

One more thing, she thought. *I have to make the cookies before I go to bed*. She headed back downstairs to make them.

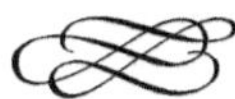

CHAPTER 28

*E*mma had gotten a very early start to the office to get the pictures without being seen. She also admitted to herself that she was again relieved to not have to talk with Tony that morning. *I'll eventually have to have a conversation with him, just not now.*

The building manager was in the hallway and saw her storing her bike. "Early this morning, Emma?"

"Yes, I was hoping you could let me into the office. I have a few things to catch up on," she said.

It wasn't unusual for her to be in early, and he said, "Of course." They walked up together discussing the weather and other pleasantries. after opening the door, he left her there, with a cheerful goodbye.

The office was quiet, and she approached her desk quickly, pulling out the chewing candy and Jake's camera before making her way over to Lauri's desk. There, she found eight vendor invoices in Lauri's folder and moved them back to her desk. She pulled the matching customer invoices from her folder. Small pieces of the cubes were chewed, one at a time, and transferred to the back corners of the invoices. She placed them at the height she had documented the previous night. The sticky candy held and she was able to take pictures of each one. The bright light streaming into the room was important, otherwise, the pictures could turn out too dark.

She glanced at the watch attached to her top and realized she had to hurry to get the papers back into Lauri's file. Flipping them face down, she wetted a small fabric square with water from her drinking bottle and rubbed it lightly on the paper to remove most of the substance. When she finished, she saw that it was still a little sticky and the paper would take a bit to properly dry. She hoped Lauri wouldn't notice.

The camera! she thought after returning the papers to Lauri's folder and hearing feet coming up the stairs. She ran back to her desk, sat down, and moved it to her lap, under the desk. It was the office manager; as usual, he barely spared her a glance as he walked by.

She took a deep breath, put the camera safely away in her bag, and thought, *I hope the pictures come out*. Realizing she was still in her split skirt, she went and changed in the hallway closet. Walking back into the office, she saw Lauri a few steps in front of her. They both sat at their desk and Lauri said a quiet, "Hello."

Emma returned the greeting, watching her discreetly. Lauri pulled out her daily file and, when there were no indications that anything was wrong, Emma pulled out her files to start her work.

A few moments later, when Lauri went to separate her invoices to be typed, she said, "These are a bit sticky, something must have spilled on them." She didn't seem bothered by it; it wasn't out of the ordinary for the raw invoices to have had something spilled on them. She continued, "Oh well, I'm typing them this morning, so it shouldn't matter."

Emma nodded, glad the stickiness didn't appear suspicious. Keeping quiet, she got her work completed and headed home. Jake had been clear about his requirements, so her first stop was his lab in the basement. She opened the drawer and stored it how she had been shown. She understood the equipment had to be handled carefully.

The pictures should be developed later that evening and she could access them with her papa in the morning. This was her first time using the device and she was nervous about the final product.

Heading upstairs, she heard Dora call, "Hi, Sister, how did it go? Will the pictures turn out?" As she exited the basement into the foyer, she saw Dora waiting for her. "It went well, but I'm unsure of the technology. I hope they come out. If not, I'll try again," she said philosophically.

Tim walked up to them and handed Emma a note. "Cole dropped this by for you today and said they want a group meeting on the findings later this week."

"Hmm, I still have to get information from Karl about the flower delivery driver. I hope to have it in a few days. I'll check in with him tomorrow," she said, thinking about what was still needed before the group meeting.

"Emma, be careful," said Dora, a note of warning in her voice.

"I will. Karl can be trusted."

Dora said, "Come eat before you have to go out again."

Emma linked her arms through hers and headed to the kitchen. Her afternoon duties were fairly routine.

That evening, Jake developed the film and indicated the photos would have to dry overnight prior to any inspection. Emma understood and let him work on their development while she sat in the sitting room with the family and boarders, working on some lace patterns. She completed her work, bid everyone goodnight, and headed to bed.

Very early the next morning, a knock at her door woke her from a deep sleep. "Just a minute," she mumbled as she rolled out of bed and grabbed her robe. Opening the door, she was surprised to find Jake there. "Jake, it's very early. Is something wrong?" she asked, pulling her robe belt tight and pushing her hair out of her face.

He didn't answer the question but instead said, "I have the pictures ready."

She knew she would have to go see them, so she said in a low voice, "All right, let me get some socks on."

He nodded and waited as she headed back to her bed, leaving her door open. She smiled slightly and sat down on the edge to pull on her socks. Standing, she gestured for him to lead the way. They went downstairs and into the quiet kitchen; no one was up yet. There was plenty of light in the room to view the pictures, Jake had turned up all of the gas lamps. She glanced down at them and saw they were surprisingly clear and the data could be read. "Jake, these are perfect. With this evidence, I will be able to move forward with the investigation," she said wonderingly.

Jake didn't smile, but she thought she made him happy. "Can I keep these?" she asked.

"Yes." Though he said yes, she thought he looked a little uncomfortable.

"Jake, I know you normally keep your pictures, but you should think of these like your work photos. You don't keep those, do you?"

"No, no, I don't," he said slowly.

"Well, you're now part of our team and your pictures are part of that work product." The information she presented made sense to him and he seemed to relax.

She gathered them up and said, "I'll take these to my room now and show them to Papa later. See you at breakfast. And, Jake, good work."

He nodded, she helped him turn off the gas lamps and they both headed upstairs.

Entering her room, she sat on the bed, knowing she would be unable to sleep. She turned up her gas lamps and compared the photos with her previously copied information. The findings were consistent; the amounts of structural steel, cement, and sand differed between vendors and customers.

Papa should be up in another hour, she thought, glancing at the clock. Hearing movement on the steps, she quickly got dressed and headed downstairs to help with the early baking. Amy, Emma, and Dora worked together to put together the pastries, biscuits, and bread that would be required for the day. Emma was rolling out the dough and pinching off biscuits to go into the oven when she heard Papa in the dining room. As he entered the kitchen, she said, "Papa, when I'm finished here, I need you to look at something for me."

"Sure, Sister, come into my study when you're ready," commented Papa absently, looking at some notes in his hands.

"Let me get the pictures and I'll meet you there." Emma finished adding the biscuits to the pan and placed them in the oven to bake. "I am on my way to see Papa," Emma commented to Amy and Dora.

Dora nodded and said, "We will keep an eye on them." She and Amy would continue working on the breakfast preparations.

Heading to her room, Emma retrieved the pictures and her notes. She made her way downstairs and laid the photographs on the desk for him to evaluate. She placed the invoices that should match -- together.

He studied the picture groupings and the differences between the two. "Hmm," he said. "There's definitely something up here. The invoice from the vendor is providing iron but the customer is paying for steel. There's a significant cost difference between the two. Steel is a better metal to build with; it's becoming the standard for all skyscrapers. Another thing that worries me is that I don't see additional steel or oak timbers to set the foundation. Without that, the concrete numbers should be much higher. See here," he said, pointing to the customer invoices, "the customer is being charged for additional steel to support the foundation but the purchase from the vendor shows a deficit in both areas."

"Papa, this is dangerous. Those buildings could collapse over time and the buildings here are partly for the less fortunate," she said, worried.

"When you and Tim chose the Baker Agency as the first location for women to be in the workplace and met with Josh Baker, did he appear to be an honest man?" Papa asked.

"We met with his assistant, but yes, he has a good reputation in the business. I can't imagine he would condone this. Papa, haven't you worked with him in the past?" asked Emma.

"Not directly, more through third parties like your office. Do you ever see him in the agency?" Papa asked.

"He doesn't come into the office. It's handled by the office manager," she said and went on to explain the separate filing systems.

"You don't ever reconcile the invoices?" Papa asked with a frown.

"No. We just type them up, multiple ones from vendors and one to the customer. One copy for the files and one to be mailed. Other secretaries place them in envelopes for mailing."

"Separate systems and separate books. How did he think he was going to get away with this? Did he think no one would notice?" Papa asked incredulously.

"I believe he thinks the women doing the work are too simple to understand what they are typing," explained Emma.

"Well, you proved him wrong," he said, proud of his smart daughter.

"Any recommendations for where we go from here?" she asked, trusting his decision on these matters.

"I'm thinking about that. We need a meeting with Mr. Baker. I think it's time, and we have enough evidence to show him," commented Papa.

"You'll set it up?"

"I will," he said, still reviewing the invoices.

"I'll let Tim and Dora know."

He nodded and looked over at her, "Tell them to keep this quiet."

"I will," she said and headed to the kitchen to let her partners know the case status.

Papa got the note to Mr. Baker organized and off that morning. The meeting was set up immediately after lunch that day.

Emma went about her normal schedule and made her way home to meet him. They took a cab to the office, she stepped down and had to arch her neck to see to the top. "His office is in there?"

"Yes, it is one of the tallest buildings that has been built. Baker's many engineering offices are helping to raise the city of Chicago to new heights."

Emma believed Mr. Baker was an honest man, but she would have to be observant of his behavior during their meeting. There was a guard in the foyer. She recognized him from Pinkerton; the security world was a small one. He was dressed in the typical black suit with a black tie and white shirt. He gave her a wink when she waved. Papa didn't need directions, so they entered the stairs and Emma realized they would be going to the tenth floor.

When they exited the stairway and onto their floor, Papa was breathing a bit ragged from the walk and had to lean on the wall to catch his breath.

"Papa, are you all right?" Emma asked, concerned. It wasn't just his breathing; his color seemed off.

"I'm fine, Emma, just a bit winded. We're not all as young as you are," he said with a smile.

She would have to keep an eye on him. As Papa got his breath back, his color returned and they headed toward the large carved doors at the end of the hall. They led to a large office space that had wood floors and intricate rugs. A male secretary saw them and waved them over to him. As they approached the desk, the secretary said warmly to Papa, "Ellis, so good to see you. Mr. Baker will be with you soon."

"How do you know the secretary?" Emma asked in a low voice as they moved to low chairs near the wall.

In the same tone, Papa answered, "He makes the initial contacts with the engineers and sets up meetings for Mr. Baker's engineering offices."

They only waited a few moments. Mr. Baker came out to meet them and, immediately, she liked his personal touch. She studied his appearance, his hair was black with streaks of grey throughout, and appeared to be in his early to middle 30s. He was also a man with an interesting face. He would have been classically handsome, but it looked like his nose had been through a few fights.

"I'm Ellis Evans and this is Emma, my daughter, who I sent you a note about this morning. I believe she has some information that will interest you."

He looked at her appraisingly and nodded. "Okay. Let's go into my office and hear what you have to say."

She didn't see anything that told her he was dishonest; his manner was open, his eye contact strong, and his voice steady. *All good things*, she thought but would reserve her final judgment until later.

They went in and sat down on the long brown couch, with Mr. Baker sitting in a dark chair across from them. He directed his question at Emma. "You want to tell me why you're here today?"

Emma took out her notebook and started, "Mr. Baker—"

"Please, call me Josh," he interrupted.

"Okay, Josh." She started going over the discrepancies she had found in the office.

When she paused, Josh looked at her in an almost curious manner and asked, "These are rather big accusations. Do you have something to back this up?"

She was relieved she didn't have just her notebook to make her case and said, "Yes, I do." She reached into her long jacket pocket and pulled out the photos she had taken of the invoices and laid them out side by side on the low table in front of him.

He sat a bit stunned at the photographic evidence. He hadn't expected anything other than conjecture. As he looked at the photos, he had to admit they contained incontrovertible proof that building supplies were being substituted without approval. He murmured, "It's funny. I gave that role to Tracey because I thought I could trust him. Prior to taking him on, I had heard things about his previous job, but I thought he deserved another chance. What to do. . ." His voice trailed off. Looking Emma in the eyes, he asked, "Emma, do you believe the engineers assigned to the office are involved?"

She gave some thought to that question before answering. "I don't think so. They are involved in the proposals and development of material costs. The office manager usually works on the initial invoice to the vendors and places the orders and then the engineers confirm the amount billed to the customer."

"Very tricky. I'll bet there are two different logbooks in his office. Do the secretaries have business training? Accounting included?"

"Yes, all of the secretaries in the offices are either temporary or permanent persons who came from the local business school. Accounting classes are required as part of our training," she said quickly.

"We'll need to restructure the office for a few weeks with new management," he said, thinking about how this would work.

Her eyes widened, suddenly worried she had inadvertently put their company in jeopardy. "Everyone will keep their jobs?"

"Yes, as long as no one else is involved in the deceit," he stated matter-of-factly.

"When will you move forward, Mr. Baker?" asked Papa.

"Call me Josh," he said absently. "Tomorrow morning. I can't let this continue." He looked at Emma and warned, "Don't do anything out of the ordinary or say anything to anyone."

"I would like to notify my partners; Tim and Dora," she stated.

"That is fine, just no one else. Is there someone in the office you would recommend over the others to help coordinate the investigation?" he asked, pondering his next moves.

One person came to mine and Emma said, "Yes, Lauri Wheeler is the best secretary in the office and would be my first choice."

"I'll trust you and will talk to Miss Wheeler. I need to bring in another person to help coordinate the efforts from the outside. I will, of course, immediately talk to my lawyers about freezing any accounts the current manager has open."

That evening, Emma told Dora about the case and to keep it quiet until after Mr. Baker confirmed it was okay. "Where is Tim?" she asked.

"He was called out to one of our businesses. He will be home late," said Dora, not offering more information. Emma watched her but didn't ask further questions. Tim stayed out late and Emma figured she would talk to them in the morning.

The next day, Dora mentioned Tim was out early on business. Emma wanted to get to the office early and didn't have time to question her. She couldn't think of anything but the office on her way in. Once she got to her desk, she sat tense, waiting for the office hours to start. She would have felt better if she had been able to discuss the situation with Tim and Dora, it just hadn't worked out that way.

Trying to behave in a normal manner, she pulled out her invoices to start typing. The office began filling with the secretaries, engineers, and the office manager. That was when things changed. Men in nice suits flooded into the office. Josh and surprisingly Tim, dressed in what appeared to be his wedding suit, went immediately to the manager's office. They were accompanied by two police officers and several discreetly dressed men.

Tim managed a subtle nod at Emma before pausing at the door. "I know most of you," he said, directing his speech to the office workers and engineers. He smiled at those around the room who knew him. "For those, I do not know, I am Tim Flannigan, and I am here with the owner of the firm, Mr. Baker. Please, stay at your desks and await further direction." He followed Josh into the manager's office.

Everyone seemed to turn into stone, staring at the manager's door. It seemed to be an eternity before the men returned, and the police officer had the office manager secured in cuffs. He looked defeated as they escorted him out.

Josh stopped by Tim and whispered in his ear. Tim nodded and said to the group, "This is the owner of Baker, Mr. Josh Baker."

Josh started with a reassuring smile to the employees, taking a moment to look each in the eye. "I would like to assure everyone that they still have their jobs." He gave them a minute to digest what he said before continuing. "This is in no way a reflection of your work in this office. We have found an accounting discrepancy that will take a while to straighten out. I would like you to work with Tim in the following weeks. He has graciously agreed to lead the audit for me. I also want to speak with Lauri Wheeler?" he asked, searching for her.

Lauri felt like her heart was going to beat right out of her chest, but she motioned to him with her hand. "Yes, sir, right here."

He looked at her appraisingly and said, "Your experience and leadership here in the office has been communicated to me and you have been selected to assist Tim with the audit. At the end of this, we will determine the final permanent positions of staffing for this firm." He looked away from her and said, "Tim, I'll leave you here to begin."

Josh approached Lauri and clasped her hands in his. "We'll speak soon." And with that, he was gone.

Lauri looked a bit shellshocked. Emma went up to her and asked, "Are you okay?"

"Why me?" she asked, bewildered at the events that had occurred that morning.

"Why not you? You are amazing at your job and they would be lucky to have you. Now, deep breath and be yourself," Emma told her.

Tim called over, "Lauri, come into the office so we can talk. Everyone else, continue with your normal duties." Tim and Lauri entered the office manager's office and shut the door.

Lauri couldn't wait any longer to start asking questions. "Tim, what's happening? Why did the police take the office manager away?"

Tim walked over to the desk and tapped the two identical books sitting on its surface. "This is the reason."

She looked at him questioningly and said, "I don't understand."

He sat on the corner of the desk and said, "You know how all of the invoices for customers and vendors are kept separate?"

"Yes," she said, frowning.

"The owner found out about the filing system and reviewed some of the invoices together. The office manager was keeping the two files separate so he could buy substandard materials and pocket the extra money. He recorded all the information in these two books. We took a chance there would be a written record here," Tim stated in a business-like manner.

"Oh, my goodness," she said, taking a deep breath and sat down on the office chair.

"Yes. These cons are limited. We didn't want to spook him, so we moved in fast. Josh has drafted a letter of explanation to go out to the customers explaining that there will be a probe into all of their projects. At this time, we do not know if the suppliers were involved or it was just the office manager. This must be kept quiet until we can figure it out. We—me and you—will work together to build one file with the proper invoices and project files. You will need to evaluate your staffing and let me know if we can get this done in a few weeks. We've been allowed to bring in more temporary help if we see a need for it," he said as he looked at her expectantly.

"This will also take weekends and evenings," she said quietly, thinking of staffing.

"Yes. You'll need to announce everyone's new job responsibilities," he said as he straightened up, away from the desk. "Let's get started. Please show me the filing system and how they are separated."

"Yes, please follow me." They headed out of the office to the file room, Lauri waved to Emma. "Emma, come with us and help pull files to start the process."

"Yes, of course." She closed the file in front of her and followed them.

As they explained the separate systems in place, Tim rubbed his forehead and said, "We'll need to pull each file and compare the differences in each one. Pull identical files for the same companies, enough for seven people to work on. Lauri, include yourself in the process."

They pulled the files and distributed them to the office employees for them to compile and organize.

Tim commented to Lauri as she started to exit the file room, "Lauri, come to the office, we have one more task." He paused before joining her and called, "Fred and Robert, I need you to come to the office for a discussion."

They entered and Tim indicated for them to sit down in the two chairs facing the desk. Tim was seated behind it, with Lauri standing next to him. The two men sat down. Fred was an experienced engineer in his thirties; Robert was in his late twenties and had trained under Fred. They both looked nervous but waited patiently for Tim to start the conversation.

"Fred and Robert, we don't think you were involved in the office manager's scam." They seemed to visibly relax at this statement. Seeing this reaction, he continued, "We would like you to stay here at Baker and help us through this mess and help us form a stronger, honest company."

Fred spoke up. "You can count on us. We really didn't know what was going on."

"I appreciate you telling me that. What I need for you to do is pull all the project files listing all the materials and highlight the ones that should have been ordered and then get with the secretaries. They will be pulling all the information into one file. I will be reconciling all the missing funds. Lauri here is your temporary office manager." They looked at one another, Tim saw and commented a bit stiffly, "Will this be an issue?"

"No, no," they said in unison.

Robert said, "Just different, that's all." He looked at Lauri and said, "I'm looking forward to working with you as our office manager."

"Thank you," she said warmly. "Let's get back to work."

They smiled back, relieved they still had jobs and headed out of the office to gather the requested files.

She walked out of the office and went over to Emma's desk. "Can you stay a full day today?"

"Yes, I'm okay for today." Emma had expected something like this. The people she normally transported documents for had been notified she would be unavailable for a while.

Lauri started by handing out the files to each secretary and said, "Has everyone gotten their duplicate files?" They nodded. "Now open each file. We want you to put the two invoices together first and then we'll be looking for differences between the two. As you pull these together, the engineers will need to review the original project files with the paperwork to see which matches the original design."

One of the secretaries spoke up. "But that will take some time."

"Yes, it will, because it takes many invoices to make a building. We want to provide data to show how much money has been stolen. If anyone has a problem with this project, please see me privately in the manager's office and we can arrange for a temp to take your place," she said in a firm voice.

The secretary who asked the question looked over at another secretary with a worried expression. She realized they were lucky to still have jobs and stopped asking questions. They got to work. It was tedious but necessary.

They all worked diligently and lunch was brought into the office as a surprise. Dora and Thomas opened the door and came in with many boxes. Emma got up and helped clear a large table near the front of the office. The food was set out and everyone started to eat.

Dora asked Emma, "Where's Tim?"

"Office," she said, taking a bite of her sandwich and nodded her head toward his closed door.

"I'll take a plate into him," she said as she gathered his food. Dora knocked softly and got a call to come in. Before the door closed, Emma heard Tim say, "Dora!"

The staff enjoyed their meal of sandwiches and fruit. Dora had also included some cookies.

Work continued that afternoon with the newly organized files being collected at the end of the day. Tim would be the one to do a final evaluation to determine the total differences for each company. Any instances of overcharging or inconsistent accounting would be cataloged.

Everyone started to get ready to leave and Lauri said, "You all did good work today. Given our progress, I think it will take a few weeks to reconcile the paperwork. At that time, we'll reorganize the office. I'll see everyone tomorrow."

Tim came out of the office and said, "Emma, Lauri, if you will wait for me, a cab has been arranged."

"Thanks, but I'm on my way out now," said Lauri. She smiled as she left for the day.

Emma went into the office and dropped onto the couch with a

sigh. She looked around and said, "I've never been allowed in here before."

As he cleaned up his desk, Tim said in a tired voice, "I would rather be working from the boarding house."

"Are you okay with doing this on top of our business?" she asked concerned about him.

"Yes, it's for a very important client and it involves us adding more employees to our business. All the temporary hires for this operation will come from us," he explained.

"That's good," stated Emma.

They locked up the file room; they'd had the locks replaced for the whole office earlier in the day. He pulled the main door shut and made sure the lock clicked into place before they left. They were both quiet on the way home in the cab. Dora and Papa met them at the door. Dora took Tim's hat and walked with him into the study, with Emma and Papa following behind.

"Long day, Tim?" asked Papa.

"Yes, as Emma can attest. We only made a small dent in the files. It looks like this has been going on for some time. I'm not sure how long at this point. I'll have to continue working long hours for a while."

"You can do it, Tim," said Dora in a supportive voice.

"Yes, I know I can. I just have to get used to the schedule," he said taking her hand.

"We can hire a secretary to help with our business until the project is over," suggested Dora.

They heard the front door open and shuffling feet. Dora knew who it was and called, "Jake, we're in here."

He came to the door and saw it was the family and asked, "Hello. Are we in here tonight?"

"No, we're just talking about Tim and Emma's day at the office," said Dora.

"Is dinner soon?" he asked. That made them laugh.

"Soon. Come to the kitchen and I'll get you a snack," she said as Jake happily followed while she asked about his day.

Thomas was not at dinner that night. Emma knew where he was and wasn't worried. He and Clair continued to spend as much time together as they could.

Later that evening, Thomas came in the kitchen door as the family sat around the table talking. "Hi, Thomas, would you like something to eat?" asked Dora.

He smiled and said, "I had dinner earlier with a friend." He turned to Emma and handed her a letter. "This is the letter you are waiting for. Alison said you could read it before sending it out."

Relieved this would start the process of getting her out of the shelter and to a safe location, she told the group as she read it, "This is good. She's kept it simple. Mentions she's missed him and missed getting to know his family. She asks that she be allowed to live with them. She covered briefly that her health was at risk in her current environment. Finally, she mentions that it must be kept quiet and details would follow if he agrees. There are some personal touches."

She turned to Thomas. "This is good to send." Before she sealed the envelope, she put a note inside for them to send all replies to the Pinkerton address. She closed it up and looked at her family and said, "We should know the timing soon." They nodded.

"I'll drop it by the post office on my way to work in the morning," Thomas commented.

With that final issue resolved, a very tired Emma and Tim turned in early.

CHAPTER 29

The next few weeks were a blur for Emma and Tim as they continued working at both the office and their other jobs. During this time, Tony and Emma didn't see each other, and she was grateful for that. There was a showdown coming up between them that she wasn't ready for.

Dora was aware that Emma was leaving early each morning to avoid seeing Tony. Unfortunately, Dora didn't have the same option and rolled her eyes when a knock sounded at the door. *I'm going to get Emma for this,* she thought as she straightened her shoulders and went to answer it. Calling to Amy, "Would you mind setting the table."

She understood that Dora wanted time alone with Tony and left the room.

Dora opened the door and waved him in. "She's not here, is she?" he asked.

"No," she confirmed, going back to the table to continue kneading her bread.

There were too many emotions for him to process; Anger, frustration, and finally pain. He slammed his hand on the table, startling Dora.

"Sorry," he said looking down at the table.

"No need to be, she can be frustrating. She has behaved this way with me, the more I pushed, the more she turned away."

"So, your advice is for me is just to wait until she is ready? How fair is that?"

"It isn't," she agreed. "I think she'll finally stop this behavior after their investigation is completed. There won't be an excuse for her to conveniently hide behind."

"She won't have forever," he said quietly.

"I know and Tony – she knows."

He stood to leave, looking a little lost. Dora watched him and wondered if she should say something to Emma. The answer to that came that evening when Tim and Emma were so tired, they could barely stay away to eat. Dora was infinitely patient with them both, holding their dinner and helping them to bed when they were too tired to move.

As the project wound down weeks later, Lauri, Tim, and Emma were reviewing the last of the files. He closed the final one on the desk, stood up, and went to collapse on the couch, saying, "That's it. It appears this was a simple scheme; it doesn't appear the vendors are involved. I believe this was a short-term event and, once the building materials were at the site, he would have cashed out and disappeared."

"Tim, what happened to all of the money?" Lauri asked curiously, knowing he was in contact with Mr. Baker.

Tim leaned back further on the couch. "Josh's lawyers seized his accounts based on the photographic evidence. The money was found in his and several of his family members' accounts. The police have kept them in custody on a variety of charges to do with fraud."

The assignment was ending soon and he was relieved. Their company had made a lot of extra money these last few weeks, but he would rather be with Dora and their business. "Lauri, how have you liked being an office manager over the past few weeks?" he asked quietly.

"I enjoyed it. I was nervous at first, but I think I was pretty good at it," she said, thinking this was when she'd learn she would be returned to the secretarial pool.

"You were very good," he confirmed. "Emma and I are recommending that you take over as the office manager here, permanently." They both smiled at her.

She sat stunned for a moment, not believing what she was hearing. Positions like this were never offered to women. "Are you sure?" she asked, her eyes darting from one to the other. She was very scared they were going to tell her it was all a mistake.

"Yes, we're sure. You're the most qualified person for the position," stated Emma warmly.

"Wow," said Lauri, not knowing what to say.

"Would you like the position?" Tim asked simply.

"Yes, yes I would," she answered immediately.

"There's still a lot of cleanup to do," he warned her. "Josh will be meeting with the building owners to assure them that changes have been made and there will be transparency in all future projects. I'll also be helping him with money recovery."

"I can handle it," she said confidently.

Tim already knew that, but he was happy to hear she was ready for the challenge.

They headed out to make the final announcements to the staff. Lauri took the lead and started, "We'll be going back to normal staffing starting tomorrow. We would like to thank the temporary workers brought in for this project, as we couldn't have gotten through the work without you. We wish you well in your future endeavors." She looked at each one with a smile.

She turned her gaze on the staff who had been with them prior to the scam being exposed. The engineers and secretaries were listening intently. "We are happy to say that we plan to be here for a long time and want you to stay with us. Our workflow will be modified and I'll have an office meeting tomorrow to discuss the changes. Our thanks to all for the long hours. We know we took time away from your families, and we appreciate your hard work."

Tim cleared his voice and said, "I am heading out, and Lauri is now your official office manager."

The room broke out with congratulations. Tim waited a moment before continuing. "Everyone here will be receiving a bonus for all the extra work put in. It will be in your next paycheck."

The workers erupted with laughter and the palpable tension vanished.

Emma and Tim were taking a cab home when she said, "Tim, that was very nice of Josh to provide bonuses to the team."

"Yes," he said. "I thought so also. He asked me to give you this." He took an envelope out of his jacket pocket, handing it to her.

Emma looked at him questionably and opened the envelope. Inside was a check for $1000, listed as a finder's fee in the memo section.

Tim smiled and said, "Yeah, mine was the same. This will go to the bank and allow us to do things we never thought we could do. What will you do with yours?"

"First, I am going to faint. Goodness!" She waved the envelope at her suddenly flushed face. "I am thinking about a few things."

Tim nodded, agreeing it would be a good idea to invest the money.

Part of it would go to the Bakery, she thought.

They both settled back to let the cab take them home, very happy they could go back to their normal schedules and see loved ones.

Tim looked over at Emma and was hesitant to start this conversation. "Emma, now that we've gotten this case wrapped up, you need to talk to Tony. He's feeling left out of this part of your life. He's pretty raw."

"I know," she said quietly. "I'm just not sure what to do about it."

CHAPTER 30

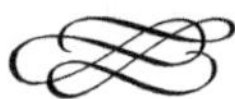

*E*mma made a decision that night to finally talk with Tony. The time he got off was approaching, she took her bike and made her way to the museum. She rode to the wall just before the museum steps, jumped off, and prepared to pick up the bike when she heard his voice. "No, I can't." He laughed at something his companion said. "I would love to accompany you, but I need to talk to Emma first." The woman continued speaking in a low tone. Emma decided it was time to let herself be seen and walked around the wall to the steps.

She couldn't tell who was more surprised, Tony or his companion. Emma assumed a pleasant expression and said, "Mrs. Smith, Tony. Tony, I thought I would walk you home."

He gave her an odd look but said, "That would be nice." He turned to Mrs. Smith and said, "I'll see you at the museum gala."

"Yes, you will. Nice to see you again, Emma." She gave her a nod and walked to her waiting cab.

"Hi," she said hesitantly.

"Hi, are you back now?" he asked shortly, looking her in the eyes.

"Back?" she asked, bewildered by the turn of conversation. "Back from where?"

"Your case, Em. I haven't seen you in weeks. I come by the house in the morning, and you're already gone. I come by in the evening, and you're not there or you're already in bed."

She bowed her head for a moment, then lifted it to look him in the eyes. "Yes, that would be accurate. I got wrapped up in my case and it became my priority."

"Here's the thing, Emma, on this list of priorities, where do I fall?" he asked, still not showing much emotion.

She didn't have an answer for that and stayed silent.

He continued. "I need someone who's there for me and I'm just now realizing that I made an agreement with you that didn't allow me any say in how our future would play out." He took a calming breath and said, "I'm finally realizing that to grow and change, I need to move on."

Emma hadn't realized they were going to have this play out here. "I think you're right. You've been building a nice career here and have a new set of people you're socializing with." His cheeks turned red at that comment. Leaning her bike against the stairs, she walked toward him, taking his hands in hers. "Tony, we just made a big commitment too early. We thought, because our friendship was so strong, that it would lead to a similar future. I think we're going in different directions."

He sat down on the steps and said, "I didn't think we would be here again. I didn't think I would change so much."

"Me either," she said as she sat next to him and put her head on his shoulder. He put his arm around her and pulled her close. "Tony, you're my best friend, but we have never had a passion that pushed any boundaries."

"Yes. I thought it would come later," he murmured into her hair.

"Where do we go from here?" she asked.

"We stay friends, but we move on in our personal lives." He paused briefly before asking, "Will you go out with Jeremy?"

He knows me so well, she thought and said out loud, "I'm not sure. Maybe. Will you go out with Mrs. Smith?" She had seen the way the widow watched Tony.

He turned red and said, "Her name is Peggy. I think so. She wants to."

Emma laughed suddenly, feeling something had been lifted off of her. "Tony, we will stay best friends. You can always come to me with anything. You'll always be an important part of my life."

"You're so important to me and always will be," he said, pulling her close for a long moment.

They sat for a while. "Walk me home?" she asked.

"Will you still bring me strudel?" he asked, some humor showing in his voice.

"Yes, yes, I will always bring you strudel." She leaned over and gave him a sweet kiss.

They stood and headed home, realizing that, after tonight, things would be different.

CHAPTER 31

A letter was delivered to the Pinkerton office the following week. Jeremy saw the return address and took it directly to Cole, who directed him to open the letter and find out if the cousin was receptive to Alison moving in with his family. Jeremy did so and saw it was a cheerful but worried affirmative. He said, "We are a go."

Cole said, "Good, then it's time to set up a group meeting. Notify everyone."

It's time to make a plan, and Emma will want to be in the middle of it, Jeremy thought with a smile.

He sent notes to everyone involved in the case to meet at Pinkerton's the following night. He received confirmation back from all. Their group was larger on this case: it involved the Pinkerton detectives who had volunteered their time, Emma, Dora, Tim, Thomas, and Clair.

The next evening, Jeremy looked around the full conference room and saw everyone had arrived. Emma approached him and asked, "Ready to start?"

"Yes," he responded. He cleared his throat and raised his voice to be heard over the noise. "Everyone, let's take a seat and start evaluating the information we have from the stakeouts. I'll list the vendor and let the operations part of the stakeout detail any information found on the type of people making deliveries to the shelter." He looked to his left and said, "Dan? You have information about the person who delivers the milk?"

Dan, a Pinkerton detective, looked at Emma. "The milkman turned out to be related to Emma."

She looked startled and asked, "Does Otto work that route?"

"Yes," responded Dan with a smile.

"Yes, he's my uncle and can be removed from the list," she said firmly.

Jeremy agreed and moved on to the next suspect. "Next is the grocery men. Jonathan has that information."

Jonathan, a Pinkerton detective, spoke up and said, "No one consistent, and there appears to be no pattern to the deliveries; different days and different times."

Jeremy prompted him, "You also looked into the mailman?"

"Yes, though it is a consistent person and on a daily route, we found no deliveries to the ladies at the shelter. Katy confirmed that he rarely stops there and, if he does, she keeps the mail and gives it to Clair."

Clair confirmed, "Yes, we don't have the address listed anywhere, so any mail is usually picked up by me and disposed of at my residence."

Jonathan had one more report. "There is Thomas, who also has access at different hours."

Clair looked a bit panicked that Thomas might get into trouble but relaxed when she heard Jeremy's next statement. "Thomas is part of the team, so he will be taken off the list."

Clair exhaled a breath she didn't know she was holding, and Thomas squeezed her hand and smiled.

Jeremy moved down his list to the flower deliveries. "The one constant delivery was the flowers; it was always the same person. Emma, can you take it from there?" Jeremy asked, glancing at her.

"Yes, I recognized the delivery name on the wagon and I followed up. A friend of mine runs that particular flower shop. I met with him and asked him to get some information for me. He was able to get me an address and a full name. They didn't think we would check it out and it turns out he also has the same last name as Ann. I think Clair can continue here," she said, looking over at her.

Clair nodded. "Emma asked me how the flowers were handled at the shelter and I confirmed with Katy that Ann is the only one who has taken over unboxing them and putting them in vases. She would also take care of debris by taking it to the outside trash location."

Jonathan assumed the conversation. "Once we realized she would move the trash out, we watched the delivery driver. He would make the delivery and then be back in the area about a half-hour later. He was seen walking around and would pilfer the trash."

Cole now spoke directly to Jeremy and Emma. "What's the plan? How do we use this?"

"Our idea," Jeremy said, seeing Emma nod in encouragement, "is to use the communication system to our advantage."

Emma added, "Our safety net here is that I think she hasn't disclosed the location until she gets paid. This is what we have planned. . ."

The group listened and contributed to the plan to get Alison safely out of the shelter. The date was settled upon and her cousin was notified by telegram.

CHAPTER 32

$\mathcal{A}$ week later, when all plans were in place, Clair was in the kitchen at the shelter talking quietly to the housekeeper about Alison.

"Katy, Alison is sick with a headache and is in her room. She needs quiet and no people visiting. We want her well enough to move tomorrow night by train. Emma will be taking her and keeping the operations small."

Ann was just outside of the kitchen, listening in. *I'll have to get the word out about the date of the move today. Pete should be here with flowers this afternoon.* She immediately went to her room to jot down the information about Alison's departure time, persons moving her, and type of transportation. She folded the note and put it in her pocket.

As usual, she volunteered to move the flowers and organized the boxes for disposal. She took the empty boxes and placed them in the trash outside, near the back door. Her brother would check the flower box and deliver the message. She was satisfied no one knew it was her selling the information about the other women in the shelter. Emma had questioned her earlier but nothing had come of it.

The next night couldn't come fast enough for her. The payday would allow her and her brother to get a new start in a new town.

The night of the scheduled move, everyone was in the sitting room and Alison was still in her room, resting. Clair had excused herself from the group and went to the hallway. Ann could hear Clair talking to someone she assumed was Emma. She smirked, sure that she was smarter than all of them. She moved closer to the door, looked in the crack, and noticed Alison was dressed as a man. She thought, *They're not so smart. I can tell it's her because her long dark hair is visible under the hat. He'll get her whether she is dressed like a man or woman.*

They moved out of her sight, and Ann heard the back door open. She assumed Emma and Alison were leaving. *Alison's husband should have her soon, and we will have our money.* She sat back in her chair, smiling and feeling great about the future.

The two figures dressed as boys exited the shelter, planning to make their way to the train station. Keeping watch for anyone around them, they headed up the alley and down the street.

A man stepped out of the shadows to follow them. He had a gun in one hand and immediately reached out with his other to grab Alison by her hair. When it came off in his hands, he froze, uncertain about what was happening.

Emma took advantage of his confusion and pivoted back on her left foot, kicking out her right leg at a 45-degree angle hitting the hand holding the gun. It flew out of his hand and skidded on the ground out of sight. At that moment, he saw he had the wrong person and went into a fit of rage. Blinded to all rational thought, he reached for Emma, eager to punish her for keeping him from Alison. She responded by taking hold of his arm and twisting it behind his back, then placed her knife at his throat.

"I think we can take it from here," said Jeremy, stepping out of the shadows. He was holding the gun that had been knocked out of the attacker's hand.

"One more thing," she said as she kneed the man in the back, forcing him on the ground. She kept it there while Jeremy tied his hands.

"Where is she?" he screamed desperately.

"Where you won't find her." Emma lowered her face to his and said in a low voice, "You won't have to worry about where she is. You'll be gone for a long time."

Jeremy gestured to one of his Pinkerton detectives and said, "Take him in. We have him for sure on assault." The husband struggled as he was being moved. "Oh, and give me that," Jeremy said, taking the wig from his loosened grip.

"You don't know who I am!" he screamed.

"Oh, we know, Mr. Lewison. We just don't care," an agent said as they dragged him toward a waiting cab.

Jeremy turned to Emma and Dora, who had walked up to stand beside Emma. "Let's meet in the shelter. Dora, good work pretending to be Emma."

"Thanks." She grinned, pulling her hat off and fluffing her hair. "Anything for my sister."

"Nice hair," Emma teased Jeremy.

He smoothed the hair on the wig down and said with a smile, "Thanks. I'll get it back to Savannah."

The triumphant group went back into the shelter where everyone waited around the dining room table. Cole was at the front, Karl sat to the left of Pete, and Ann sat across from them next to Clair. Tim was at the far end of the table and several Pinkerton detectives stood around the room. Lily was also in the room, looking confused.

Emma immediately noticed Karl and went over to kiss him on the cheek. "Thanks for bringing in Pete," she said in a loud voice so Pete could hear.

Pete's confused face turned red at the comment. He turned to Karl and said, "I thought we were here to bring in a special flower order." He studiously avoided his sister's hard gaze.

Dora went to sit by Tim. "Did it go okay?" he asked.

"Yes, it was exciting," she said.

Tim looked worried, she smoothed his brow and reassured him, "Don't worry, this is just the one time. It was a bit *too* exciting for me." He smiled and pulled her close as they waited expectantly for the bad guys to be revealed.

"Emma, do you want to start?" Cole asked expectantly.

"Yes," she said and moved to the front of the table with Jeremy and Cole. "Please, everyone, sit. We appreciate you being here for the case closure."

"Case? What case?" asked Lily. "Why am I here?"

Emma glanced at Lily and said wryly, "Not to worry, we'll get to you soon enough."

Lily let that sink in and realized she still might be in trouble. She tried to make herself small in her chair.

Emma turned her attention to Ann and said in a conversational tone. "Ann, I understand you have a real interest in flowers and like to set them up after they are delivered." It was more of a statement than a question.

Ann, feeling she was being somehow cornered, weakly said, "Yes, I set them up in the sitting and the dining room." She waved her hand toward the arrangement located in the center of the table.

"They are nice," Emma agreed. She turned her gaze toward Karl. "You do provide beautiful flowers." He smiled in response, and she let her gaze slide to Pete. "Pete, nice to meet you. I know Pete is your first name. What would be your last name?"

He didn't answer and looked down at his hands. "Ann," Emma said, shifting her glance over to her, "would you happen to know Pete's last name?"

Ann's true nature seemed to come out and she said coldly, "I don't know what you're talking about." She could feel the money slipping from her hands; her plans were all coming apart in front of her.

"Hmm, okay, let's make this easy," Emma said. "Your last name is Langston. You are Ann Langston and you are Pete Langston. We know you are brother and sister. We also know you were using the flower boxes to move messages back and forth."

They still looked defiant as she continued. "What? You don't believe me?" She pulled four pieces of paper out of her notebook and unfolded each to read out loud to the group. "The move is scheduled for Tuesday this week, will send times and location in the next note. Oh, and here is the time Alison will be moved." She paused and looked up at Ann, then Pete. "We got you. What do you have to say for yourselves?"

Pete, the less confident of the two, started talking and Ann tried repeatedly to stop him, but he continued. "I started delivering flowers to the shelter six months ago and I noticed Alison Lewison was on the stairs during one of my deliveries. I told my sister who I'd seen and she saw an opportunity to make some money."

Ann finally got a word in and directed her disgust at Pete. "You idiot, there's no way they could have the messages unless you. . . you didn't take the notes with you?" she asked incredulously.

Pete put his head down on the table and wouldn't answer his sister.

Clair stepped in. "By selling Alison's location to a known abuser, you may have killed her and put the other ladies here at risk."

"So?" said Ann belligerently. "Why should we care about her? We wanted the money."

Clair had had enough. "Money? Seriously, you had your brother beat you up so I would take you in, and it was about money? We strive to protect these women and you undermine everything we stand for. You disgust me." She left the room without looking back.

"I think we have enough," Cole said to Jeremy. "Let's take them in."

"What are we being charged with?" Ann asked, still defiant.

"How about facilitation of assault?" answered Jeremy.

That seemed to take her down a peg as agents escorted her and her brother out of the room.

"Lily, don't you go anywhere," Emma warned, noticing her trying to slink out. "Thomas," she called. "Can you bring in those books?" He came in and set them near Emma.

"Those are mine. What are you doing with them?" Lily asked.

Cole took it from there. "Interesting thing about these books, they're all listed on police reports as missing. All were taken during various social events in the last year. So, you say these are yours, Lily?"

"Well, uh. . . uh. . ." Lily was floundering, not knowing how to answer.

"Hmm, let me see." Cole opened each book. "Yes, I can confirm these are first editions and their value is quite high. That will get you significant jail time."

Emma asked, "Were you even beaten up, or was it a setup like Ann's?"

That seemed to finally make Lily open up. "Yes, I was," she said defiantly. "I was working as a maid at the parties you mentioned and my partner would take things to sell. I knew the books were important, but he didn't believe me. He just started hitting me until I couldn't stand because I stole the wrong items."

Clair had walked back in and heard Lily. She understood mistakes and said, "Cole, can we work something out?"

He nodded. "If you tell me your partner's name and where he's selling the merchandise, I'll see what I can do for you. You will also need to return the books."

Lily looked at Clair and said, "Thank you for helping me even though I deceived you. When I get through this mess, I would like to help out here, if you will have me."

Clair could never turn away from her women. "I'll be here," she said.

Lily stood and, ready to face the consequences of her actions, asked, "Do we leave now?"

"Yes," said Cole quietly. "We'll interview you and see what can be worked out."

Clair hugged Emma and Dora as they prepared to leave in a cab Cole had called for them. They met it a few blocks down the street, not wanting to bring any additional attention to the shelter.

Emma commented, "That was an exciting evening; two cases closed."

Dora said, "I can see why you enjoy this, the unexpectedness of it all."

Emma settled back in the seat. "Yes, but it's more than that. It's the puzzle. Putting the pieces together and seeing if they fit. In these two cases, they fit."

Dora asked, "And Alison?"

"Taken by Papa over land in a wagon. I got a telegram confirming that Alison is safe and he is on his way back," answered Emma.

Tim asked, "Will they charge Lily?"

Emma considered that. "No, I think they'll make a deal with her and we'll probably see her back there at some point."

CHAPTER 33

A few months later, after everything had settled down, Emma was getting a bit bored with no cases to work on. Dora called to her as she was walking down the stairs for break-fast. "Emma, you have a note; it was delivered earlier."

She offered her thanks and made her way into the foyer. She looked over at the stack of letters sitting on the small table, flipping through them until she found the one addressed to her. Opening it, she read it silently.

Dora walked up and hugged her from behind, laying her head on her shoulder. "Who's it from?"

Emma answered absently, "It's from Cole. He has a case he would like my help on."

Dora released her and looked over her shoulder at the note. "When does he want you?" She was thinking about Emma's current temp jobs.

"It says he'd like to meet this afternoon. I'll let you and Tim know if I need coverage," Emma said, excited about the prospect of a new case. She went back upstairs to finish getting ready for her day.

That afternoon, she rode her bike over to the Pinkerton office. She tapped on Cole's door and was called in. "Good afternoon, I got your message," she said.

"Emma, thanks for coming in. Have a seat," he said, pulling out a case file and studying the information in it. "I'd like you to work as an investigator on a case for us."

She sat down in the chair in front of his desk and asked curiously, "Why me?" She had worked many cases, but this was the first she was asked to take the lead.

He looked up from the file. "It involves a woman whom I believe you already know, Millicent Carlyle Landon."

"Yes, I've known her since I was a kid. Is she all right?" asked Emma, concerned.

"That's what we're being hired to find out. Her grandfather Benjamin Carlyle has requested our services."

"Why did he feel a need to call us?"

"He believes Millicent may have made a mistake in getting married. She's cut off all contact with him and has requested her inheritance be given over in larger advances."

"That is troubling. As I remember, she was very social, though she could be a bit scatterbrained," commented Emma.

"Yes, and Mr. Carlyle has inquired on his own but isn't making any progress, so he contacted us. He asked specifically for you to help out on the case."

"I remember Mr. Carlyle. He's a very nice man. We met them when Papa was helping with his home here and in New York. You say he doesn't live in Chicago anymore?"

"He moved a few years ago and now is at an age where he can't travel easily."

Dear one commented, "So, she just headed to New York?"

Narrator said, "Well, there was a lot of discussion with the family if she should go alone. Emma did point out she had already made several trips by train by herself."

Tim volunteered to take her to the train station. He was placing her bag in his wagon as Papa and Dora walked her down the stoop. "You will be extra safe," said Dora. "I don't know what I would do without you."

Emma reasoned with her, saying, "It's just a trip to New York. You and Tim have been there without any problems."

"I know, but I was with Tim," she explained.

Papa interrupted Dora and said, "Sister will be fine. She's ready for this step."

Emma hugged him tightly and said, "Thanks, Papa. Now, enough worrying. I need to be on my way."

Before she moved to the wagon, Dora reached up to touch Emma's cheek. Emma clasped that hand tightly to her and said, "I'll be fine." She smiled at her and turned to climb into the wagon. Tim leaped up beside her and clicked at the horses to get them moving.

Papa and Dora waved as they drove away.

When they got there, Tim reminded her, "Be extra cautious and don't stray too far from your private compartment."

"I will. Thank you, Tim." She leaned over and kissed him on the cheek before jumping down. He handed her the carpetbag and clicked at the horses to move forward.

Emma noticed a group of older ladies whispering and watching her. She realized they'd seen her kiss Tim goodbye—all while dressed as a boy—and it gave her a good laugh. She turned around to the still whispering women, winked, and threw them a kiss. That seemed to scandalize them and they whispered furiously to one another.

Emma was laughing as she strode off and climbed the steps to the train. She walked down the long hall to her private compartment. It was expensive, but it would keep her protected from unwanted visitors. She also made sure she spoke to the porter and slipped him a tip to keep people away from her room.

Settling in, she unpacked her books for a good long read. While the train prepared to pull out, she glanced at the titles on her lap. These included: *The Adventures of Huckleberry Finn, The Strange Case of Dr. Jekyll and Mr. Hyde,* and *A Study in Scarlet.* Choosing *A Study in Scarlet* to begin, she opened it to the first chapter to start reading.

Her trip would take about a week and would include two different trains. One from Chicago to Buffalo, New York, via New York, Chicago, & St. Louis Railroad Company, commonly known as the Nickel Plate Road (NKP), and a transfer in Buffalo to New Jersey. The final leg to New York City would be a carriage. It had been arranged with her client to take her over the bridge and into the city.

Tony was still on her mind, even though they had been broken up for the past few months. It was his comment about Jeremy she kept dwelling on. *Was Jeremy more than a friend to her?* She put her head back on the seat and finally admitted to herself that she had stayed with Tony because she didn't want to lose him as a friend. He was her best friend, but not the person she was in love with.

Another thing he'd mentioned, that she should have checked in with him when she took on new cases. That bothered her. *Does a relationship give a man that kind of power over me, to have to check in before taking a job? I don't think I'm relationship material, but Jeremy. . .* She sat there thinking about him, letting the book rest in her lap.

A sudden knock startled her and caused her to check for her two knives before approaching the door. She cracked it open and was flummoxed by the person in front of her. She opened the door wide. "Jeremy, what are you doing here?"

The porter was in the hall and looked over, worried he had let

Jeremy knock on the door. Emma nodded to him. "It's okay, I know him."

As he leaned in, she grabbed him by the sleeve and pulled him the rest of the way into her compartment. "Well?" she asked, bewildered by his appearance. Jeremy smiled in that way that always made her knees melt and didn't say anything. She frowned and said gruffly. "Sit down already. Talk."

"I'm going to New York City," he said, still smiling.

"That, I figured out," she said wryly.

"Pops has a custody pickup that needed to be done and I volunteered," he said, hoping she was happy he was there.

"And?" she prompted.

"And I always wanted to go back to New York City," he said. He'd been born there and had lived there with Cole when he was little.

"And?" she prompted again.

"And you were going, so I thought I would tag along," he said, letting his voice trail off, wondering if he had made a mistake.

"Are you here to provide some type of protection for me?" Her voice grew strained. She had thought they had gotten past this in their relationship.

He decided to take another direction and answered, "No, I was just hoping for some company and, if anyone is protecting anyone, it's you protecting me."

That made her laugh. He always made her laugh. She stopped with her questioning.

"Did I see Tim drop you off? Was Tony busy?" he asked curiously. He was interested in all things involving Emma.

"Yes," she said, quietly. "We're done. Tony needs someone who will be there for him, and that it isn't me. We will continue to be best friends, but no more."

Jeremy wanted to grin and shout, but he knew she would not appreciate it, so he kept a sober look on his face.

"Let's talk about something else," she suggested.

"All right, how about your case?" he asked.

Emma started thinking about what data she could share. She pulled out her notebook and unfolded the telegram she had tucked into it. She read it out loud: "From, Benjamin Carlyle. Emma, I need to speak with you in person about Millicent. I am worried that she has gotten into trouble. Send me a telegram with your travel dates and I will have your train met."

She finished reading and said, "The gentlemen who sent the note is an old family friend and his granddaughter, Millicent, just married at the beginning of the summer. She has somewhat disappeared from the social scene but does turn up at the dressmaker occasionally. I don't know the husband well, but I did meet him at their wedding. He's in his thirties and the grandfather believed he would be a stabilizing influence on her."

She paused for a moment and then continued. "The more I think about it, the more I realize I haven't seen Millie since the wedding. I initially questioned if there was an actual case here, something to investigate? Cole and I decided it was worth visiting Mr. Carlyle to get further information before I start an investigation in Chicago."

"Interesting. You say you knew her previously?" he asked, brushing back his brown curls off his forehead and settled onto the seat next to her.

"Yes, I wasn't able to see her before I left, but she's usually a little silly and not serious. She might be accidentally involved in something, however unlikely," she answered.

"You said you know her husband?" he asked.

"I know of him—successful businessman, nice looking, and kind of quiet. We were acquaintances. We went to some of the same events, but I wouldn't say we were friends. I did speak with him at his and Millicent's wedding."

~

The wedding

"Emma," she heard Millicent call. She had been admiring the wedding cake, wondering if it tasted as good as it looked. Looking over she saw the bride and groom. "Come meet my new husband, Donald Landon." Emma walked toward the couple, they were resplendent in their finery.

"Donald this is Emma, she made my dress."

"It is nice to meet you. It is beautiful work," he complimented her. He reached out his hand to take Millicent's and said, "We must see to our other guest."

"That's a lovely ring," Emma commented, noticing the distinctive design on the gold band that included a ruby stone on his right hand,

He looked down at it briefly and said in a quiet voice, "Thank you. It is the only thing I have from my father."

"Congratulations again," she said as they walked off.

Present day-Emma and Jeremy

"What about you? Who are you picking up?" she asked.

"My pickup? Sam Cummings. He's a known counterfeiter and was caught making money in Chicago and was sent to New York to testify in a case against the Whyos Gang. He's also agreed to provide information in our counterfeiting case in exchange for leniency."

"Counterfeiting, that sounds interesting. What kind?" She leaned toward him, wanting all the details.

"Mostly paper money. He's been doing this for a while, but he started getting greedy and was printing way too much and got caught. It also turns out his bosses in the gang were not aware of the amount. He jumped at the chance to help us; he knew what would happen if they got to him first."

They continued discussing the cases and then shared dinner

from Emma and Jeremy's bags. The days flowed into one another, with the majority of time being spent together, only sleeping in separate compartments. They read, talked, and generally enjoyed each other's company.

The train switch from Buffalo to the New Jersey line was easy and they ended up sharing a compartment. That leg of the trip took just a day to complete.

"Could you step out for a moment?" she asked, indicating for him to exit so she could change clothes.

He grinned and said, "Well, I can stay if you need help with any buttons."

"Oh, you! Out!" she said and pointed to the door. After it closed behind him, she turned the lock and pulled out her red split skirt, high-necked black blouse, and a long black jacket. She unpacked her hat and confirmed her knives were in place. She was tying her boots when she heard a knock. She reached up to release it and said, "You can come in, Jeremy."

He sat down next to his bag and enjoyed Emma's company a while longer as they waited for their final stop. As they were descending the train steps Emma asked over her shoulder, "Do you have transportation waiting?"

"I don't. Could I get a lift?" he asked hopefully, casually waving off the man who was there to pick him up.

"Hmm, do you need to confirm with that gentleman first?" she asked, hiding a smile with her hand, having seen his gesture.

He turned red, realizing he had been caught. "Yes, I'll be right back." He paid off the carriage and went back to accompany Emma to hers.

Emma started to climb up on her own. "Emma," he murmured, "may I help you?"

She realized she was acting like a boy and smiled at him. She turned to him and said sweetly, "Please." He grinned and lifted her into the cab.

The driver turned to them and said, "The trip will take a few hours and we'll be stopping to give the horses water. The cab has been arranged by Mr. Carlyle, so no directions to that location are necessary."

"We'll have one additional stop that will require an address. Jeremy," Emma prompted, "where do you need to be let off?"

He unfolded the address and gave it to the driver, who nodded and said, "That shouldn't be a problem. It's on our way."

Their ride was pleasant; they talked quietly, enjoying the view and each other's company. As they reached Jeremy's stop, he went to climb out and Emma stopped him with a touch of her hand. "If you have time, would you like to see some of the city with me before we head home?"

He tilted his head and said, "That would be great. My job should be coming together soon and then I'm headed home on the same train as you. I'll drop you a note." She nodded and waved goodbye as she told the driver he could head to the Carlyle residence.

As they drew up in front of the imposing townhouse, she took in the red brick structure that stretched down most of the block. The driver indicated she should enter through the kitchen door. The discretion didn't bother Emma, and she made her way around to the back. She knocked on the door and the maid who answered looked a bit surprised. Emma introduced herself. "Hello, I'm Emma Evans. I'm to stay here and meet with Mr. Carlyle."

The maid blinked and said in a solemn tone, "Oh, they didn't tell me you were so young." She motioned for Emma to follow her and showed her to her room. "Mr. Carlyle will expect you to be down in thirty minutes for lunch." The maid pointed out the water closet and said she would bring fresh water for washing to the room.

Emma cleaned up with a washrag but would not be able to wash her hair prior to lunch. Brushing it, she took time to rebraid it before changing into a dark blue walking suit with a button-up jacket and high neck red shirt. The clothes were the ones she wore routinely to her office positions.

Once dressed and refreshed, she headed down at the time indicated by the housekeeper for lunch. She slowly descended the grand staircase that wrapped around into the foyer. A footman stepped out as she neared the bottom of the steps and said, "Please, follow me to the dining room." Emma did so, admiring the elegant wallpaper, sumptuous rugs, and paintings hung on the walls.

As they entered the dining room, Mr. Carlyle stayed seated. Emma was able to see why she had traveled to see him here; he could not travel to see her. Mr. Carlyle was in a wheelchair and was very pale.

"Mr. Carlyle. . ." she started.

"Emma, come here," he said with a very friendly smile.

She walked to him. "Hello, Mr. Carlyle," she said, taking his hand in hers.

"Thank you for responding so quickly to my request. Now, please, sit down. We will eat first and then discuss why I have brought you all this way."

He indicated for the butler to pull out her chair. She smiled and sat down. They ate their meal, keeping the conversation light, discussing families and what was happening in Chicago and New York.

As the meal came to a close, he waved to a male servant to move him into the study. He looked over his shoulder and said, "Please, join me, Emma."

She nodded and followed him. The study was imposing, with full bookshelves and a large dark desk, settees, and chairs. Light colors of blue and white were used to accent the room. Emma would have loved to inquire about the books, but knew she wasn't there for that.

He tapped the settee arm, and she responded by sitting down. "My granddaughter, as you know, married Mr. Landon about six months ago. Since that time, they have cut off almost all communication with me." He waved a hand. "I do get the occasional note, but no visits and no telegrams. I am concerned about Millie; this isn't like her. She is normally full of information and will talk your ear off."

"Well," Emma mentioned, "there may be a reason. She's newly married and they may want some quiet time together."

"You are right and, if it were just that, I would leave it alone. But it is also the money. They have already run through her annual allowance (this was just March) and Millie will be able to access her inheritance when she turns twenty, which will be later this year."

Emma nodded slowly and asked, "Would you mind if I took notes?" He nodded and she pulled out her notebook.

He continued. "I have our business manager coming over this afternoon to discuss the money that has been requested."

Emma thought, *Money could be the key to the investigation.* As she completed her notes, the butler entered to announce Mr. Beeker was there to meet with them.

A rather average-looking man with hardly any hair walked into the room. "Geoff, please come in. Emma has arrived and I have been going over my concerns with her."

He followed Mr. Carlyle's direction and moved over to the settee to join them. He set the books he was carrying down on the table in front of them.

"Emma, this is Geoff Beeker. He is our financial manager. Geoff, this is Emma Evans, a family friend, and the private investigator Pinkerton sent."

Emma thought she saw a movement of an eyebrow, and maybe his eyes widened slightly when he was introduced to her. He covered well, and the signs were only detected briefly.

"It is nice to meet you, Emma." He nodded his head toward her and looked at Mr. Carlyle. "Shall I get started?"

"Yes, please do begin. Emma, you may continue to take notes," stated Mr. Carlyle graciously.

Geoff opened the books. "Millicent's spending has been somewhat erratic as of late; normal spending on dresses and such, but now also a new person is getting paid out of her finances, a house staffer named Roger Smith. I have enquired about his actual position, but I do not get satisfactory answers."

"What has she said in response to your inquiries?" Emma asked him directly.

"She has indicated to me that her household staff had to be let go, that they no longer performed the services she needed. She also indicated this Mr. Smith was now head of the household and would run the household accounts with significantly fewer people."

"What!" Mr. Carlyle roared, showing a different side to his character that Emma hadn't seen before and causing her to jump a bit.

"Yes, this occurred just after the couple got back from their wedding trip," Mr. Beeker answered.

"Why wasn't I informed?" Mr. Carlyle asked sternly.

The tone didn't seem to bother Mr. Beeker, and he answered in a calm, controlled manner. "Sir, you mentioned that this was her time to grow up and take a hand in her finances. Also, I would have expected some financial spending from her new husband, but there hasn't been anything on the accounts." He directed his next statement at Emma. "One of our biggest concerns is that the wedding dates moved up her inheritance date from twenty-five to twenty and that date is only three months from now."

Emma was busy documenting the information in her notebook: *Millie has not been in touch with her grandfather, out of the ordinary; Millie was married in last few months; household help let go since wedding; a new mysterious person on the payroll; inheritance coming up in three months.* She closed her notebook and said, "I know where I can start. I can track down the help who was let go."

"Also, look into this Mr. Smith, please," Mr. Carlyle requested.

"Also, Mr. Smith," she agreed, nodding at him. "Mr. Beeker, you mentioned her normal spending is for dresses. I also think I can start there; I work for them occasionally providing lacework."

Mr. Carlyle looked satisfied and said, "Well, that sounds like a good start. I would like to set up a weekly telegram with updates from you. Mr. Beeker will send your fee each time the telegram is received. Will that work?"

Emma nodded and said, "Sir, I'll do my best for you."

Mr. Carlyle smiled. "Okay then, dinner is at 8pm. I will not be available tonight, but I will see you for a final dinner tomorrow."

"Thank you, sir. I'll get started as soon as I return to Chicago," promised Emma.

He had returned to his role as the gracious host and asked, "Did you want to see any of the city while you are here?"

"Yes," Emma said. "I want to see everything. If it's okay, I have a friend I would like to meet in the morning. My train is scheduled to leave the following day."

"That will be quite all right. You may use my carriage," he offered.

"Thank you, sir," she responded sincerely. She looked over at Mr. Beeker and said, "Mr. Beeker, it was nice to meet you."

"You also. Good evening, Mr. Carlyle, Miss Evans," Mr. Beeker said as he exited the room.

Emma said, "Goodnight," and headed to the foyer. She saw the butler and asked, "Can you get a note to the Warren hotel for me?"

"Yes, miss, I can do that for you."

She opened her notebook and hastily wrote the time and address to meet. Handing him the note, she said, "Thank you."

"You're welcome."

She went up to her room to take a bath, wash her hair, and rest. Her dinner was delivered to her room that evening. The maid put the tray on the desk and said, "Miss you received a note." She handed it to her and left the room, quietly closing the door behind her.

Emma opened it and smiled broadly. Dropping back on the bed she thought, *Tomorrow will be a good day.*

CHAPTER 34

The next morning, as she was eating breakfast, the maid mentioned the carriage would be available when she needed it. Emma finished and went back upstairs to change into a green traveling suit with a longer jacket and a high-necked lace shirt with lace around the hem to match. Picking up a stylish hat, she pulled out her hat pin/knife and examined it in the light. All of her hats had been modified to allow her to carry various sizes of knives. Sliding it into the special slot, she pinned the hat in place and made her way downstairs.

As she reached the foyer, she noticed a very familiar lanky man with curly brown hair on the far side of the room. "Jeremy, I'm so glad you were able to come over this morning," she said as she rushed over to kiss him on the cheek.

As she stood on her tiptoes, he took the opportunity to adjust the kiss from his cheek to his lips. The kiss could not be defined as sweet; it was more of a slow drop. He pulled back and said, "Well, good morning to you also." She gave him a slow smile in response and held out her hand to take his. They headed outside to retrieve their carriage.

He helped her in and, when asked for directions, they said they wanted to see as much of New York as they could. They started off, and the first thing Emma noticed was the road was made of a different type of material from the ones used in Chicago, which were usually masonry blocks or cobbled stones. She asked the driver, "Sir, excuse me."

"Yes?" he asked, not turning around.

"What are the roads made of here? They have a smooth black look to them," she inquired.

The driver looked around and said, "It's a new substance called asphalt. It was installed about. . ." he took a moment to scratch his beard and think before he continued, "about 1877 when Battery Park and Fifth Avenue were completed. The benefit is that it makes the ride much smoother." That was confirmed a few minutes later when the carriage moved from the asphalt onto stones and blocks.

They rode past the wealthy district, marveling at the ladies' detailed dresses, the well-dressed men in hats and nice suits. As they passed an older man wearing a top hat and a monocle, Jeremy tapped Emma's shoulder to point him out. The man noticed their attention and tipped his hat as they passed. They gave him a big smile and a wave in response.

Next was Navarro Flats, a massive apartment structure on Central Park South at Seventh Avenue. It was an amazing sight to see where so many people lived in one place. They rode along to the Hoffman House Hotel, and she leaned over to say to Jeremy in a low voice, "I hear they have a bar. I'd like to see it."

He wanted to see it also. They asked the driver to stop and then climbed down from the carriage. They entered the lobby of the hotel. It was a grand place, elegant with large paintings dominating the walls, the floors covered with colorful rugs and couches anchoring them. As they made their way to the bar, he whispered to her, "You won't be allowed in, but I think you'll be able to sneak a peek."

She nodded and grinned at him in response. He walked in

front of her and she was able to stand in the doorway and get a view of the nude paintings hanging on the walls.

"Sir, do you have a reservation?" said a tall man in a suit, blocking their path. "Women are not allowed here," he added, looking down his nose at her.

"No, no, we don't want to come in. We just wanted to check on the time," said Jeremy.

They turned and walked away slowly down the hall and started laughing as they turned the corner and exited the hotel. They found their driver and continued their tour of the western side of the city.

One of the locations they wanted to see was Madison Square, a genteel neighborhood. The attraction wasn't the buildings in the area; it was a statue. Well, part of a statue—the arm and hand holding a torch. It was the new Statue of Liberty that had been given to the United States by France. Her hand, holding the torch, had been on display in Madison Square Park in New York City from 1876 to now. *The World* newspaper had been advertising to get enough money donated to have a pedestal built for it. They stood marveling at its size and shape, knowing it was only a small piece of the entire structure.

They continued their tour by way of the new structure being built over the Hudson River. It would eventually call it the Brooklyn Bridge; it was a massive structure to behold already with the supports in place. It would be another two years before it was usable for traversing from Brooklyn to New York City, but it would be a marvel when complete.

She looked around at the skyscrapers starting to take shape and thought for a moment of how much impact Papa had. He continued to design and consult on buildings in Chicago and here. The design differences between the two cities were startling. Chicago balanced the visual with the practical commercial design, producing large, square palazzo-styled buildings, hosting shops and restaurants on the ground level, and containing rentable offices on the upper floors. In contrast, New York's skyscrapers were frequently narrower towers which, being more eclectic in style, were often criticized for their lack of elegance.

Their driver let them off in the shopping district so Emma and Jeremy could stroll through different stores, trying candies and other small items. Emma picked up a scarf and lace appliqués for Dora. As she moved on to the next store, the sidewalk grew busy and crowded with children. Something brushed against her pocket and, without thinking, Emma grabbed the arm of the pick-pocket, twisted it behind his back, and pushed him into an alley. Jeremy followed closely behind and leaned on the wall to watch the interaction.

"Hand it over," she said, holding out her hand to the blond ten-year-old.

"I didn't do nothing," he said petulantly.

"I'm pretty sure you do plenty," said Emma.

"Let me go," he said gruffly as he continued to wrestle with her, trying to dislodge his arm.

She held him firmly and said, "First, you hand over my purse."

The young thief hesitated only briefly, then used his other hand to hand over the bag.

Emma dropped his arm but did keep a hand on his sleeve. "You know, you're not very good at this particular skill; I wasn't even paying attention and could detect your fingers lifting my purse."

"How would you know?" he said, looking her over dismissively.

"How?" she asked wryly and opened up her hand to show the boy the items she had lifted from his pocket.

"Hey! Those are mine. How did you do that?" he asked incredulously.

Jeremey straightened up from the wall, walked over to them, and said, "She is a *good* pickpocket. You should take her advice and find another occupation." As he looked, he noticed this didn't appear to be a regular street kid; he had clean clothes and nicer shoes. Bending down in front of him, he asked kindly, "Where are your parents?" When he didn't answer, Jeremy leaned closer and tilted the boy's head up. "Where?"

He squirmed a bit and finally said, "Working."

"And where are you supposed to be?" prompted Emma, handing him back the items she'd taken

"School," he acknowledged, sliding his belongings back into his pocket. He continued to look down, clearly guilty.

"Why aren't you there instead of here? This is a dangerous business you're trying to get into. These people don't play and won't like you trying to take their profit," stated Emma.

"I don't like school," he snapped.

That got Emma's attention. "Why not, little man?"

"It's boring. Math is okay, but the reading is so boring."

Emma and Jeremy laughed at that, and Jeremy said, "So, a life of crime begins with a boring book? "

Emma's mind was working, and she drummed her fingers on her lips. She asked, "What's your name?"

"Mark Sutherland," he stated simply.

"If I send you some books guaranteed to keep you interested, will you read them and write me what you think about them?"

That seemed to catch his interest. "What kind of books?" he asked topic.

She listed a few she knew would be interesting. "*The Adventures of Huckleberry Finn, Treasure Island,* and *Around the World in 80 Days.*" She watched his eyes light up at the titles.

"How do I know you won't just disappear and not send them?" he asked suspiciously.

Emma pulled out her notebook, wrote her address, and her name. She asked for his. After she documented the information and tore out the sheet to give him, she said, "If you'll hold off from any more pickpocketing and missing school for at least three weeks, I'll send you the three books as soon as I get back home to Chicago."

"And if you don't send them?" he asked.

"Then our contract is broken," she said simply.

He tilted his head and said slowly, "That's a deal," and stuck out his hand to shake hers.

She covered up her smile with her other hand as she shook. He was released and looked like he would run off when Jeremy asked, "Off to school?"

He looked a bit guilty but said, "Yes, a deal is a deal." He ran off.

"Do you think he will stick to the agreement?" asked Jeremy.

"I think so," she said, feeling they had made a small difference. "I'll send the books when I get home," she promised.

They made their way to the cab and had the driver take the long way back to the house, by way of the bay. It was noisy and dirty but very interesting to see. It made her smile, and she turned to Jeremy to say, "This is one of my wishes, to travel and see more than just Chicago. This is a good first step."

"I'm glad I was with you for this first trip," he whispered as he pulled her close to him. He started a smile that slowly worked its way across his whole face. He continued to hold her until they reached their final stop. Hopping down, he reached up to assist her. As he swung her around, he said, "I'll meet you here in the morning, and we'll have that pick up at the police station before going to the train." Jeremy knew Mr. Carlyle wanted to have a final dinner with her that evening. Leaning down to kiss her, he said, "Goodbye," and climbed back into the cab to head to his hotel.

Emma's evening meal involved a final conversation with Mr. Carlyle and a promise of a telegram the following week. He said a quiet goodnight and they parted to go to their separate bedrooms.

She woke early the next morning and got organized to begin her day. Pulling out her notebook, she made final notes on Mr. Carlyle's case. Lastly, she made a separate note to send the books back to Mark.

Closing the carpetbag, she did a final look around the room.

That's it, she thought. A knock sounded on the door. "Yes? Come in," she called.

The young brown-haired maid came into the room and said, "Miss, breakfast is ready, and you have a gentleman waiting for you in the foyer."

"Thank you, I'm coming down now," she said, taking her bag in hand and following the maid.

"Oh, and Mr. Carlyle said your gentleman is invited for breakfast," the maid commented as they walked toward the stairs. "I will leave you here," she said and hastened to other duties on that floor.

Glancing toward the foyer, she spotted Jeremy waiting. "Good morning," he called up to her.

"Good morning. Do we have time for breakfast?" she asked as she reached the final step and lowered her carpetbag and hatbox down to the base of the stairs.

"Yes, we don't have to pick up that item for another hour," he said, looking at his watch.

"Good, Mr. Carlyle invited you to eat," she said cheerfully.

"Nice," he said. "I can always eat. Is your bag okay here?"

"I think so. They'll move it if it gets in the way."

They went to the dining room to eat and were told Mr. Carlyle wouldn't be joining them. Their breakfast was an enjoyable meal. Afterward, they made their way to the police station in a cab Jeremy had hired. During the trip over, he told her that, when they went in, she would wait in the outer offices while he took custody of the counterfeiter.

Within the station, Emma was waiting and observing the comings and goings of the officers when she overheard some policemen discussing the Whyos gang. *Hmm,* she thought, *Jeremy mentioned the counterfeiter was a member of that gang.*

She listened in as the police discussed their history. Formed from the remnants of several defunct Five Points outfits, the Whyos were one of the most dominant New York street gangs from the 1860s to now. The group had started as a loose collection of petty thugs, pickpockets, and murderers but, by the 1880s, they had graduated to more high-class crimes like counterfeiting, prostitution, and racketeering.

She thought it odd that they went in through the front door of the station for Jeremy's pickup. *Shouldn't this have been a more secretive operation?* she asked herself. Then, she surmised, *I've never been involved in a prisoner transport, so maybe this is how it is normally handled.* All things considered, Jeremy was in control of the situation.

She watched as he appeared, leading a man in handcuffs. Jeremy took off his jacket and draped it over the man's hands to hide them. The counterfeiter also had a hat pulled low on his face. They would have to be extremely careful transporting him and would be accompanied by police officers to the train station. He nodded to her, and they exited the station to a waiting carriage. Surprisingly, the train trip was uneventful as they traveled from New Jersey to Buffalo. She sat across from the counterfeiter, trying to take in his clothes and mannerisms. There was nothing about him that indicated he was a criminal.

The final move to the Buffalo train was handled quietly, and they made their way to their separate compartments. Entering her room, Emma removed her hat and turned to throw it on the seat when she detected movement out of the corner of her eye. Someone grabbed her by the neck and pulled her back to him. Letting him think she was scared, she made a distressed sound, planning her next move. The train started forward, and she used the momentum to push him back into the far wall. He had not expected her to fight back and loosened his grip, allowing her to break free.

Why am I always being grabbed by men? she thought as she swung around to kick him in the face. She bloodied his nose and stepped back to retrieve her hat knife from the seat.

He took a moment to use the back of his hand to wipe the

blood from his nose. He was very angry but in control of himself. She also realized he held a gun in his other hand.

"Gun beats knife. Drop it," he snarled at her.

She could see he meant what he said and dropped the blade onto the carpeted floor.

"Move over here and sit down," he ordered, motioning to the seat. "You're going to get that policeman in here with us," he directed.

She didn't say anything, she just continued to look at him. A sudden knock at the door startled her and, as she glanced over, her attacker was suddenly close to her ear. "Tell him to come in, understand?" he whispered.

"Emma?" called Jeremy.

"Yes," she answered. "Just a second, Tony."

The man waved at her to tell him to come in and positioned himself by the door.

"Tony, you can come in now." She knew Jeremy would understand her warning.

Seconds later, he burst in, but what was surprising was that Jeremy was accompanied by the counterfeiter. She didn't have a chance to think. They were on the man, trying to get his gun away. The room was small, and Emma had to climb up on the chair to keep from being crushed. She took the opportunity to remove her hidden knife from her thigh sheath and jammed it into the attacker's shoulder. That stopped him long enough to allow them to wrestle the gun away. Jeremy held it on him while Emma yanked her knife out of his shoulder. Jeremy looked at him consideringly and said, "Mr. Johnny Dolan, I assume?"

Emma knew immediately who he was talking about and kept a close eye on him. He held a hand on his cut shoulder to stop the blood flow, he looked at them and down at his shoes.

Planning, Emma thought. *I know what he is going to do.* "Jeremy, you should take his shoes."

Dolan looked at her, surprised.

"His shoes?" Jeremy asked, nonplussed.

"Yes, I believe there's something special about them. And don't let him take them off himself," she added.

Dolan's looks turned from surprised to exasperated. They got the shoes off safely and handed them to Emma.

"There is this." She tripped the mechanism, and blades popped out.

"That would have been unexpected. How did you know?" the counterfeiter asked, looking at her in amazement.

"Funny thing, I had a similar idea a few years ago and I heard about a certain someone who wore this type of shoe. I decided it was just too dangerous. Though, I wouldn't mind keeping these for the design," she said hopefully.

Jeremy shook his head no, and she shrugged. She pulled out her notebook to sketch the mechanism, before handing them to him for safekeeping.

The counterfeiter, introduced to her as Fred Snider, Lieutenant in the local New York City police department, moved Dolan to the other room to be held until they reached the next stop. Once he was secure, Jeremy returned to explain things to Emma.

She started with the question, "So, where's the actual counterfeiter?"

"He's in Chicago testifying before the court. He was moved a few weeks ago to a safe house," he explained.

Emma smiled. "It was a setup; the talkative policeman at the station, the daylight movement. All to get Dolan."

"Yes," he acknowledged. "We weren't sure he would go after us, but there was a chance. We didn't expect him to go after you."

"As usual, he thought the woman would be the weak point," she said wryly.

"Well, he didn't know you," he said with a smile.

They continued to talk quietly until the next stop. Jeremy said, "I need to get them off here." As they exited the train, she noticed many policemen surrounding the station. They took Dolan into custody and placed him in a wagon to move him back to New York. Lieutenant Snider would stay with him as an escort. The men waiting gave Dolan a funny look when they realized he wore no shoes.

Emma and Jeremy both settled back into her room. "Well, that was exciting."

"Yes, it was, wasn't it?" He grinned.

She grinned back. They were such similar people. "Want a sandwich?" she asked. Jeremy had ordered a basket of food from the hotel, it was waiting for them when they arrived at the train.

"What were you going to do with the shoes?" he asked as he ate his lunch, watching her sketch.

"Study them to see if there is a safer way to contain knives in my shoes. I thought I might get with Papa about the design," said Emma thoughtfully, taking a bite of her sandwich.

He just smiled. She was always planning. He continued to ask about her case with Mr. Carlyle, and they spent a pleasant and quiet rest of the trip home.

CHAPTER 35

The morning they arrived in Chicago, she met her arranged cab and asked Jeremy if he needed to be taken anywhere. He indicated he had transportation and they separated with a soft kiss.

The cab dropped her off at the boarding house and she bounded up the stairs, happy to be home. She slammed the door open as she entered and ran to the kitchen. Dora met her there with a hug.

"How was your trip? Any problems?"

"Not a one," Emma said, pulling off her hat and undoing her hair. She ran her hands through it, the strands had gotten a bit matted due to the humid air they were experiencing this summer.

Dora noticed and said, "Well, you head up for a bath and hair washing. We can talk about it after you rest."

Emma agreed and headed upstairs with her carpetbag, all her energy gone. After five days of train rides, she wanted nothing more than to take a long hot bath. She lit the gas lamps in the room and wondered if they would have electric lights soon. The demonstration she had been present for in 1878 involved devices with 2,000 candlepower and was created by a spark of current across two carbon rods. *It would be exciting if the technology evolved enough to allow for lighting in residential homes.*

She drew her bath and washed her hair before lying down for a nap. It would still be damp at dinner, but at least it would be clean.

So nice to sleep somewhere that isn't moving, she thought drowsily as she fell asleep.

Dora came in a long while later and nudged her shoulder, saying, "Sister, time to get up."

Emma stretched, yawned, and asked, "Time already?"

"Just about," Dora acknowledged.

Emma patted the bed. "Climb in with me."

Dora hesitated only briefly to remove her shoes and climbed into the warm bed next to her sister. "Ready to tell me about the trip?" she inquired, laying close.

"Yes. Jeremy was there," Emma said softly.

That startled Dora. "In New York?"

"Yes, but also on the train with me," said Emma, looking intently at the ceiling. "Separate rooms, of course," she added, slanting a gaze at her.

"Of course," said Dora with a laugh. "So, tell me, why was he there?"

Emma went on to discuss Jeremy's reason for the trip and the outcome on the way home.

"Well, that is certainly exciting. Did you get to see some of the city? I would hope more than I did," she teased her.

"I did see much more than you did," Emma said with another laugh. "I bought you a few things." She reached over to her side table, next to her, to retrieve the gifts and handed them over to Dora.

"I love these," she said, looking at each one. "So, Jeremy, what's happening there?" inquired Dora curiously.

"I don't know, but I'm enjoying being with him. You know, Dora, I feel different when I am around him," said Emma.

"How so?" she asked curiously.

"When I was with Tony, I always had to be reminded to be in the moment with him. Otherwise, I was always looking for cases, making observations, and never really relaxing and enjoying our time together. With Jeremy, I was able to sit back and focus on us," she stated wonderingly.

"That is different for you," she acknowledged. "Did you enjoy it?"

"I did," she admitted. "I almost forgot to mention Mark Sutherland."

"What, another gentleman?" Dora asked incredulously.

"No, not quite." She went on to describe how she had met him and her promise.

"It sounds fun and something Papa will approve of. What books will you start with?" she asked, curious about the little boy in New York.

"I was thinking *The Adventures of Huckleberry Finn, Treasure Island,* and *Around the World in 80 Days.* I need to write him a letter. Could you ask Tim to take them to the post office today?"

"So quick. You mentioned three weeks of school first?"

"Well more than two will have passed by the time the books reach him. I don't want him to back out of our contract."

"I will leave you to write your letter," she said as she rolled off the bed. "When you're done, can you come help with tonight's dessert?" Dora inquired, turning back to her before she exited the room.

"I can," she promised. Watching Dora close the door, she stretched broadly and rolled to the side of the bed. She got up to refresh herself with a damp rag and ran a brush through her still-damp hair. She sat at the desk to write the letter before getting dressed.

Dear Mark,

This letter is to begin what I hope is a long conversation about adventures and books. As part of our agreement, here are the books I promised. I want to hear any questions from you about the characters and their adventures. I trust you will hold up your side of the agreement and send me a letter back, confirming you are attending school. I look forward to hearing from you.

Sincerely yours,

Emma.

She folded it and got dressed. Taking it with her to the study, she looked around for the books she wanted. The books were located, she bundled them with brown paper and tied the package with twine. She took the letter and books to the kitchen, where she knew Tim would be working.

Tim was exactly where she thought he would be. She leaned over to give him a quick kiss hello on the cheek. "Welcome back, Emma," he said, absently looking up from his books.

"Thanks, Tim. I'm glad to be home," Emma stated with feeling.

"Are those the books I need to get out today?" he inquired, nodding at the brown package.

"Yes," she acknowledged.

"Great, let me get on my way, I wouldn't want to delay anyone's education," he said wryly as he headed out.

"What do you want me working on?" Emma asked Dora.

"Cheesecake, the ingredients are laid out for you," Dora stated. Amy caught her eye and gave her a wink. Emma started working on it.

She completed the cake and placed it in the oven. It was getting close to dinner, and she wanted to run up to her room to clean up. People's voices could be heard through the door on their way to dinner, she hurried to finish dressing and left the room. She ran into the twins, Taylor and Franklin on the stairs.

"Emma, you're back!" they exclaimed.

"Yes, I am," she said and accompanied them downstairs to the dining room.

"Can you tell us about your trip?" Franklin asked.

"Not just yet, but maybe at dinner. Now, help me set the table," she requested.

Taylor and Franklin started pulling out the plates and glasses while Emma got the silverware. Everyone pitched in to move the platters and, as dinner started, Emma let the conversation flow around her. They were all asking the same questions and wanted details of the train trip and New York City. She took time to describe how the train ride was long and the sleeper compartments were wonderfully comfortable. "New York is like Chicago, very noisy and busy. I did get to see some marvelous buildings that I know Papa had helped build." She smiled fondly at him. He sent her a similar smile.

The twins demanded to know about the Hudson River and the new bridge they had heard about. She tried to remember what she had seen and heard. "It was so big, growing out of the water. I would like to see it when it's completed." She looked over at Jake and said, "I may have to borrow your camera on my next trip."

He nodded, "We can work on that."

The women wanted to know about fashion, particularly hats and bustles. Emma confirmed both were bigger. Dinner drew to a close and Emma, Dora, Tim, Jake, and Papa moved into the kitchen to help Amy with the dishes.

Once done, Papa mentioned he would be in the study and looked over at Jake. "Would you like to come with me?"

Jake looked a little conflicted when he said, "I think I would like to hear about the new case, but I can come to sit with you after."

Papa nodded and headed to his study.

Emma pulled out her notebook and started detailing the oddities of the case: money being spent by Millie, limited communication from her to the grandfather, household help being let go. "I think there's something odd there, but I'm not sure it's sinister or dangerous."

Jake asked, "Any photography work on this job?"

Emma mulled that over and said, "Not just now, but I think we can utilize it later in the case."

Jake nodded and sat back to listen to the details.

Dora asked, "What's the first step?"

"Well, first will probably be evaluating the information with Cole, since this is a Pinkerton case," she said.

Tim said, "If we want to be used again, we will need to follow their rules. Agreed?"

Everyone nodded, understanding how important this job was to them.

Emma stated, "I'm thinking I need to locate the household staff who were let go. They may have some observations for me."

Dora said, "I can help with that. Millie's previous cook always had a weakness for Cousin's bread. I'm sure that wherever she ended up, she is still getting it delivered."

Emma made a note to go to the bakery for the information and said, "I can do that in the morning. I will drop by there first."

"The interview with Cole should be your priority," reminded Tim.

"Yes, I'll go right after the bakery. Hopefully, he has time for me. Also, Millie's current man of business is John Darko. Do you know him?"

"I know of him. He has a reputation as an honest man of business. I can look more into him just to be sure," said Tim, making a note in his logbook.

"Another thing, her husband's man of business, we need to find out who that is and see where the money is going," said Emma.

"I can do that," commented Tim.

"Now for Millie, I need some one-on-one with her. Dora, has Mrs. Simpson asked for any assistance for her shop? Or any lace orders?" she asked.

Dora flipped through her logbook and said, "Now that you

mention it, there is some sort of cotillion coming up and she did request some temporary help starting this week."

Emma looked at Tim and asked, "Can I be spared a few weeks from the office work?"

He nodded and said, "Your replacement is doing well enough to stay if you're ready to move on."

"I think I am, though if more auditing is needed in other offices, I can make some time," she offered.

They ended the meeting and Emma went upstairs to read and relax as the evening wound down. She slept well that night and awoke refreshed to begin her day. After she got up, she washed her face and got dressed, leaving before the sun lit the sky. The weather was cold that morning, she shivered and sank into her long coat as she rode her bike to the bakery.

Coasting her bike into the back area of the bakery, she hopped off and parked it close to the back door. The smells wafted over to her. *Yum, a wonderful way to start my morning.*

Cousin spotted her as soon as she came in and gave her a big hug. "Hi, Emma, here to work?" he teased. She was one of his most requested bakers and, if he could get her to make something special, it would be a good day.

"I can be," she teased back. "But I also need some information about someone who orders a specialty bread from you."

"I can help with that; my customer list is in the office. Do you want help looking?" he asked, already making his way back to his baking station.

"No, I can do it," she said with a smile, seeing that Cousin was already rolling out the dough to make bread. With the smell of yeast in the air, she made her way to the office and opened the door. It was as neat as he was in life, everything in its place. The wooden file box sat on the desk. He had the files set up by types of baked goods. Dora had provided the cook's first and last name and specialty bread, she pulled out her notebook and looked for the matching card. She found the card she wanted almost immediately and realized that Mille's previous cook had an order due to be delivered that day. Making note of the address in her notebook, she exited the office and asked, "Cousin, can I make this delivery for you today?"

He glanced over and said, with a gleam in his eyes, "Maybe, but you'll have to work for me this morning. I have a large pastry order and some staff are out sick."

She smiled wryly. Having known he would trap her into baking this morning, she had prepared to stay. "I can stay until 10am," she promised.

"You can use your old workstation. The daily list is there," he said, waving his hand toward it. Emma removed her coat and borrowed an apron to cover her clothes. She looked at the card and saw Berliners, Bratapfels, and several cakes. She got to work and enjoyed temporarily being back.

"How is Chloe?" she asked Cousin, curious why she hadn't seen her that morning.

"Good, just tired. The baby's due any day and she's home resting," he replied.

Emma nodded and continued to work and fill her orders. By 10am, she was tired but happy; she occasionally missed working at the bakery. Cousin gave her the bread order and, with a big hug of thanks, she left to begin the first step of the case. Heading out the back door, she put the bread in her tote and rode over to the Pinkerton office.

Once there, she hopped off the bike and placed it on her shoulder to climb the entrance stairs. A Pinkerton detective met her at the door and, instead of a lecture, he just rolled his eyes at her as he took it. He said over his shoulder, "Mr. Tilden is busy with a client just now if you would like to wait."

"I can wait," she called back.

"I think Jeremy is in his office," he said innocently.

"Really," she murmured. "Maybe I'll go there first." With that, she turned and headed in that direction. She knocked, entered his office, and saw a relaxed Jeremy with his feet up on his desk, reading a file.

He looked up, expecting to see one of the Pinkerton employees, and realized it was Emma. He tried to stand but didn't seem to remember his feet were still on the desk and fell backward in his chair. "Hello, Emma," he said with as much dignity as he could muster as he straightened up and got a firm footing on the floor.

She laughed out loud at his antics and said, "Hello, Jeremy."

He let the dignity go and started laughing with her. "Are you here to see Cole?"

She nodded, walked over to his side of the desk, and leaned back against it. It put her in arm's reach of Jeremy. "My team recommended I keep Cole in the loop since this is a Pinkerton case."

"Probably for the best," he acknowledged. "Pops should be available soon. Come here, let's talk about something important."

"And what would that be?" she asked coyly and held off for just a moment and then allowed herself to be pulled into his lap.

"Us?" he asked, sounding distracted.

"Is there an us?" She murmured the question into his neck.

He tilted her head back and said, "I think so," and gave her a slow, wonderfully long kiss. He was lifting his head to add to their conversation when the door opened and Cole strode in.

"Emma, I'm sorry if I kept you waiting." He stopped abruptly when he saw them. "I hope I'm not interrupting anything," he said wryly.

"Well, I found something to keep me busy," she said, slanting a gaze at Jeremy.

"So, I see." Cole chuckled. "Emma, come to my office. Jeremy, I think you have things to do?" He looked at him pointedly, and he reluctantly relinquished Emma.

"Yes, Pops," Jeremy said, wishing she could stay longer.

She waved goodbye to Jeremy and followed Cole back to his

office. They sat on his couch, and Emma covered the information provided by Mr. Carlyle and his instructions.

"A weekly telegraph, I think we can handle that," he said.

"I've met with my team and we have some leads." He nodded for her to continue. She covered: the help, money manager, and seamstress.

"That sounds like a solid start. I would say let me know of any significant changes in the case and confirm with me before any undercover work," he cautioned.

"I will," she promised. "My priority is to build the background information first, prior to the first contact."

"Do you expect to make contact with Millie this weekend?"

"I'm hoping to."

"Okay, let's regroup on Monday and see what the next step will be."

"Agreed," she said, closing her notebook and prepared to stand.

Cole stopped her by saying, "Emma, thanks for the help on the transport from Chicago."

"No thanks are necessary, I enjoyed it," she said with a smile.

"Yes, I can see you did," he murmured.

"I'll be on my way."

"Thank you for coming in," he said as he watched her go. *If Jeremy had any sense, he would grab hold of her and never let go.*

As she exited the office, the Pinkerton detective who had stored her bike brought it out and carried it down the stairs for her. She thanked him as she hopped on to head to her first lead in the case. The maid lived in one of the more expensive districts and the paved roads made for a smooth ride. The address indicated it was a single-family home about three blocks up. She slowed to a stop, climbed off the bike, and parked it near the kitchen door. The bag that held the bread was slung over her shoulder, she removed it and tapped lightly on the door. A small older woman answered the door, her gray curls escaping the white bonnet on her head. "Hello," she greeted in a singsong voice.

"Hello," Emma replied. "I have your bread order from Cousin's." She showed her the bread she was carrying.

"Oh, how wonderful. Thank you for bringing it by. I just love their bread. Come in, please," she said, taking it and placing it on the table.

"Thank you. Would you mind if I stay and speak with you for a moment, Miss Grisham?" asked Emma, pulling out her notebook.

"Do I know you?" she asked, taking time to look hard at her.

"I don't know if you remember me, but I did stay at Millie's house one weekend years ago," Emma said, hoping to stir a memory.

"When you were a girl," she finished for her. "You were much younger and didn't eat much while you were with us, as I recall."

"That would be me, Emma Evans. Please, call me Emma."

"Call me Genny."

"Genny. . ." Emma started.

Before Emma could answer, Genny asked her rather abruptly, "Are you here about Miss Carlyle?"

"Yes," she said surprised. "I'm inquiring for her grandfather. He's very concerned, especially when he heard you and the other staff were no longer in place."

"Yes," she said, looking down at the table. "So much happened at once. We were so happy about the marriage, we were hoping the couple would start a family soon. That wasn't what happened and as soon as Mr. Landon moved in, the staff started to disappear. We were told the help that left had stolen items or they were untrustworthy. After a while, it just seemed they wanted us all gone. Roger himself wanted me out, about ran me out of the house. Sadly, I haven't heard from anyone I worked with." She looked dejected and said, "I didn't want to leave, but the situation wasn't working. We tried to talk to Miss Carlyle directly, but she deferred only to that Roger person."

"Roger?" Emma inquired.

"Roger Smith. He showed up right after the wedding and took

over the running of the house. We never saw Mr. Landon once he showed up; he was the only person allowed to see him. Miss Carlyle never left her room except to shop, and Mr. Landon was always locked in the library on business."

"Do you feel that Mrs. Landon is in danger?"

"I never saw anything, but we were cut off from any contact with her, so I can't be sure."

"Are there any other household staff members who might have more information?"

"Yes," she said hesitantly. "Susan Baker, her personal maid, was with her every day, but she is out of the country, visiting family. Roger told me." Emma wrote it all down in her notebook.

Emma took a moment to evaluate her notes. *If Millie was married in the last few months, where is her new husband and why has no one seen him? I need more information on Roger -- where did he come from?*

She closed her notebook and thanked Genny for her time. As she made her way home on her bike, she mulled over the information.

The next step, she thought to herself, *is to make contact with Millie.*

Emma worked temporary jobs making lace at a local fancy dress establishment. More affluent women were able to get dresses made for each season and kept up with new styles coming in from Paris. Emma was known locally for her lacework, a skill she had learned from Miss May. It was time-consuming work and she only accepted a few jobs a year due to the intricate natures of the patterns.

She stopped by the shop. It was quiet when she entered, and she waited in the salon. The owner walked out of her office and saw her. She immediately went to hug her and said, "Emma, how are you? I haven't seen enough of you lately."

"I know, I've been busy. Dora mentioned you need me for some work over the next few weeks?" asked Emma.

"Yes, with the big event coming up, we need some detailed lacework."

"I think I can arrange that," she said. "But can you also do me a favor?"

The owner looked curious and said, "Of course."

"Can you tell me if Millicent Carlyle-Landon has one of the appointments this weekend?" Emma asked innocently.

The owner went to her appointment book and flipped a few pages before saying, "Yes, she has an appointment on Saturday."

"Would you mind assigning me to work with her?"

"That works well for me. She has picked an intricate lace overlay for a few of her dresses," replied Ms. Simpson.

"Please confirm with Millie and let her know I'll be available this Saturday afternoon for her dress design session," requested Emma.

"I will." She had known Emma long enough to not ask any additional questions.

"Can I see the dresses she is interested in? So, I can start the design work?" Emma asked.

Mrs. Simpson pulled out the custom drawing boards for Emma to evaluate. Emma looked up from her notes and said, "I'll put together some ideas to recommend to her this weekend." Before she exited the shop, she thanked Mrs. Simpson for her help and headed home.

Upon reaching the boarding house, after a quick hello to Dora, Tim, and Amy, Emma moved to the sitting room. She pulled out her lace design books to begin sketching several types of overlays that would go well with the dresses Millie was interested in.

After dinner that night, she filled in the team on what she had learned from the housekeeper and detailed her upcoming Saturday seamstress appointment.

Tim nodded. "Good work, Emma. I also spoke with John Darko. He's still handling Millie's accounts and hasn't seen any inappropriate spending from her or the household."

Emma was taking notes. "Did he say anything about the change in staff?"

"Just that he indicated the money to pay them had been shifted to Mr. Smith." Emma started to question that, but Tim continued, "And before you ask, I did inquire about Mr. Alto. He refused to see me, and his secretary indicated he no longer has Mr. Landon as a client. He was rather rude about it."

"Hmm, several suspicious items with Mr. Landon. One, no one has seen him since the wedding and, two, his money is unaccounted for," said Emma.

"Sounds like the beginning of a puzzle, the corner pieces starting to fall into place. I think we wait for Emma's meeting with Millie?" suggested Tim.

"Yes," the team agreed.

CHAPTER 36

Saturday morning, Emma completed the details on her lace designs and got ready for her appointment with Millie. It was not something she was looking forward to. Millie had never really liked her, she had only contacted her when she wanted something. She inhaled and exhaled, trying to calm herself, and went downstairs.

She called from the foyer, "I am going out now."

Steps could be heard running in from the kitchen. Dora hugged her quickly and said, "Don't let her get to you."

"I won't," she promised and headed to the salon, taking the trolley downtown. As soon as she entered, she saw Millie and realized almost instantly there was something different about her. Standing in the doorway, she paused to make her observations. Her mannerisms, manner, even the tone of her clothes bespoke a more subdued woman than she remembered. Yet, in her eyes, there seemed to be something of the girl still there.

Emma decided it was time to make herself seen. "Mrs. Landon, how nice to see you again," she called.

Millie ran over to hug her. Emma stood very still in her embrace; they'd never had this type of relationship previously. While she hugged Emma, she said, "Millie, not Mrs. Landon. I was so thrilled to hear you were available for my lacework."

Mrs. Simpson noticed Emma and Mrs. Landon were ready for the appointment; she motioned to her assistants to set up the drawings in the large salon.

"Mrs. Landon, Emma, let's get settled in the salon," directed Mrs. Simpson. "Emma, let me take your coat." Emma handed it to her, she gave it to her assistant to hang up.

They moved into the salon and sat down on the plush sofas; the assistants brought out easels to display each dress design. Emma pulled out her design notebook to begin the consultation, she started by showing her the designs. "We have used the lace as you see on the first two drawings of a tea gown, confections that had lace drape over the bodice and again on the edges. The other drawing is a fitted day dress, with lace relegated to the sleeves and a limited bustle."

Millie's response was positive, but not like the orders previously when she wanted to keep adding embellishments to the gowns. This time, she accepted the sketches as is.

"When can I expect my first fitting and a viewing of the lace appliques?" asked Millie.

Mary, the head seamstress, had joined them and stated, "In about three weeks, we'll have pinned muslin designs for an initial fitting."

"The lacework will take an additional month," added Emma. Millie looked a bit pensive about the timing but didn't comment further.

"Would you like some tea, Emma?" asked Millie.

Emma nodded and Mrs. Simpson left them to attend to her next customer. The tea was brought in and the door closed to allow them some privacy.

Emma decided to ask some direct questions. "Millie, how are you doing?"

Millie seemed to struggle a bit with that answer and then finally replied, "I'm fine."

"I only met your husband once at your wedding," she began.

Millie interrupted with a giggle, sounding a bit more like her old self, and said, "He travels, you know."

"Yes, and I understand you've gotten new staff for the house?" asked Emma, watching her closely.

She glanced a bit coolly at Emma. "I think that is *my* business."

Emma understood immediately she should back off that line of questioning. Instead, she asked in a light, conversational tone, "Have you spoken to your grandfather lately?"

"No, I do owe him a letter. I've just been so busy," she admitted.

Emma made mental notes for the first telegram to send to Mr. Carlyle.

Millie seemed calmer as she finished her tea. Emma let the conversation move back to fashion and parties. As the appointment came to a close, Millie hugged Emma again and promised, "I will see you soon." She collected her things and exited the shop. Emma watched from the window as the two men waiting by her private cab immediately straightened to assist her.

Turning slowly away from the window, Emma retrieved her design book and stood.

"That seemed to go well," Mrs. Simpson said, as she entered the room.

"Yes," Emma commented. They reviewed the lace designs proposed and she formally accepted the job, with a promise of an initial deliverable for four weeks from that day.

Placing her drawing book into her shoulder bag, she made her way home, walking instead of taking the trolley. The afternoon had cooled off considerably, but she didn't notice, her mind occupied with Millie. "Is there a case here?" she asked herself. "Or just a worried grandfather?"

Arriving at the boarding house, she hesitated before going in. She sat outside on the stoop, making notes about what she had learned. Millie's behavior was different, but that may be attributed to getting married and growing up. There was also her agitation when she asked her about the staffing changes. Emma needed firsthand knowledge of who was working in that house to determine if Millie was safe.

She completed her notes, making her way inside. Taking off her hat as she entered, she placed it in the closet, then headed through the foyer and dining room to enter the kitchen. Dora and Amy were putting together a stew that already had the kitchen smelling of herbs and meat.

"Hi, Dora, Amy," greeted Emma.

Dora absently cut a piece of bread and added butter before handing it to her. "Is everything okay?"

"After dinner," she mumbled as she ate. Dora nodded and continued preparations.

That night, with their smaller group, Emma said, "I think we've done what we can without knowing what's happening inside Millie's house. I need to meet with Cole and discuss going undercover."

"Has something happened?" asked Dora.

"No, at least, not yet," she replied. She went on to describe her meeting with Millie and her plans to follow up. "It was more than just her words that bothered me; it was the absolute change in her demeanor. It might be her husband's influence. I do remember finding him a little standoffish at the wedding, but I thought that would change with time. I'm also worried that Millie is nineteen and, when she turns twenty, she's expected to receive her full inheritance from her grandfather. I need to get into the house to see what is going on there." She paused a moment, thinking, and asked the group, "How do I do that? Large homes like Millie's need all types of help, but if this Roger is limiting the number of servants, how do I get in?"

Dora spoke up. "They're probably using Moore Services. They're the main supplier of household help here in town. If they're not allowing people to stay permanently, there may be a temporary position open. I know the owner and I'm pretty sure we can work something out."

"Wonderful. Can you get with her soon?" asked Emma.

She pulled out her calendar and said, "I'll make it a priority."

Tim commented, "Won't Millie know you by sight and make an undercover job difficult?"

"Not if I get with Savannah. She'll have some ideas to hide my identity. I also need to review my plans with Cole. I plan to catch them both after church tomorrow," said Emma. Emma and Savannah had gotten to know each other when Emma borrowed the wig for her undercover work at the shelter.

"Emma, invite them to Sunday lunch and we can talk after," Dora suggested.

The group agreed and retired to the sitting room. Emma worked on her lace, Tim and Dora tackled their books, and the others sat and talked quietly.

CHAPTER 37

$\mathscr{A}$fter church on Sunday, Emma waited for Cole and Jeremy just outside the main doors. "Jeremy," she called when she saw him exit with Cole.

"Emma, how are you?" asked Cole. Jeremy held out his hand as she approached. She took it and let him pull her in close.

"I'm good. We were hoping," nodding to where Papa, Dora, and Tim were standing, "that you both might join us for lunch."

"I think that can be arranged," answered Cole. Jeremy gave an enthusiastic, "Yes."

Cole smiled broadly and said, "We'll need to drop by the house to change clothes and then will be over directly."

"Wonderful. See you both there," Emma said.

"Definitely," Jeremy said as he leaned down to give her a soft kiss goodbye.

Emma and her family got their wagon and headed back home. Once inside, she joined Dora to help with lunch. Amy had Saturdays and Sundays off to be with her family, and the family dinners could be quite large with additional guests.

Sunday lunch consisted of baked chicken, potatoes, and assorted vegetables. The bread had been freshly baked the day before and was cut for the table. Emma was working on the finishing touches for dessert. She finished it and put it on the side counter for later.

As lunch was being pulled together, Emma heard a knock at the front door. Tim, sitting at the table, said, "I'll get it." He headed out of the kitchen.

Emma and Dora could hear Tim and Papa in the front of the house, greeting their guest. *Conversations are always lively with this group*, thought Emma.

Jeremy stole his way into the kitchen and winked at Dora as he snuck up behind Emma. She had seen him out of the corner of her eye and was not surprised when he wrapped his arms around her. She turned and said lightly, "Hello, Jeremy."

"Can't surprise you, can I?" he asked playfully. She just smiled at him in response. "After lunch, want to take a walk, maybe go to the park?"

"Hmmm," she pretended to think and finally said, "Yes. Now, out of the kitchen. You're too distracting."

"I am? Good. Dora, everything smells wonderful," he said on his way to the door.

"Thanks, Jeremy. Lunch will be soon. Get with Tim and help him set the table. When you're done with that, come back for the platters," Dora said in her commanding voice.

Jeremy nodded and went to do her bidding.

Lunch was indeed wonderful and everyone had their fill. As it was cleared away, Cole asked, "Can we close the doors for our meeting?"

Papa and Jake excused themselves while Tim pulled the pocket doors closed behind them.

Cole started, "Well, Emma, I would assume you're ready for some undercover work?"

"Yes." She briefed him on the information they'd learned.

Cole sat back in his chair and said to the group, "Good work and thorough. Emma, the position you were speaking of, you're sure it will be available?"

Dora answered for her. "Yes, I was able to get a confirmation from my contact for an assistant cook position focusing on household baking. She'll pick up her uniform and card on Monday and then meet the house manager."

"What about Millie, won't she recognize you?" asked Jeremy.

She looked at him and said, "My thought was that Savannah could help out with a wig, I have some glasses and perhaps some makeup."

Jeremy nodded and said, "She enjoyed helping with the shelter case. I think she would feel the same about this one."

"Great," said Cole. "Just one thing. I rarely send one person in undercover. We normally have a backup in case of emergency." Emma started to talk, but Cole continued without allowing the interruption and looked directly at her. "Emma this isn't a comment on your skills. It is procedure."

Emma stopped and realized she shouldn't take offense. If she wanted to work a Pinkerton case, she had to follow their rules. "You're right. I'll follow the appropriate procedure."

Cole looked satisfied with that answer.

"Pops, I think I have an idea. Emma, does the house have a garden in the back?" asked Jeremy. Some of the bigger houses had intricate gardens.

"Yes, it's very large and very detailed," answered Emma.

Cole understood what Jeremy was saying and commented "Yes, I see. We could replace the gardener with you for the time Emma is in the house." He looked at her and asked, "Would that work for you?"

Emma nodded in agreement and said to Cole, "Papa and I have the house plans in the study. We would like to show them to you and Jeremy." Cole, Emma, and Jeremy moved to join Papa in the study.

The doors were pulled closed. Papa had laid the blueprints on the desk. As they studied them, Emma began pointing out the major rooms in the house. "The study, located on the second floor, has a secret room and a staircase leading to the basement," Emma said, pointing to the west wall. Papa handed her a pencil and she drew in the location. "There's also a dumbwaiter in that room with access to the kitchen and basement."

Cole looked at the drawing consideringly and said, "Emma, how do you know about this? Have you been in the house?"

"That's an odd story," said Emma. She looked at Papa, and he nodded encouragingly for her to continue. "Millie and I weren't friends when we were younger. We knew each other, but we didn't have a lot in common. Honestly, I think she felt she was above us because Papa had worked for her family. It was surprising when she sent me an invitation to spend the weekend with her."

"Why did you go?" asked Jeremy.

She shrugged and said, "I accepted because I was curious about why she wanted me to visit, and it had the added benefit of allowing me to see the inside of her house."

"Did she show you this secret passage?" asked Cole.

"No," she said, tilting her head, thinking about that weekend. "No, we were playing at hiding and finding. In this case, Millie was hiding and I was looking for her. Honestly, I went into every room in that house, looked through all closets and under the beds. I still couldn't find her."

"How did you finally find her and uncover the location of the secret staircase?" asked Jeremy curiously.

"It was her laughing," she said simply. "She finally came out and showed me how smart she was for hiding there."

"I'm surprised that she showed you," said Papa.

"I was also," she acknowledged.

"Did you have a chance to go back after that weekend?" asked Cole.

"No, her parents passed away soon after that and she moved to her grandfather's house. Once she married, the house passed to her and Mr. Landon."

The group discussed the final plans and their meeting drew to a close. Cole stayed after to spend some time talking to Papa.

Jeremy looked over at Emma and put out his hand. "Walk?" he suggested.

"Yes," she said softly taking his hand.

As they made their way down the street, he suggested, "We might want to see if Savannah is available this afternoon to confirm she can help with your disguise."

"Agreed," she said. "Though I will miss our alone time."

"Well," he pulled her close for a kiss and murmured, "we can work on that also."

They were laughing and enjoying each other's company when they ran for the trolley. They talked and held hands all the way to Savannah's apartment in the theatre district. On the way there, Emma said to Jeremy, "Will she be mad we're together?"

"Savannah and I, we're just pals. She's interested in one of the stagehands working backstage on her current show," said Jeremy with a laugh.

Emma smiled and relaxed, enjoying their trip. They hopped off the trolley and made their way to Savannah's apartment.

She answered on the first knock and said sincerely, "Jeremy, Emma, hello and welcome. This is a nice surprise. Come in."

"Thank you. We have a favor to ask," Jeremy said as they made their way into the sitting room.

Savannah watched and realized something had changed between the two. She smiled, knowing this is what he had always wanted. "Is there a case I can help with?" she asked intuitively.

Emma grinned and said to Jeremy, "I like her." She went on to describe the case and what types of changes might be needed to her appearance.

Savannah mulled it over and said consideringly, "A wig for sure. You mentioned you have glasses? Some makeup can be used to change the look of your lips. You mentioned this is for an assistant cook position?"

"Yes."

"Well, for that, you might need some acting lessons," she commented.

"Acting lessons?" Emma questioned.

"Have you ever observed the staff in a house, the type Millie has?"

"No, not really," she admitted.

"They would not meet their employers' eyes for one thing. For another, they try to stay invisible."

"That works for me. I'll remember to do both."

"And only speak when spoken to and only in hushed tones."

Emma pulled out her notebook to take notes. "I'll study these. Thanks for the advice."

"Okay, let's go to my room and I'll get the wigs out." She gestured for Emma to follow her. Jeremy stayed in the sitting room with a book he'd picked up when they entered.

"We need something dark, maybe reddish." Savannah pulled out the shorter wig. "It will be like the shelter case, but this one will have more pins since it won't be as temporary as the last one." She pulled the wig onto Emma's head and asked, "Will you be able to do this on your own?"

"I think so. If not, I can get Dora to help," she commented.

Savannah explained the makeup as she applied it to her face. The different layers caused her lips to look thinner and her cheeks fuller. Emma looked in the mirror in amazement; she didn't recognize her reflection.

"Let's show Jeremy," she suggested.

They walked into the sitting room and for a moment, he didn't know it was Emma. He said in an incredulous voice, "That's perfect."

"Let's go back and put the items into a bag for you to take home," said Savannah.

Emma took off the wig and used a wet rag to wipe off the makeup. "Promise we will get together for dinner soon?"

Savannah said, "I'm looking forward to it."

Jeremy winked at Savanna and thanked her.

They parted ways, promising to give her all the details once the case was over.

"We still have time to take a cab over to the park," he said hopefully as they left the building.

"That would be nice."

They hailed a cab and headed there. Sitting together, they enjoyed each other's company. Jeremy dropped Emma off at the boarding house in time for dinner. She asked him in, but he had to complete some office work before starting his undercover position with her the next day. They kissed goodbye and Emma headed inside.

She picked up her lacework and went in to sit with the family and boarders. The lacework would take up her evenings for a while. Working diligently, she was able to complete some of the scallops for the tea dresses and started working on the more complicated overlays.

CHAPTER 38

The next morning, Emma readied herself for the day; she put on a plain gray dress and moved to her makeup table. The wig was next. She sat down, pinned up her hair, and pulled the wig over it. Next, she applied her makeup and slid on the ugly wire frame glasses. Taking a good look at herself, she thought, *What a picture you make.*

Gathering up the things she might need, she slid her notebook into her skirt pocket and stowed her knife into its thigh sheath. The clock dinged, reminding her that she had to get going before any of the boarders noticed her. She headed downstairs and slowly opened the door to the kitchen.

Dora saw her in the doorway and waved her in. "Amy is getting the wash, so we have a moment. Eat some breakfast and you can leave out the back door."

"Thank you," Emma said as she ate. "Well, what do you think?"

"I wouldn't have recognized you," admitted Dora. She got up to get Emma's lunch pail, handing it to her. With a hug, she said, "Probably no bike today. Too many people might recognize it."

"I thought of that. I'll catch the trolley this morning," Emma said as she shrugged into her dark blue jacket. "I'll see you this evening." Exiting out the back door, she walked quickly to the trolley stop and only had to wait a moment for it to appear. The trip was fast, and she jumped off as they reached her destination. The employment service was a few additional blocks from the stop, she used the time to go over her notes.

The buildings had the addresses posted clearly on the outside. She located the correct one and entered, following the signs to the agency. The agency door was painted an imposing black; she slowly turned the knob and entered the room. People were lined up on both sides of the long room; some looked bored, some hopeful—all wanting jobs.

She approached the secretary sitting at the desk. "Hello, I'm Molly Mullins. I believe Mrs. Stevens is expecting me?"

He checked his card list and said, "Yes, she is expecting you."

"Can you point me to her office?" she asked.

He looked surprised that she didn't know the way and indicated the door with his hand. "You may go in now."

Emma entered and a woman she assumed was Mrs. Stevens sat at the desk. She was an imposing figure all in black, with her hair pulled back into a tight bun. "Mrs. Stevens?" she began.

"Yes, don't tarry. What do you need?" Mrs. Stevens asked rather impatiently.

"Dora recommended I speak with you," Emma stated.

Mrs. Stevens took off her glasses, looking her over, and said, "Well, yes, that is something I wanted to discuss. I'm doing this as a favor and don't want this business to reflect badly on me."

"I understand. I am qualified for the position and I'll work hard," she assured her.

That seemed to mollify her. "I would do anything for Dora. Let me know if the situation changes. Remember, no complaints from the client," she said firmly.

"I will remember," Emma assured her.

"I have a uniform for you. You'll need to change here and head straight over." She stood and walked to a closet, pulled out a black and white maid's uniform, and handed it to her. "You may change down the hall, the small room on the left," she directed.

Emma changed and placed her gray dress in her bag. Heading out of the building, she hailed a cab; Millie's house was a significant distance from the service agency.

As they neared the townhouse, she realized it was bigger than she remembered. It took up half a block and had an intricate stone exterior. The imposing ivory columns towered over the cab as it approached.

Service people were expected to enter from the back, so she took her bag and paid the driver before making her way to the kitchen door. She knocked and waited. A woman opened the door, also wearing a black and white maid's dress. When the woman didn't say anything, Emma said, "Hello, I'm Molly Mullins from the agency." When the maid still didn't say anything, Emma continued, "I'm here to bake and assist with the cooking."

The maid reached out her hand and said, "Do you have your employment card?"

Emma reached into her pocket and handed it over to her. The kitchen-maid did not smile or show any expression at all. Her figure, if you could call it one, was more of a rectangle shape- seeming to come to a point at her head and wide at her hips. Her overall demeanor gave her an air of doom. *Not a great way to start this job*, Emma thought.

She waved her in without comment and finally said, "You can put your things in that closet there," indicating the small door behind her. "I am working on lunch. You can help with the afternoon tea. I will need two types of desserts: a cake and small pastries."

Emma nodded and asked, "Where would you like me to set up?"

She looked at her for a long moment. "Roger will want to see you first. Stay here," she warned as she exited the kitchen.

"I guess she went to get Roger," Emma mused as she looked for supplies to place on her workstation. One of the cabinets she tried had what she needed. The kitchen door opened as she started to pour the flour. She hesitated and placed the bag on the station, waiting for him to speak.

He was a tall man with a trim waist. He appeared to be in his late thirties; he had thin black hair and a small mustache. "It says here," he said reading her card, "that you bake and will assist Mrs. Miller?"

Remembering Savannah's instructions, keeping her voice and eyes lowered, she answered, "Yes. I've worked in many households as a baker and assistant cook."

That seemed to satisfy him. "You will not be allowed outside the kitchen without an escort. Mrs. Miller will brief you. If you cannot adhere to these rules, you will be replaced." With that, he turned and exited the room.

Kind of an odd duck, Emma thought. She looked at Mrs. Miller and asked, "Rules about leaving the kitchen?"

"Yes. You must be escorted to the lavatory and you are to be accompanied if you take a tray outside of the kitchen. If you want to stay, you will pay attention to my instructions," she warned softly, but not unkindly.

Emma started working on the cake, wondering about the other household help. "Isn't there anyone else working here?" she asked.

Mrs. Miller sent her a look and said, "Roger brings in people to clean as needed. I'm the only one allowed to deliver the tray to Mrs. Landon."

Emma decided it was best to work and not ask any more questions.

The cake came together quickly and she moved on to the pastries that would be needed for the afternoon tea. The rules about exiting the kitchen were strictly enforced; each time she needed to visit the lavatory, she was escorted by several men located in the hallway outside. *There is no way I am going to be able to access the study with all of the security here.*

Suddenly, she heard yelling outside the backdoor; it seemed Roger was very angry about something outside. Looking through the window, she realized he was yelling at Jeremy.

"What do you think is going on?" she asked Mrs. Miller.

"The garden is off-limits to anyone but the gardener, Mrs. Landon, or Roger," stated Mrs. Miller in a firm voice.

Roger slammed in the door and Jeremy followed behind him, his head lowered. "You are only to work on the things I tell you to and you are to leave other areas as they are. Do you understand?"

Jeremy nodded and said, "Yes, sir."

"I still don't understand what happened to the last gardener and how you happened to take the job," he muttered as he left the room.

Jeremy sent Emma a crooked smile and asked for some water. He raised his eyebrows in a silent question, making sure she was okay. She nodded to him that she was fine. When he exited, she was told by Mrs. Miller, "Go down to the basement to get some preserves for me."

Finally, thought Emma. Trying to remember the last time she had been in this area of the house. She turned on the gas lights as she made her way down the stairs. *First the preserves.* She moved several jars to the stairs and walked toward the narrow door leading to the hidden staircase. A lock had been added to it; it appeared to be a new addition. She reached for a small pin from her wig to open it. It sprang open quickly and she peered in, the stairs were caked in dust; clearly, they hadn't been used recently.

"Are you lost down there?" Mrs. Miller called from the top of the stairs.

"On my way up," she called back. She picked up the preserves and went back upstairs.

Over the next few days, Emma worked hard and didn't do anything suspicious, trying to gain Mrs. Miller's trust. The plan seemed to be working, she gave Emma a key and asked that she come in early the next day to make the bread.

The next morning, Emma entered the house in the early hours. The grounds were very quiet, and the men were already stationed in the hallway. She notified them she was in the kitchen and started the bread, leaving it to rise as she went down to the basement to access the hidden stairs again. This time she entered and made her way slowly up the winding stairs. Her portable gas lamp lit the way.

There were several landings. At the final one, she accessed the switch that allowed her entry into the study and extinguished the lamp. The door swung open and surprisingly the room was not dark, the curtains on the windows were open, letting the early morning light in. She started searching for anything that might tell her what was happening in the house. The desk drawers were all unlocked but contained only blank papers.

The door to the hallway rattled and she heard a scraping noise, like a key being inserted into the lock. This forced Emma back into the hidden staircase. With a deep shuttering sigh, she made her way down the stairs in the dark. She exited into the basement, secured the lock, and turned to head back upstairs to the kitchen. *Wait -the last time I was here I saw the dumbwaiter. Where was it?* She looked around and saw the sliding doors on the far wall.

Do I have time? Emma asked herself and went to stand in front of it. *I have to try.* It was locked, but she easily picked it and slid the two panels open. She lit her lamp and used it to illuminate the interior; slowly putting her hands inside to feel around. There was something in there, she touched it briefly and pull her hand back out. Her palm was covered with a white powder. She put it to her nose and thought, *What's that smell? Lime? Why would there be lime here?*

More information is needed, she thought and climbed into the space, her lamp in front of her, she came face to face with . . . *a man?* A scream got trapped in her throat and she crawled backward, almost falling back into the basement. Taking two steadying breaths, she forced herself to move closer to and touch him. Slowly raising her hand, she ran her fingers down his face, curiously it didn't feel like skin, it felt like leather. *The lime must have reacted with the body. Could this be the missing Mr. Landon?* She pulled her hand back and placed it on her chest, as though to prevent her heart from leaping out. *Out! Out! Out!* she thought and pushed herself out and back into the basement.

Beginning to feel faint, she bent over, trying to catch her breath. *You have to pull yourself together. I need to know if it is him. How . . .? The ring,* the one she admired at the wedding. Forcing herself back into the dumbwaiter she tried to find his hands. His arms were twisted behind him, grimacing, she leaned him toward her to get the access she needed. They were stiff and didn't come loose from their position easily. "Please don't break off," she muttered. Then she heard a sound that she didn't want to hear, it was the sound of paper tearing. She tried to ignore it as she continued to pull on his arm.

The hand became visible and she saw the ring was still in place. Pulling on it, the paper tearing got worse until the finger broke off. The ring slid off quickly and she placed the finger into his hand. Pocketing the ring, she climbed out, closed the dumbwaiter, and put the lock back on with a shaky hand.

The preserves! She immediately went to get some preserves and headed upstairs to the kitchen. The room was empty as she entered and moved them to the counter. A wave of nausea engulfed her and she barely made it to the kitchen sink before she threw up. She washed her face with shaky hands and recovered enough to go to the lavatory in the hallway to fix her makeup and put a cold compress on her neck. The guards there escorted her to and from the lavatory, they didn't seem to notice her distress.

Back in the kitchen, she began to put the loaves in the oven. The rolls were next, she had them ready to go in as soon as the loaves came out. Taking a break, she sat down, breathing deeply to settle her heartbeat as she tried not to dwell on what she had seen. Once she felt steadier, she got up to start work on the pastries for breakfast.

Mrs. Miller entered soon after. She looked over at Emma and said approvingly, "Smells good in here." She didn't notice anything out of ordinary with Emma appearance, the heat of the kitchen had helped with her color

"Thank you," Emma said quietly, not making any further conversation.

Mrs. Miller sent her a look but didn't try to engage her.

Jeremy came in for water about an hour later and sent her a look. She shook her head and mouthed, *Later.*

He nodded as he drank and went back to work in the garden. The day went by quickly, she stayed busy, trying not to think about what she'd seen.

Walking home, almost in a daze from the day's event, she noticed someone was following her. She ducked into an alley and waited for the confrontation. The shadow could be seen hesitating and she took the opportunity to nab him by the collar, pulling him into the alley. It was Jeremy. "At least there's no knife this time," he commented wryly as he kissed her.

"Jeremy," she tried to get in between kisses.

"Yes," he murmured as he moved to her neck.

"I found Mr. Landon," she said quietly.

"Really, where is he?" he asked curiously, not stopping his kissing.

Emma placed her hands on his face, looked him in the eyes, and said, "Concentrate. Mr. Landon is dead. I found his body in the basement dumbwaiter." She let her emotions take over and cried tears she'd had to stifle earlier.

"His body! Oh, Em," he said incredulously, pulling her in for a hug. "Are you sure?"

She put her hand in her pocket and fingered the ring. "I'm sure."

"Okay, let me think a moment. This has moved into dangerous territory. I'm not sure we should continue and put you at risk."

Once she had cried herself out, she said passionately, "I'm not at risk and I would like more time to find a way to get Millie out of there."

"Let me discuss this with Cole and make sure he's on board with continuing. I'll stop by tonight," promised Jeremy.

"All right, please let him know I want to continue. We need more evidence."

"I will," he said reluctantly. He pulled her close and walked her home.

That night he came by and talked with the concerned family. "Cole agrees with you Emma, but he wants you to check in with me more often with updates on how you are doing."

"Will you be safe?" asked a worried Dora.

"I won't take any unnecessary chances, but I want to continue. We need to find out what is going on there," said Emma.

Everyone agreed to move forward with the case.

CHAPTER 39

The next morning, she was up early again and made her way to Millie's house to make pastries for breakfast. Opening the door to the hallway, she let the men stationed there know she had arrived for the day. They seemed more relaxed with her than they had previously and even waved when they saw her. She completed a set of pastries and took them out to them, she even managed to get a smile out of them.

Mrs. Miller arrived and, as usual, started her work without much talking. The day went well, with baking filling most of Emma's hours. She was thinking that tomorrow, she would check out the hidden staircase again.

With her day over, Jeremy walked her home and kissed her before parting. Once inside the boarding house, she went into the dining room and made notes for tomorrow's activities.

A smell wafted by her and she headed to the kitchen to check on dinner. She pushed open the door and could see Dora and Amy were working on preparing a stew. Amy was industriously working on cutting carrots and onions and Dora was peeling potatoes. Emma sliced off a piece of bread and added some butter to it.

Dora asked in a worried tone, "Well, how did it go today?"

"Fine, just a lot of questions. More questions than answers at this point."

"Is Millie safe there?" she whispered.

"I think she's more valuable to them alive, at least right now," she whispered back.

Dora whispered back furiously, "Can we just go get her out of there?"

"That's easier than it sounds. There is no overt abuse and Millie has a reputation for being a bit silly. I think I'll just keep researching and try to figure out what is going on. Want some help with dinner?"

"Definitely. Start the dumplings so we can add them to the Eintopf stew." Emma got to work on making the dumplings.

Narrator: Eintopf is a one-pot stew using unused ingredients so no food goes to waste. The stew would go a long way to feed the boarders. Broth, vegetables, potatoes, and beef.

Emma set the dumplings into a bowl and covered them with a cloth. Next, she helped pull the chocolate pies out of the oven, that Amy had put in earlier.

"Emma, we got word today, Chloe had her baby, a small girl, healthy," said Dora with a bright smile.

"Oh, that is wonderful! What is her name?" asked Emma, looking over at her.

Dora's face softened and she said, "Mary."

That was their mama's name, the news made Emma's eyes well up with tears, she let them fall and went to hug Dora. "That is lovely, I will make her a christening gown," she promised.

"I plan to take some food over tonight if you would like to come with me," Dora suggested.

"I would," she said, happy she could put the case out of her mind for a little while.

After dinner, she and Dora went to visit the Baby Mary. They carried the Eintopf stew and bread for the new tired parents. Chloe and Cousin's mothers were there when they arrived.

"You brought dinner!" they exclaimed.

"There is plenty for everyone," commented Dora.

"Thank you," they said and moved it to the kitchen.

"How is Chloe?" Emma inquired after them.

Before they could answer, Cousin stepped out of the back room with a swaddled baby in his arms. "Would you like to see Mary?" he asked, pulling the blanket away from her face.

"We would," said Dora, and they approached slowly, as not to scare the baby.

"Oh Cousin, she is beautiful," commented Dora.

"Well, she had to live up to her namesake," he commented.

That comment caused the girls to tear up again. "Can I hold her," asked Dora.

"Of course," he said as he carefully handed the baby to her.

When she was in Dora's arms, Emma reached over and touched the tiny hand. "How is Chloe?"

"She is fine, just tired. This little one wore her out."

They knew they needed to let them rest, so they headed home with a promise of a return visit in a few days. Dora was quiet on the way home and Emma let the silence settle around them.

As they entered the kitchen, the case was back on Emma's mind again. She looked around to see if Jake had gotten home yet. He hadn't been at the table with them that evening. He sometimes worked late, as cases demanded. The front door opened and she could hear scuffling steps going past the sitting room. Dora smiled and went to the kitchen to help him get his dinner. Emma let him eat before approaching him.

"Jake," she said as she sat next to him at the kitchen table.

"Yes," he asked, not looking at her.

"I need your camera for my current case. The smaller one."

"Okay, when?"

"I'd like to use it tomorrow and get you the pictures to develop as soon as possible. I'll see if Jeremy can drop the camera off tomorrow at your work."

"That will be fine."

She smiled and said, "Thank you." And headed back to the sitting room to work on her lace projects. The amount of time it took to create it, was the reason she only accepted two or three jobs a year. Though this particular job was more of an investigation, she didn't want to disappoint her friend and owner of the dress shop.

She worked for the first hour, setting up the initial pattern that would be repeated with the additions of scallops. While her fingers were busy, she listened but stayed out of the group conversation. She heard absently that the twins had a long day in school but enjoyed recess. Tim joined the group, sitting close to Dora, making her blush with his teasing.

Emma thought to herself, *What is going on at Millie's? How do I find out?*

She paused a moment, set her lacework down, and said, "Tim, could you meet me in the study?"

"Sure," he said and kissed Dora before standing to follow her.

They entered the study and he closed the doors. Pulling out her notebook, she asked, "If this is some type of con to take Millie's money, what types of documents should I be looking for?"

Tim thought for a moment and commented, "Logbooks, I think. Even illegal activities need to be documented."

"Where would they be? In the desk?" she asked.

"No, somewhere hidden, I think. You would be looking for a safe. Probably not anything obvious. Look for something heavy and probably big."

CHAPTER 40

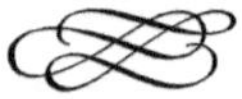

$\mathcal{T}$he next morning, she was once again alone when she started her pastries. *This would be the best time to access the staircase and enter the study.* Finishing her work, she headed to the basement and made her way there. *If there are logbooks, they would be here.*

She remembered what Tim had said and looked for the safe or something that might house one. The desk caught her eye. *Too obvious, and it's not locked,* she thought and continued her search.

She looked past a large globe several times but then thought about what Tim had said about the size of hidden safes. Going over to it, she found it met the requirements, large and heavy. Twirling it around, she looked for a compartment or opening of some type. Her hand encountered a small indention, and she used her fingers to open the panel, revealing a combination lock.

Dear-one: How does Emma know how to open combination locks?

Narrator: She lived with two amazing women (Miss Amy and Miss Marjorie) who were accomplished burglars. Emma worked with them to get an understanding of different types of locks and how to open them.

. . .

Emma worked the combination, leaning her head close to listen for the click as she found each number. The safe sprang open on the final one. Reaching in, she discovered Tim was right—the logbooks were inside.

She pulled them out. There was just enough sunlight with the shades open and her portable lamp to allow for the pictures to be taken. Leaning them against some of the large books on the bookshelves, she grabbed the camera, taking as many pictures as she could. They were written in some kind of code; she would get with Tim to try to decipher it.

She replaced the books in the safe, took her camera, and made her way back down the hidden staircase to the basement and then up to the kitchen. Hearing voices, she hid the camera under her apron and slowly opened the door. Mrs. Miller wasn't alone; Roger was also there.

"And where have you been?" asked Roger when he saw her enter. "You're not allowed out of the kitchen without approval."

"I sent her to the basement to check the inventory for preserves so I can determine when we have to start canning again," Mrs. Miller said, covering for her.

Though shocked at the help she received, Emma said, "Yes, we're running low on fruit but have enough vegetables."

Roger looked at them both, but since he had no reason to doubt Mrs. Miller, he said, "Just make sure you don't go where you aren't supposed to," and left the kitchen.

Emma moved and had her back to Mrs. Miller as she placed the camera in her bag before she started pulling the ingredients for a streusel. "Thank you," she said quietly to Mrs. Miller. She nodded to Emma and went back to peeling potatoes.

Emma waited another moment before saying, "Why did you do it?"

"I'm here for reasons of my own," she explained simply. Not

sharing anything further, they went on cooking together companionably.

Jeremy knocked at the door and Mrs. Miller found a reason to remove herself while he was there. Emma slipped him the camera and said in a low voice, "Get this to Jake at the police station and ask him to develop the pictures by this evening."

"I will. Is everything okay?"

"Yes, I think we have an ally in Mrs. Miller. She covered for me just now."

"Interesting. I need to get moving so no one realizes I'm not in the garden." He looked around and gave her a quick kiss before he exited the room. Mrs. Miller returned and didn't ask any questions. They continued to work together in a companionable manner, the rest of the day.

On her way home, Emma slipped into an alley and removed her wig, and wiped her face. She kept her coat closed and slipped back out to return to the boarding house. Emma met Jake and went up the stoop with him. "I was able to get those prints ready for you," he said.

"Great, are they readable?"

"Yes, I could make out the individual line items," he said as he handed them over.

She clutched them to her chest. *This could be it*, she thought and carried them into the house.

She called, "Tim, can you meet me in the study?"

Tim called back, "On my way."

Emma had spread out the pictures for Tim to evaluate. "Pull the door shut behind you." He did so and walked over to the desk.

"It's definitely a code. Give me some time to look at this," he said absently. Tim continued to pour over them that evening and into the night. When Emma woke the next morning, she found him in the dining room. He had his jacket and vest off and his shirt sleeves rolled up.

"Have you been up all night?" Emma asked incredulously.

"Yes. I broke it a couple of hours ago. They're using a simple replacement code, but it was hard to tell what they were replacing." He had the photos with him and pointed to one, "Here, you see that they are importing units much bigger than they are selling. The profit margin appears quite high."

"Do you have any idea what it is?"

"Based on where it is coming from and the quantities, I think it may be opium."

"I think we should turn over the information on the drugs to Cole. He'll need to investigate further." She paused. "Tim, can we tell when the next shipment will happen?"

"That, I can tell. It looks like the ships dock about every four months and one is due to arrive soon. I think we can set up a sting to see who meets the ship and takes custody of the drugs."

"Do you think the main people will be there?"

"I think the person behind this is very controlling and will want to make sure their product is delivered. Do you have an idea of who it is?"

"Roger is the best suspect at this point. I think it's also time to get Millie out of there," she insisted.

"I agree. Can you approach her at the house?"

"That will be the hard part. Millie rarely comes out of her room. But Mrs. Miller could help me with that. She delivers her meals. I'll see if I can talk with her tomorrow."

"Emma, are you all right staying in the house until we can check it out?"

"Yes, this is too important not to follow through on. I will give Jeremy an update this morning."

CHAPTER 41

She briefed Jeremy and Cole before going to work. Cole had prior experience with drug shipment and knew who to contact about the ships that were coming in. Emma and Jeremy headed to the house to begin their day.

Emma had not seen Millie in all the time she had been in the house. There was only one way to get access and she needed Mrs. Miller's help. "Can I take the tray up today?" Emma asked her.

She sent her an odd look but answered, "Yes, you can. I'll let the guards know."

Emma set up the lunch tray and headed out of the kitchen. The men looked at her questioningly and Emma said in response, "Mrs. Miller asked me to take Mrs. Landon's tray up today."

They glanced over her shoulder and Mrs. Miller said, "Yes, she can go up." They nodded and let her go ahead.

As she headed upstairs with a guard, she had the tray perched on her right hand and shoulder. She knocked lightly and was told to come in. The guard stepped back and waited as she entered. Millie sat at the desk in her room, her back to the door. She was dressed in a light afternoon tea gown.

Emma started to say, "Millie. . ." but before she could get it out, she noticed the book Millie was writing in. The shock made her freeze; it was a logbook, just like the ones in the safe.

It was Millie! She's in charge! How could I have missed that? Women can be criminals, too, Emma reminded herself. She had been naïve on this one.

"Yes, why are you still here?" Millie asked without turning around.

"No reason, madam," she murmured, as set the tray down, and left. She immediately started downstairs to the kitchen.

This isn't about saving Millie anymore. It's now about stopping the illegal activities and taking Millie into custody, she thought.

Someone grabbed her arm and turned her around. Fighting against her instincts to react to the attack, she found herself face to face with Roger.

"What are you doing up here? You know you're not allowed out of the kitchen."

She didn't struggle but instead behaved in a docile manner and lowered her eyes. "Mrs. Miller told me she was busy and that I should take up the tray for Mrs. Landon."

"You will come with me to talk to Mrs. Miller," he demanded.

He half dragged her downstairs. Emma didn't see Mrs. Miller as she was thrown into the kitchen, but she did hear a bang and saw a pan hit Roger's head.

As Emma took in the picture of Roger splayed across the floor, she looked at Mrs. Miller in amazement. "Wow," she said, she took the offered hand and pulled herself up from the floor.

"Grab his ankles," said Mrs. Miller in a low voice, as she lifted him and put her hands under his arms. They moved him toward the basement door and down the stairs.

She pulled out a rope, handed it to Emma, and said, "Make yourself useful."

Emma tied him up and pulled out a handkerchief to tie around his mouth.

"Who are you?" she asked in amazement.

"I am Donald Landon's mother, and I know these people have stolen my son's money and probably killed him," she said grimly.

"Mrs. Landon—" started Emma.

"Hannah," she interrupted.

"Hannah, I'm so sorry, but they have killed your son. I found him more than a week ago," she said gently.

"Where?" Hannah asked in a shaky voice.

She indicated the dumbwaiter with her head. Hannah started to go over and Emma said, trying to stop her, "Please, don't look. He isn't what you remember."

She hesitated, wanting to see her boy but decided Emma was right. Instead, she asked, "How can you be sure it's him?"

Emma put her hand in her pocket and pulled out his ring.

Hannah took the ring, studied it, and asked quietly, "Are you here to stop them?"

"I am, and I think we finally have enough to get Millie and take down her operation," she said bracingly. "But now, since we have Roger, I expect we need to move a bit faster."

"Agreed," Hannah said, wiping her tears, as she slipped the ring into her pocket.

"Let me check in with the gardener. He's working with me."

Hannah and Emma headed upstairs to the kitchen. Jeremy was there, looking around when they came up from the basement. He started to talk but stopped when he saw Emma had company.

Emma saw the look and said, "It's okay, you can talk in front of her. She is Mr. Landon's mother. Mrs. Landon, this is Jeremy Tilden. He's part of the team helping to bring this illegal operation down."

Jeremy was shocked but shook himself out of it. "Em, we got word the ship is coming in tonight."

"Well, that's a relief, because there's an issue." She went on to describe what they had done to Roger.

He looked resigned and said, "I'll get the team organized. We don't want to arouse any suspicion, so don't change your schedules and leave at your normal times."

"Oh, and one more thing. . ." Emma said, delaying his exit.

He raised an eyebrow and waited.

"Roger isn't the one in charge," she said.

He frowned, "He's not? Then who is?"

"Millie," she said simply.

He looked nonplussed for a moment and then said, "Women are moving into everything these days." He started out of the kitchen.

"I'd like to be there," said Mrs. Landon, that stopped him.

Jeremy started to say no, but Emma said, "She deserves to be there. I will bring her with me." When he looked worried, she said, "We'll stay in the background."

Jeremy headed out to get everyone in place. Mrs. Landon and Emma followed Jeremy's directions and left the house at their regular time. They had checked on Roger and he was still secure in the basement. Once Millie left to go to the ship, the Pinkertons would have him picked up.

Millie watched them leave the house. *Finally*, she thought. Getting dressed, she organized her logbook for the delivery and exited her room. "Roger!" she called from the top of the stairs. When no one responded, she started down and ask the guards at the base of the stairs where he was.

"We don't know. He hasn't been around for a while," one responded.

She frowned and thought, *This is my enterprise, after all, and my money. I don't need him.* She said out loud, "Fine, we'll go without him."

The two men gave her an odd look but followed her orders. Normally, Roger directed all things in the house, but it looked like that was changing.

"Get the buggy ready. We will be leaving at 10pm to go to the docks," Millie said.

She returned to her room until it was time to leave. At the appointed time, she exited in a dark dress and a hat covering her hair and made her way downstairs.

The guard stepped up and said, "The carriage is waiting for you."

"I'll need both of you with me and bring your guns."

They did as they were told and climbed on the top of the carriage. Millie rode by herself inside. She wasn't worried; the men with her had been through this process many times. She thought, *It's probably time to get rid of Roger. I can run this operation on my own.* She sat back, feeling very confident and in charge of the situation.

They pulled up to the predetermined position and waited for their contact to appear. She heard a knock at her carriage door and opened it to descend. A lanky man with a cap pulled over his eyes was there. She said curtly, "Well, don't just stand there. We need to confirm my items are here and ready to be transported."

Jeremy pushed up his hat, pulled out a gun, and pointed it at her, saying, "Yes, your items are here and the delivery people are now in our custody." At that moment the Pinkerton detectives surrounded them and took the two men on the carriage into custody.

Millie tried to slip into her previous persona and started to cry. "These men have kept me locked in my house and I had no one to turn to. Roger forced me to do this, all of it."

"This Roger?" Cole asked, pulling the tied-up man out of the shadows.

Millie seemed stunned to see him there. She wanted to demand where he'd been, but couldn't. She kept crying to cover her anger.

Jeremy was called over by Cole to bring Roger to the police detective. He looked at the young officer assigned to Millie and said, "Watch her. I'll be right back." The officer nodded and stayed where he was.

The issue, thought Emma as she observed Millie being taken into custody, *is that the officer appeared to believe everything she is saying to him.* She just shook her head when he gave her his handkerchief. *Good grief,* she thought and kept a sharp eye on Millie.

As Millie reached into her bag, Emma knew what would happen next. Grabbing her clutch knife from her skirt pocket, she threw it. The blade pierced Millie's hand, causing her to drop the gun she was in the process of pulling out of her purse.

Jeremy was on his way back and immediately grabbed the gun in one hand and the moony officer's collar in the other. He glanced toward Emma and sent a silent, *Thank you.*

Emma responded by saying, "I was never one to stay out of the fray."

Millie heard the comment, looked her way, and asked, "Just who are you?"

Emma took off her wig and wiped her face with her arm, Millie recognized her immediately and said, "You bitch!"

Emma looked at her and said softly, "So, now you know."

Once Millie was finally in cuffs and Emma's knife safely returned to her pocket, things started to calm down. The Pinkertons completed the final roundup of the drugs and people.

Millie just couldn't wait to rip into Roger when he was close to her again. "You are so incompetent. I have to do everything myself."

"Does that include killing my son?" interrupted Hannah, coming out of the crowd of detectives.

"Your son? What do you have to do with this? What is she talking about? I don't know the cook's son," Millie snapped, bewildered.

"Actually, you do," commented Emma. "She's Donald Landon's mother."

Going pale, she said, "His mother? But he said she was dead."

"He chose to tell people that. We didn't have the best relationship, but that doesn't mean I didn't love him. Why did you have to kill him?" Hannah asked.

"I didn't kill anyone," she said defiantly.

"They found the body, Millie," commented Roger laconically.

Millie blinked, she immediately changed her story, and said, "That wasn't murder. That was an accident."

"We'll see," said Jeremy.

"She did it!" blurted out Roger. "She was behind everything."

"You keep your mouth shut!" she shouted.

"I just did as I was told," he said. "We knew each other from her honeymoon. She knew I was moving this merchandise and she said she had a deal that would benefit us both. She said we just had to take care of one thing. That thing turned out to be moving her dead husband into the dumbwaiter and placing a lock on it in the basement. He was already dead when I got there, at the bottom of the steps."

Millie sneered and said, "Well, it just figures you would turn out to be a worm of a man." She turned her ire back to Emma. "I knew you were trouble when you started asking me questions at the dressmaker. It was Grandfather, wasn't it? The money. He always kept a tight hand on my money, and I knew it would be worse as I got closer to my inheritance."

Emma didn't answer and watched as they took Roger and Millie away, both preoccupied and glaring at each other.

Cole, Jeremy, and Emma stood together, watching them leave. "What will happen now?" Emma asked.

Cole responded, "Millie killed Donald and was the leader of a drug-smuggling operation. Prison is the least of her worries."

"So," Emma said contemplatively, "how should we word the telegram to Mr. Carlyle?"

That made Cole and Jeremy laugh out loud and Cole said, "You are my kind of agent."

They left the area together to head home after a long day.

CHAPTER 42

few weeks later, Emma was at the courthouse; she was
there as support in the trial. Benches lined both sides of
the long hallway, and she was startled to see a wheelchair positioned nearby. Looking forward, she made eye contact with Mr.
Carlyle. She had known he would be there to support Millie, but
she hadn't expected to speak with him.

He indicated for his helper to roll him over to her. As the
helper pushed him closer, Emma felt trapped, but she knew she
had to face him. "Hello, Mr. Carlyle," she said quietly.

"Emma," he said. He waved off his helper; he wanted privacy
for this conversation. "Emma, I want to speak with you." She
waited for him to start yelling at her or accuse her of framing
Millie.

Instead, he said in a quiet but firm voice, "Emma, I do not
blame you for anything you found at the house or Millie's arrest."

She gave him an incredulous stare as he continued. "When I
brought you in, I had my suspicions that Millie was involved in
something nefarious. Why?" he asked when he saw her look.
"Millie has always had a dark side. She could hide it under that
rather silly surface, but I had reports of bad behavior from the

help working at the house. I had hoped her marriage would redirect her."

"Well, it did that," she said.

"Yes, I am afraid she is a throwback to my father. He was not a good man. He benefitted from many illegal activities. When he died, I was finally able to move us into the legal side of things. Millie's parents died when she was about twelve, and I just found I couldn't say no to her."

"How did they die?" she inquired softly, sad this man had lost so much.

"They were on a family holiday at our country house. Millie enjoyed running around in the fields and collecting flowers. I got notified that her parents had eaten something bad and died."

"What did they ingest?" she asked curiously.

"White Amanita bisporigera mushroom, it is deadly if ingested. They died so quickly; we didn't know what had happened initially. The local doctor thought to check the leftovers from the dinner and found the poisonous mushrooms."

"Did Millie eat any of the mushrooms?" she asked without expression.

"No, she doesn't like them at all and has always refused them. After that, she seemed to change. Outwardly, she was the same cheerful, silly girl, but when she was home, she was quiet and very studious."

"What did she study?" Emma asked curiously.

"Herbs mostly. She carried the *Culpeper's Complete Herbal* book with her everywhere, making notes in it."

Something clicked in Emma's head. "Mr. Carlyle, I have to see someone. Will you be okay here?"

"Yes, my man is nearby."

She left him to find Cole. He was at the courthouse observing Millie's case and had checked in with her earlier that day. She found him around the corner and said to him in a low voice,

"Cole, I think we need to speak to David. I have some information that is pertinent to the case."

He saw that she was serious and said, "I saw him in a side room, preparing for today." They walked over and Cole knocked on the door. A voice called for them to enter.

"Emma, Cole," greeted David Williams, prosecuting attorney for their case.

"David, Emma has some information to share with you." He nodded at Emma to begin.

"I was speaking with Millie's grandfather just now and he mentioned something that made me feel we weren't seeing the whole picture. I think Mr. Landon's death means more than we thought. Remember," she said as she looked at Cole, "when I told you I was invited to her house for a weekend when I was a kid?"

"Yes," replied Cole.

"Well, what I didn't mention at that time was that Millie was very pushy about what I ate, so much so that I stopped eating that weekend. I had to sneak some bread and butter from the kitchen."

"What was she trying to get you to eat?" asked David curiously.

"Well, she kept saying she had picked herbs just for me, herbs she would add to my dinner once it got to the table. The pressure was intense, and her personality would change when I said no. If her parents hadn't come home, I'm not sure I could have held out. About a month later, I heard her parents had died. We didn't know it at that time, but Millie's grandfather just confirmed that they had accidentally been poisoned by mushrooms that were in their dinner."

Making up his mind, David said, "We need to get the doctor to check for poison in the husband." He left the room immediately to get that started.

"Good job, Emma," Cole said as they waited to hear the results.

David also contacted the court immediately and ask for a continuance. He also took the time to amend the charges to add the murder of Donald Landon.

Donald's mom, Mrs. Landon, was at the court and was notified that the additional charge was being added. She looked satisfied that her son would get his justice.

Emma pulled out her notebook and said, "Cole, I think we also need to check to see if the staff who 'disappeared' actually went on to other jobs. It always bothered me they weren't around to be questioned."

"Emma, do you think she. . ." Cole felt this couldn't have happened and no one noticed.

"I don't want to think that, but now I'm wondering why the garden is so protected. Did the help 'disappear' there? Could you ask Jeremy to meet us at Millie's house, in the garden?"

Cole sent a note over, and the three of them arrived at the house within the hour.

"Over here," she said when she saw Jeremy approach. They gave him the background on the case.

Jeremy said, "I think I know where to start. If I'm right, we'll need shovels. Also, I know where the mushrooms are located."

They sent word to David and made their way to the beautiful rose bushes located at the back of the property. "This location is perfect for covering up fresh dirt around the bushes. Also, there's plenty of room if she wanted to add more bodies," stated Jeremy grimly.

Cole sent a runner to get some Pinkerton detectives to join their group and bring shovels. The men were digging and, after a few moments, found something. "Over here!!" One of the policemen called. Emma, Cole, and Jeremy ran over. Bodies, one after another were uncovered. It looked like most of the household staff had met their end in that garden. The police chief was notified immediately to come to the house to take over the investigation.

While they were waiting for him, Jeremy pointed to the hidden spot where the mushrooms were being grown. It was the only overgrown section in the garden. They examined the area and

Cole squatted down, using his handkerchief to break off some of the mushroom caps.

"We'll have to have these tested, but I believe this will be what killed those people."

Emma hesitated when they were ready to depart. "Emma, are you ready?" asked Jeremy.

She leaned into him and said, "Jeremy, I need to check Millie's room for that book."

"Do you know where she has hidden it? The study?" he asked, knowing she had found the logbooks there.

"No, I think it is probably in her room," commented Emma. "Millie wouldn't want that out of her control."

"Let's go up," he said. As they entered the house, Emma glanced around and took an umbrella from the stand. He didn't ask why she needed it, and they made their way to Millie's room.

They entered the room and Emma said, "I have an idea." She used the tip of the umbrella to tap on the wooden boards. Jeremy realized what she was doing; she was listening for a hollow sound, indicating a hidden compartment. As she tapped under the desk, she heard what she was looking for. "Here," she said, pointing to the floor. They knelt and Emma pulled out her clutch knife to pry up the board. "Ah-ha," she announced. The board lifted to reveal a hollowed-out spot. She put her hand in and pulled out the book.

"We need to get this to David," said Jeremy, impressed that she had found it so quickly.

"Agreed," she said as they exited the room and headed to the police station. They got there in time to meet Cole. Jeremy asked, "What's going on?"

"David is in the interrogation room waiting for Roger. We will wait out here while they question him," he said.

They would have liked to go in to observe, but they understood that wasn't possible.

As Roger was brought into the interrogation room, he looked

around and said, "Are we having a party?" The prosecutor, police chief, and assortment of policemen filled the small space.

"Roger, we have some additional questions for you," David said.

"Okay," he said warily.

David watched him closely as he stated, "We've looked under the rose bushes in the garden."

Roger couldn't decide whether he wanted to stand or to sit. He finally sat and said in a pleading tone, "I really didn't know what was going on. I know that sounds odd, but I would go on a trip to set up opium buys and another member of the staff would be gone when I got back. I was told they took other positions. By the time I understood what was happening, the only person I could save was the cook. That's when I set up the protocols for exiting and entering areas."

"Why did you stay if you knew she was a murderer?" asked David.

"We were making too much money. I kept thinking one more score and then I would get out. I also thought I could control her," he admitted.

"Would you be willing to testify about the additional bodies?"

"Do I get the same deal for limited jail time?"

"About that, we'll need to add some time for not reporting the crime in a timely manner."

Roger nodded, understanding he had to take responsibility for his actions. He thought, *Maybe the cook will say some positive things about me. After all, I saved her life.*

The charges were amended for a second time to include the additional murders. Millie's defense attorney appeared stunned at the amendments. He looked at her, but she just stared forward and would not answer his questions.

David submitted a new witness list to the court:

- Gardener: Jim Brown was found at a family member's house. He was also arrested for disposing of multiple bodies.
- Jeremy Tilden: for his knowledge of the mushroom and rose bushes.
- Dr. Knight: doctor who examined the body of Donald Landon and confirmed poison as the reason for his death.
- Dr. Morison: retired doctor who examined Millie's parents and determined their death was from poisoning.
- Miss Grisham: previous housekeeper for information on disappearances.
- Roger Smith: accomplice of Millicent Landon.

Cole and Emma entered the court and made their way to the seats on the prosecutor's side. The judge had yet to enter and the jury was out on a break. David nodded when he saw them and was about to say something when the judge appeared and the jury took their seats. The case started again with Jim Brown, the previous gardener, as a witness.

Prosecuting attorney David Williams asked, "Mr. Brown, can you tell us if you kept the white Amanita bisporigera mushroom growing in Mrs. Landon's garden?"

Mr. Brown looked very nervous and avoided looking at Millie. "Yes, I tried to tell her they needed to be removed, but she said she wanted to develop and oversee them."

The prosecutor asked, "Did she harvest them?"

Mr. Brown answered, "She did. She told me it was for experimentation purposes."

The prosecutor asked, "Can you tell us about the bodies we found under the rose bushes at Mrs. Landon's home?"

"She just told me they died and we should bury them," Mr. Brown said lamely, clearly not sure how to answer the question.

The prosecutor continued, "Mr. Brown, you didn't think that was suspicious, not notifying the police that someone had died?"

"Well, yes, but she was an upstanding lady. I thought she was being nice, burying them there," said Mr. Brown, looking uncomfortable.

The prosecutor gave him an incredulous look and asked, "She was such an upstanding lady that she just needed to get rid of bodies?" Mr. Brown didn't respond to the question; he just sat and stared at his hands.

The judge asked the defense attorney, Jeffery Cumming if he wanted to question the witness. He had a few questions, but there was little that could be done to contradict the gardener's testimony.

The prosecutor asked for the next witness. "Jeremy Tilden, please."

Jeremy was escorted into the court and took his seat next to the judge. The prosecutor started his questions. "Mr. Tilden, you were the gardener for the last week. Did you notice the mushrooms there?"

"Not initially," admitted Jeremy. "I was there to monitor activities inside the house."

The prosecutor continued with his questions. "What types of conversation, if any, did you have with Mrs. Landon?"

"Very little at first," he said. "She contacted me when she found out I was a short-term replacement for the gardener. She was adamant about the garden; she didn't want it touched."

The prosecutor followed up, trying to confirm he had seen the mushrooms. "Was one of these a patch of mushrooms?"

Jeremy answered, "When I brought up that she had a patch of bad mushrooms, she said they were pesky and should probably be removed at a later date."

The prosecutor asked, "Did she mention the rose bushes?"

Jeremy nodded. "She mentioned I was to trim them only and not disturb the beds."

The defense attorney said, "I choose not to question this witness at this time."

The next witness called was Dr. Knight, the doctor who had examined Mr. Landon's body. He was an older man and slowly made his way to the stand.

The prosecutor waited patiently for him to be seated and asked, "Dr. Knight, can you tell me what you found when you examined Mr. Landon's body?"

The doctor glanced at the judge and then the prosecutor and asked, "May I use my notes?"

The judge asked to see his notebook. He reviewed it and handed it back. "You may use them."

The prosecutor prompted, "Doctor?"

"Yes," he said, reading, "I noted that he had excessive drool that had dried from his mouth, leaving a trail to his shirt. I also noticed an abnormal skin color that is similar to when the liver fails."

The prosecutor had a follow-up question. "Doctor, what was this color?"

"Yellow."

The prosecutor continued the same line of questioning. "Doctor, did you examine the four bodies buried in the garden?"

Dr. Knight confirmed, "I did."

"What did you find?"

Dr. Knight glanced back down to his notebook. "The same as I found when I examined the husband's body. Once we cleared the bodies from the flowerbed, the yellow coloring was obvious."

"What did you deduce?" asked the prosecutor.

Dr. Knight closed his notebook with a snap. "Poison. By ingesting mushrooms, in all five cases. "

"Thank you, doctor."

The Judge looked at the defense attorney and asked, "Would you like to question the witness?"

The defense attorney looked at a loss for a moment and leaned over to ask Millie a question. She shook her head vehemently in response. He looked at the judge and said, "No, I do not have any questions for this witness."

The judge said, "You are excused." Dr. Knight stood and exited the courtroom.

Dr. Morrison, the retired doctor who had examined Millie's parents after they passed away, was called next.

The prosecutor asked, "Doctor, what did you see when you examined Mr. and Mrs. Carlyle?"

Dr. Morrison stated, "Excessive drool, abnormal skin color, and complaints of severe cramps."

"What did you deduce?"

"Poison, by ingesting mushrooms," answered Dr. Morrison.

The defense attorney stood and asked, "Dr. Morrison, can you tell us how the mushrooms got into their food?"

"No, the cook said there were no mushrooms served with the meals that day," he answered.

"Thank you," said the defense attorney and sat down.

The previous housekeeper, Miss Grisham, was called next. She entered very nervously and sat in the witness stand. The prosecutor asked, "Miss Grisham, you were the housekeeper when Mrs. Landon was first married?"

Miss Grisham replied, "Yes, I was the housekeeper for Mrs. Landon for a long time, since she was a girl."

The prosecutor continued, "What can you tell us about Mrs. Landon's interests as a young girl?"

"Well, she was always in the garden and always bringing in clippings to include in the dinners," she commented.

"Did you include them in the dinners you were preparing?"

"Only if I recognized them. Otherwise, I told her it might be dangerous," she answered honestly.

"Your witness," said the prosecutor.

The defense attorney stood up, walked around his desk, and asked, "Did you ever see her put anything into the food, something you told her not to?"

"No," Miss Grisham stated simply.

"Thank you," said the defense attorney and sat down. Millie leaned over to whisper something to him. He smiled and patted her hand reassuringly.

Roger Smith was called as the next witness. He walked in and was escorted to the stand by an armed policeman. He did not shy away from Millie's gaze and actually smiled at her. The prosecutor asked, "Mr. Smith, how did you get involved with Mrs. Landon?"

"We met on a cruise. It was her honeymoon," Mr. Smith stated, continuing to smile.

"Where was Mr. Landon during this meeting?" asked the prosecutor.

"Mrs. Landon said that he was sick and confined to their room," said Mr. Smith.

"Did you ever see him?" asked the prosecutor.

"No, I did not," Mr. Smith stated quietly, his smile slowly fading.

"Why were you on the ship?"

"I was setting up some operations overseas."

"Were these illegal operations?" asked the prosecutor, looking at the jury. They looked both fascinated and repulsed.

"Yes," Mr. Smith admitted. "Drugs."

"You willingly admit you were involved in illegal activities?" asked the prosecutor in a deliberate manner.

"Yes, I am going to prison for these activities."

"And you were involved with Mrs. Landon?"

"Yes, we got very close on that cruise and I shared my business enterprise. She wanted in on the deal and said we could use her house as a base of operations."

"What about her husband?"

"She said he wouldn't get in their way, that she would take care of it."

"Did you know what she meant by that?"

"No, I didn't. A few weeks later, she notified me that I could move in and said she needed help cleaning something up. When I got there, her husband was lying at the bottom of the steps."

"Were the servants in the house?"

"She had told them they could have a holiday."

"Did she tell you what happened to him?"

"She said he was beating her and fell down the stairs."

"He would never do that!" stated Hannah Landon, jumping up from her seat in the gallery.

The judge looked annoyed and said to the gallery in general, "We can't have any disturbances from the courtroom while proceedings are taking place." Hannah sat back down next to Emma and held her hand.

"Did you think she was telling the truth?" asked the prosecutor.

"Objection, this man is not a doctor," stated the defense attorney forcefully.

"Judge, Mr. Smith can provide his observation of the man, the general condition, without being a doctor," answered the prosecutor calmly.

The judge said, "Yes, he may provide his observations as to what state the man was in when he arrived. Please, continue."

The witness did so. "He had a yellow color to him and he seemed to have liquid coming out of his mouth."

"Did he appear to have any broken bones?"

"Not that I could see," he said simply.

"You also mentioned in your statement that, at this time, there was additional staff in the house and you noticed they started to disappear."

He shook his head. "It was odd. No one gave notice; they just went away. I started to get suspicious when Mrs. Landon thought nothing of them leaving."

"You told the housekeeper, Miss Grisham, to get out of the house in a rather abrupt manner. Why?"

He looked toward Millie and then back at the jury. "I was standing by the back windows and was watching the garden when I noticed something odd. I looked closer and saw the gardener moving something that appeared to be a body. That night, after he had gone home and Millie was in her room, I went out with a shovel. I dug until I found the body. It was the upstairs maid, Renee." Crying could be heard coming from the gallery.

"Thank you. Your witness," said the prosecutor to the defense attorney.

The defense attorney stood and asked, "IF you saw this happening, why didn't YOU notify the police?"

"I felt I was stuck. There was no way to get out of the arrangement without turning myself in. I stayed," he said honestly.

The defense attorney sat down, showing no expression.

The prosecutor had a follow-up question. "Mr. Smith, what measures did you put in to protect the household staff when you realized there was a danger?"

"I put in special precautions that no one was allowed with Mrs. Landon alone at any time. I also reduced the staff to only four persons and limited their access to the house." He looked at the jury and said beseechingly, "I protected them as best I could."

The judge called for a ten-minute break and Millie seemed to be looking around the courtroom for someone. Emma followed her gaze to where her grandfather normally sat; it was empty. Emma wondered where he was. Millie asked her lawyer something and he nodded.

Cole walked up to where Emma was sitting and sat down next to her. "Have you seen Mr. Carlyle today?" she asked.

"No, not this morning, but I can have one of my men find out if he will be here."

Emma nodded.

Cole called over to one of his men, "Go to Mr. Carlyle's hotel and check on him." The man nodded and headed out of the courthouse.

The judge looked at the defense attorney and asked, "Do you have any witnesses?"

"I had one witness," said the defense lawyer. "I call Millicent Landon to the stand."

Millie stood elegantly, her pink lace dress providing an innocent picture. Emma smirked briefly and thought, *She is wearing my lace today.*

Millie made her way to the stand confidently, certain they would believe everything she said.

The defense attorney asked, "Mrs. Landon, what are your current interests?"

"Currently, I am interested in fashion."

"Were you also involved in the illegal operation with Roger Smith, that he testified to earlier?"

"I didn't have a choice after my husband died." She took a moment to deliberately wipe a tear off her face. Emma watched the jury and could see she was getting to them, that they were buying "the poor helpless girl" act.

"Do you have any knowledge of mushrooms or other flora or fauna?" asked the defense attorney.

"No, none at all. I don't like to get my hands dirty," she said directly to the jury. They laughed in response.

"I rest my case, judge," the defense attorney said and sat down.

The prosecutor stood and asked, "Mrs. Landon, you indicated you have no knowledge of mushrooms or other flora or fauna?"

"Yes," Millie answered, knowing she could convince these men of anything and get out of the trouble she was in. She could see she was winning in the jury's faces. Even with the evidence presented, she could still come out of this.

The prosecutor saw the look on her face and knew she thought she had won. He was about to prove her wrong. "Judge, I have something to put into evidence," he said as he walked back to the table and pulled out a book from his briefcase.

"Judge, I have no prior knowledge of this evidence," the defense attorney protested.

The prosecutor answered, "I just received it this morning."

"Please, hand it to me." He handed the book to the judge to review. He examined it closely, handed it back, and said, "It is fine. Please enter it into evidence."

"Judge, may I confer with my client for a moment?" asked the defense attorney.

Millie had paled considerably when she recognized the book. The defense attorney walked over to her; he whispered questions she refused to answer. She just stared straight ahead.

He returned to his table and sat, unsure what Millie would say next.

The prosecutor asked, holding up the book. "Is this your book?"

Millie didn't answer the question and just stared forward. The judge leaned over and asked the question for him. She glanced at her attorney; he nodded that she had to answer.

She realized she had no choice and stared back at the prosecutor. "Yes, that's my book."

The prosecuting attorney nodded and proceeded to open it. "As I see here, there is writing in the book. Is this your writing?" he asked and showed it to her.

She stared at it and slowly nodded and said a quiet, "Yes."

"Thank you. Now, if I look further into the book, I see you have marked multiple pages for different types of mushrooms, including those found in your garden. We have your gardener on record saying you asked specifically for these mushroom clippings. You also mention recipes. Can you tell me what these recipes are for?" Again, he showed her the book.

"Different types of soup recipes," she said in a low voice.

"What types of soups?" he prompted.

"Mushroom."

The court hushed at that final answer, knowing she had

murdered those people. The prosecuting attorney knew he had completed his case and stopped with his questions.

There was nothing more that could be said, so her lawyer didn't try. Millie stood and made her way back to the table. She didn't seem as elegant and grand as she had when first taking the stand.

The prosecuting attorney started his closing statement. "You have seen here through witness testimony that Millicent Landon was not only involved in the drug smuggling as testified here by her house manager and assistant Mr. Smith. We have also presented evidence that Mrs. Landon murdered her husband and four household staff members with poisonous mushrooms. The evidence showed she has poisoned before and gotten away with it. I implore you to find her guilty of all charges presented."

The defense attorney stood. "Mrs. Landon is a young, innocent woman who was taken advantage of by men who coerced her into participating in illegal activities after they killed her husband. Mr. Smith is trying to use an innocent young girl to hide his illegal activities and the fact that HE murdered those four people and placed them in the rose garden."

The jury was instructed to deliberate and return with a verdict. Emma, Jeremy, and Cole sat on the hallway benches outside of the courtroom. They only had to wait about three hours. The judge returned, along with the jury, stating, "You have reached a verdict."

"We have," said the jury foreman. Millie stood, looking straight ahead. "We find her guilty on all counts."

The judge nodded and said to the jury, "Thank you for your service." He looked down for a moment and raised his eyes to look at Millicent. "Millicent Landon you are sentenced to be hung by the neck until dead." Millie's hand fluttered lightly around her neck at that remark.

Cole told Emma later that Millie's grandfather died without knowing the final verdict.

Emma chose not to attend Millie's hanging. Some of the victim's families did attend. Emma had the closure she needed at the trial. She and Jeremy did appear at Millie's funeral, though no one else was present.

Millie's grandfather had requested no services for himself.

On the day of the funeral, Emma received a note from Mr. Carlyle's lawyer that he would like to see her that week. She sent back a confirmation of the time and date she could meet him.

"What do you think that's about?" asked Jeremy when she told him.

"I don't know. It could be anything."

Jeremy just smiled when he saw her drumming her fingers on her lips. *Planning,* he thought.

ABOUT THE AUTHOR

Kimberly Mullins is the author of series of books titled "Notebook Mysteries". Her stories are based on historical events occurring in 1800's Chicago. She holds a BS in Biology and a MBA in Business. She lives in Texas with her husband and son. When she is not writing she is working as a Process Safety Engineer at a large chemical company. You can connect with her on her website www.kimberly mullinsauthor.com.

Photo Credit: Blessings of Faith Photography

 twitter.com/kremullins_kim

www.ingramcontent.com/pod-product-compliance
Lightning Source LLC
Chambersburg PA
CBHW070630100726
47907CB00007B/1930